# IMPOSTER

## AN ASH PARK NOVEL

## MEGHAN O'FLYNN

IMPOSTER

Copyright 2019



Distributed by Pygmalion Publishing, LLC

*For those who feel, deep in their souls,*
*that they don't belong:*
*You do.*

**1**

———

DEATH. It was an impossibly loud thing, an eerie, high-pitched silence that dominated even the chattering people on the sidewalk just outside. He could feel it weighting his shoulders. He could taste it, sweet and metallic on his tongue and overlaid with the musty stink of shit. He'd seen hundreds of bodies, and every one still hit him in the gut—especially when the deceased was a child.

Petrosky stopped near the middle of the living room, a room like any other in the neighborhood save for the corpse hanging from the living room rafter. The boy couldn't be more than fifteen—skinny, his black workout shorts bagging off his bony hips, a fake-faded green T-shirt draping his shoulders like a poncho. His slight frame made it worse, somehow, as if the universe was actively attacking the vulnerable. And his head... Thick dark hair, half-slitted brown eyes now marred with broken blood vessels that made him look like he might at any moment start crying crimson tears.

*Poor kid.* "Who found him?" Petrosky glanced at the slippery pile of bodily fluids—mostly the kid's intestinal contents—now congealing on the floor beneath the boy's bare toes. Petrosky's own stomach clenched, hot and achy.

"Parents," Jackson said, kneeling near the floor to the

right of the body, far outside the dark puddle. She'd been here half an hour, but Petrosky's partner was still crisp and pressed like she'd just stepped out of a "How to Detective" manual: tailored gray suit, sensible shoes, her tight black curls shorn close to the scalp, even shorter than his own thinning salt-and-pepper locks. He peered down at the floor where Jackson was looking. Was that a tiny scrape in the gleaming wood? But no, these floors had scrapes all over—"hand-scraped hardwoods," that was what his neighbor, Billie, had called them when she was jokingly trying to convince him to install them at her place. Petrosky thought the fashionably beat-up boards were as strange a fad as faded clothing.

Jackson straightened. "Parents and the younger brother came home this morning from a two-day visit with Mom's sister in Lansing. Figured he'd be okay alone for a couple nights, but..." She shrugged, mouth relaxed, face blank—professional. But her dark eyes were as tight as Petrosky's shoulders.

A breeze tickled his neck, and he turned toward the buzz of voices filtering in from the yard, like the clucking of hens—louder now. "Was the window open when you got here?" Detroit and the surrounding metropolis were always muggy in August, but this week Ash Park had been especially sticky even out here in the historic district. He couldn't see anyone leaving the window open overnight.

"Yeah. One of the first responders opened it because of the..." She gestured to the sheen of nastiness on the floor. A white L-shaped couch stood behind the puddle—behind the swinging body. Not a single gooey drop on it. At least the kid hadn't still been kicking when he'd shit himself. The beige wingback he'd probably stepped off of—his last fully conscious act—wasn't so lucky; it lay upended, two of its wooden legs slimed with fluids. As were the boy's legs, the flesh around the heels stained purple, his toes stiff, drips of black and brown dried in fetid streaks from beneath the edge of his workout shorts to the bottom of his soles. But he could still see the port-wine birthmark on one pale, white thigh, deep reddish-brown and stark against his otherwise graying flesh. "Judging by the blood settling and the rigor, it's been less than twenty-four hours—probably last night, early this morning."

Jackson nodded. "We'll know for sure once the ME gets here."

Petrosky grunted assent, his eyes on the kid's face. His neck. Usually, hanging victims had moments of instinctive defensiveness once the suffocation began in earnest—a struggle against the ligature. Most had claw marks on their throat.

But not this boy. The child exhibited the expected bruising around the rope itself, lines of angry blue-black, but none of the claw-like scraping Petrosky had anticipated. *Huh.* Had he taken something to dull the pain before he put his head through the noose and stepped off that chair?

The clucking sound came again, from outside: the droning of voices. The neighbors? Sounded like more than the few horrified middle-aged women he'd seen loitering on the sidewalk—the kind who looked like they should have Chihuahuas in their purses. But with a case like this, there would be strangers out there soon enough, prying into every little crevice like scavenger birds tearing at a decomposing raccoon. "Where's the family now?"

"They're with friends a few houses down—the neighbor was rounding them up when I got here. That guy didn't see or hear anything unusual, not that you'd expect him to."

Right—suicide was often a silent affair. Like depression. Petrosky nodded, but he could not drag his gaze to his part-ner's face. The kid's bloody eyes. The purple line on his neck. The breeze sighed, and Petrosky got a nose full of shit—shit and death. You never got used to that. Never. He coughed.

"You dying, old man?" Her voice echoed off the curved wooden staircase to his right. The beige curtains on the bay windows at the far end and the plush white carpet on the exposed second story landing absorbed the hiss of his breath, but not the sounds of the room.

"Not today." *Probably.* But he'd give his left testicle for a jar of VapoRub—not like he was using them for much else at the moment. He finally pulled his eyes from the kid and peered up at the rope instead, new rope from the shiny braid. How long had the boy struggled before giving up? Maybe Petrosky didn't want to know. "What about Scott?"

"On his way. I already told the officers outside that no one enters this room but Scott and the ME."

*Good.* Evan Scott was the best forensic guy they had, still practically a kid, but a genius kid. Petrosky squinted one last time at the rafters, following the rope over the beam, then to the wooden banister where it was secured, then turned back to the body. A deeply purple tongue protruded from between the boy's lips, so swollen it didn't look like it should ever have fit into his mouth.

"Goddammit," Jackson muttered from the far side of the room, behind the couch, her hand on one of the floor-to-ceiling curtains the color of Petrosky's pasty ass. She frowned through the slit she'd opened in the draperies. "We've got company."

Petrosky edged around the couch to peer over her shoulder at the backyard: lush grass surrounded by an eight-foot fence, and bordered on the inside with thick conifers and oaks, a glistening swimming pool in the middle. Over the top of the fence, someone's fat face appeared, but the man dropped when he met Petrosky's glare. If the lookie-loos thought they were going to climb over the fence into the backyard, they had another thing coming. And from the street...

On the other side of the room, the thickly curtained windows faced the driveway on the side of the house. Petrosky pulled one curtain back in time to see an older model Range Rover squeal up to the curb, back doors winging open before it was even parked. A man with a belly like a basketball under his shirt flung an enormous camera onto his shoulder and stepped onto the emerald lawn.

"Ah, the vultures are here." But he'd expected that. When a kid in an affluent neighborhood offed himself, they had to at least get a sound bite for the evening news. Or more than a sound bite, because it was *this* kid.

And suddenly everything was too loud, too vibrant. Little needles prickled at the base of his brain and tingled down his back and along his arms like a memory trying to slither from its prison. *Focus, Petrosky. No time for nonsense.* But that's what he'd told himself yesterday too. He cleared his throat. "You think Acharya's on his way?"

"If there's a story, he is. Guy went primetime after our last case." Jackson raised an eyebrow. "You *want* to talk to the journalists now?"

"Hell no." Petrosky sniffed. "I was just curious."

Jackson dropped the curtain and sighed. "Let's go talk to the parents. We'll meet up with Scott and the ME later on today after they toss the bedroom—I don't have the stomach for it right now."

At least they didn't have to make the death notification. Those conversations always brought to mind the day he'd been on the receiving end, and Julie... His daughter had been about the same age as this boy when she'd died. When she'd been murdered. He swallowed hard.

"Why'd they call us?" Jackson said. "No ligature marks at the wrists or ankles, no additional bruising that would indicate a struggle—probably a standard suicide."

"It's a little more complicated than that." Petrosky let his gaze drift back to the body—that horribly purple tongue.

"Why?"

He finally met her eyes. "This is Gregory Boyle, the kidnapped and miraculously returned wonder boy."

**2**

---

THE NEIGHBORHOOD WAS quirky-rich and uniformly non-conformist—brick or stucco, wide porches or modern walk-outs, tiger lilies or tulips, or rounded hedges—but all of them retained the pretentiousness that pervaded any little city which had art fairs. Or farmer's markets. Artisanal coffee shops selling organic pickles that someone made in their basement. But today the front sidewalk was choking on the fancy boots and high heels of TV's finest, who descended like locusts as Petrosky and Jackson stepped onto the lawn.

A blonde with blue eyeliner shoved a microphone in Petrosky's face. When the metal brushed his lips, he backhanded it, and his smarting knuckles were well worth the look on the journalist's face when the equipment went flying, narrowly missing hitting another reporter in his smarmy mouth.

"Hey!" she squealed.

"Fuck off," Petrosky snapped. "All of you."

Another reporter—a dark-haired man with just as much makeup—yelled, "Is Little Greggie really dead?"

Little Greggie. The press had called him that—*shit, seven years ago?*—when he first went missing. Actually, it had been his parents who coined it; Gregory Boyle's mother had let the nickname slip on the six o'clock news, and it had stuck.

But now the words were obscene. Gregory wasn't little; he was a buck-forty and five-six. And he was dead, his grieving parents hiding from these assholes at the neighbor's place—where Petrosky and Jackson were going now.

The male reporter lunged forward, and Petrosky grimaced at the microphone wielding prick, the reporter's eyes wide, excited to get an answer to his question, even if it was bad news. Maybe especially if it was bad news. "Have a little goddamn respect you sonofa—"

The steady pressure of Jackson's hand on his arm drew him off, away from the throng. Thank god, there was Scott's car—a used Cadillac, a little pretentious, but at least he'd bought domestic. The reporters withdrew and headed for Scott instead as he exited his vehicle, apparently deciding the kid would be more likely to talk to them than Petrosky. They were wrong about that. Scott was just more elegant with his evasion.

Jackson glanced Petrosky's way as they headed up the walk toward the neighbor's, toward a family who would never be the same again. "What's your deal today?"

Petrosky shook his head. "I'm fine." He wasn't. His chest was tight—a steady, vicious pressure since he'd awoken. Maybe it had started yesterday. Or even last week. "I'm definitely better than Scott is right now."

"What do you think Scott will do to get them off his back?" Jackson asked when they were out of earshot.

"Last time, he pretended to only speak Spanish and accidentally ended up with someone who spoke fluently. He'll probably use French."

"Of all the languages—"

"Want to bet on it? Loser has to put bees in Decantor's car." Detective Decantor was a good guy, but if he didn't stop with the J-Lo and pop culture references, Petrosky's "thicc" ass was going to "pop a cap." Or something.

"Bees? What the—"

"He hates bees. Loves that one rapper, though, and that guy has a rather insectile face. Pretty ironic if you ask me."

"*I* hate bees, Petrosky."

Their footfalls tap-tap-tapped against the sidewalk. He raised an eyebrow.

"And no, you are not putting bees in that man's car."

Petrosky stepped around a teal fire hydrant. *Who paints a fire hydrant teal?* "He's definitely going French. I saw the app on Scott's phone."

"You were betting with inside information? You're a goddamn cheat."

The drone of the reporters had quieted with distance, as had the tension between Petrosky's shoulders. He glanced up the block in time to see Evan Scott raise his hands, his mouth moving rapidly, and the reporters cocking their heads—confused. *Way to go, kid.* Petrosky turned back to the sidewalk and squinted at the road ahead. Where was the neighbor's place where the Boyles were staying? They were already five houses down.

"Gregory Boyle—was he the one kept in a warehouse?" Jackson asked.

Petrosky nodded. "I think so." Gregory Boyle had been seven when he'd vanished on his walk home from school one afternoon. He'd been held captive for five years, and then *poof*, he'd shown back up. Petrosky didn't remember much else about the case, though it had been all over the news at the time. "Kid's been home…two years if memory serves." But these days, his memory was hazy. Usually on purpose. "To be honest, I always thought he pissed the kidnappers off, so they booted him." He smiled, but it felt hollow even to him. *Fake it 'til you make it* was only good advice for people who were good at pretending to be happy. On his best day, Petrosky looked like he'd rather smother someone than chat. Which was how he preferred it.

Jackson stopped abruptly, and Petrosky followed suit, narrowing his eyes at the house looming before them. The Boyles' place had been modern—angular and hard on the outside despite the tree-trunk rafters and plush beige carpeting on the stairs. The neighbor's house was a stucco bungalow that was easily five times the size of Petrosky's house with a rounded upper balcony and an enormous half-circle front porch that mirrored the second story. No front stairs to the entrance, just an oversized double door with carved window surrounds that made it look like trees had become sentient and were trying to devour the building.

Petrosky dropped the door knocker and listened to the echo reverberate through the foyer.

"I hate this part," Jackson muttered. Her mouth was tight, tighter even than when they'd been in the presence of the dead boy. He peered over his shoulder at the Boyle house—*reporter shitheads, all of them*—eight houses up the block. Yeah, this home was much too far away for the inhabitants here to have heard anything, even if the boy had been throwing chairs around with abandon instead of just quietly kicking one over.

*Thunk.* Petrosky turned.

A tall, thin black man opened the door—wiry glasses and a bald head shiny enough to reflect the sunlight. His face was drawn.

Petrosky flashed his badge. "We're looking—"

"Kennedy, Damon Kennedy." The man stepped back and waved them into the foyer. "Please."

Petrosky and Jackson stepped over the threshold into a high-ceilinged foyer, a long wooden bench on the left wall, the enormous mirror above it reflecting…plants? He peered at the wall to his right. Floor-to-ceiling greenery, some kind of living vine. Bright, airy kitchen beyond the foyer in front of them. A hall to the right past the plants led somewhere not readily apparent—maybe Narnia with all this greenhouse shit.

"This way, Detectives," Kennedy said. "The Boyles are in the living room."

They followed him over a rustic wood floor, not shiny, not pretending like the floors in the Boyle house—the wood here was ugly and scarred and somehow more proud for it.

Kennedy left them at the living room entryway and headed back up the hall toward the kitchen.

The air tightened the moment they stepped through the arch. Mrs. Boyle sat with a boy of about twelve on the living room sofa, the couch curved at the exact angle of the back bay windows and all puckered up with tawny buttons in the same rustic fabric as the rest of it. Mr. Boyle stood, arms crossed, beady eyes squinted in agitation or pain, beside an enormous coffee table that looked like driftwood. Rough, like the thing might give you a splinter if you touched the top. Abrasive. Petrosky liked it.

Mr. Boyle approached when they flashed their badges. "Ron Boyle, my wife, Adrian." He nodded to the woman, but his arms stayed crossed, brow furrowed beneath his thinning black hair—his bristly mustache made up for what he lacked up top. "Did you cut him down yet?" He practically spat the words, more angry than sad.

*Interesting.* "The forensic team and our medical examiner are there now, working the scene, making sure we have all the pieces we need. Did they tell you that you might have to get a hotel for the night?"

Ron nodded, dark eyes run through with ruby spiderwebs. "Damon said we can stay here until this…nasty business is taken care of."

*Nasty business?* What a way to refer to your teenage son's suicide. Jackson had stiffened beside him—she clearly didn't like the vibe in here any more than Petrosky did.

"What kind of evidence could you possibly need?" Adrian Boyle asked, her voice low and steady from the sofa. Sandy hair, freckles across the bridge of her nose, cleft chin, square jaw. She stared at them with dry eyes, her fingers like talons on her knees. "He killed himself, just get him down so we can bury him." Not an ounce of inflection in her voice. Shock, surely, but he didn't like the way her nostrils flared, or the gaze of the pre-teen boy at her side—eyebrows slightly raised as if he were trying not to roll his eyes, the face of a child listening to an hour-long algebra lecture. Petrosky frowned.

"We'll have the medical examiner transfer him to the funeral home after the autopsy is complete," Jackson said. "But in a case like this, I'd wait before you make arrangements."

Adrian shook her head. "We don't want an autopsy."

Petrosky and Jackson exchanged a glance.

"Why not, ma'am?" Jackson asked.

"Because I said no!" Adrian's eyes flashed fire, her voice a harsh bark—forced, like she was having trouble getting the words out. "He's my son, and I can refuse."

*The hell you can.* And the rage in her face, the spittle on her lip... The grief response was complicated, but most parents didn't go straight to feral aggression. "I assure you, our team is working as fast as they can," Petrosky said instead of arguing the point.

The youngest member of the Boyle household—their only child now—sighed.

Ron Boyle shook his head and grumbled: "We've had a long week, Detectives, we just want to...oh, I don't know." He threw his hands up and turned away from them toward the fireplace, fists clenching and unclenching.

*What the hell is wrong with these people?* Petrosky's shoulders went rigid. He didn't think the guy would throw a punch, but Ron's back was so tight beneath his white T-shirt it looked like his tendons might snap. This entire interaction had been an exercise in weirdness.

"We just have a few routine questions," Jackson said slowly, her eyes on Ron's back. "What time did you arrive home?"

The man turned, his jaw more relaxed—resigned. "About eight."

"That's pretty early to be leaving a vacation. You had to get up at what? Five-thirty?"

"Yeah, I have...*had* a business meeting this afternoon, so what?"

Jackson nodded. "Was the front door unlocked?"

Ron narrowed his eyes and shook his head. "No, I had to unlock it."

So Gregory had locked himself inside before he put the noose around his throat, not that this was unusual—most people locked up when they were home alone. "No signs of forced entry?" Petrosky asked. "Nothing missing that you saw?"

"I only saw him," Ron said. "I didn't look at anything else."

"Did you touch anything?" Often parents ran to the body, grabbed their child—fucked up the scene. If they had to deal with forensic contamination here, it was better to know where to look for it.

But Ron was shaking his head again. "No. He was obviously dead. I barely stepped into the room." He sniffed. "I opened the door, saw him, Adrian screamed, and we turned around and closed the door before Stevie could see. Called you from the front lawn. Took you long enough to get here, by the way." His jaw hardened once more, eyes bright with fury as if they'd tried to piss him off with their tardiness. *Huh.*

"You're just doing this because it was Greg, right? Little Greggie?" The brother, the twelve-year-old, wrinkled his nose with distaste and whirled on his mother, eyes glittering. "You wouldn't care if *I* did it."

Adrian turned to the boy in slow motion, mouth open in a small shocked *o*. "Of course we would, Stevie, of course." She wrapped an arm around him, he tried and failed to shrug away, and now her eyes did fill as if she were more moved by Stevie's accusation than her other child's death. She addressed Petrosky and Jackson. "Gregory was…he had some issues. Obviously, we have some…complicated feelings to work through."

*Complicated? That's it?* The hairs on the back of Petrosky's neck prickled, though the kid having issues should make it easier to confirm suicide. Jackson pulled her notepad from her jacket. "What kind of issues, Mrs. Boyle?"

"Just…he seemed more upset…got into some fights at

school." Adrian Boyle straightened, Stevie still clutched against her side, and brushed a hand through her sandy hair as if her arm weighed a thousand pounds. "His grades were good, but he'd stopped caring as much, especially in the last…six months. He spent a lot of time…by himself."

Petrosky nodded, the *chht-shh* of Jackson's pen a steady drone in his ears, but far better than the clucking journalists on the Boyles' lawn. Ron Boyle scratched at his hearty mustache and leaned back against the mantel.

"When did this all start?" Jackson asked. "This personality change?"

"Maybe…a year ago?" Adrian said. Her gaze dropped to her lap again. "He had been happy for so long. When he came home, he was just glad to be here with us…excited to play with his brother…and then…" She swallowed hard.

Jackson made a note on her pad. "Was there a trigger that you're aware of? Something that changed for Gregory?" She was asking the usual questions, but her words felt different today. Tentative. They weren't just looking to confirm a suicide—they had to rule out homicide because of Gregory's history with some serious bad-guy kidnappers, though Petrosky couldn't see a kidnapper showing up to off a victim two years after they'd let him go home. This was probably a waste of time, but the way the Boyles were behaving…

Adrian pursed her lips and shrugged. Sluggish movements as if she were stuck in invisible quicksand. "No trigger…I don't think. He was just…upset, like I said. Kinda withdrawn. But we did everything we could…sent him to the school counselor…I signed him up for 4-H clubs, for Boy Scouts…for anything I could think of. Wholesome activities. He refused to go to any of them. And he kept on…being upset."

*Yeah, he kept on being upset because Boy Scouts doesn't cure depression.* Nor did any number of wholesome activities. Gregory had to have been severely traumatized by his kidnapping and five years of captivity, and puberty might have worsened matters too—no matter how he appeared just after his return, trauma sometimes showed up in unexpected ways. How could they ignore that, pretend it was something you could cure with a camping trip? "Define upset," he said now.

"Just what I told you," she said.

"Crying?" Jackson asked.

"No."

"Nightmares?" Petrosky said.

Adrian frowned. "Not that I knew about."

From the fireplace, Ron shook his head. "He never talked about any of it," the man said. "Never told us a thing."

So either the Boyles had allowed their traumatized child to keep everything bottled up, or they were holding back now—probably both. Were they embarrassed about his depression? Ashamed they hadn't been able to help him? Both reactions were common after a child's suicide, not necessarily suspicious. He didn't want to imagine this boy sinking further into despair until he thought suicide was the only way out, but it happened. Petrosky had been there himself, precariously close to swinging from his own rafters —well, if rafters were guns, and the rope a bullet straight into his gray matter. If he could just piece together an escalation, see a pattern to Gregory's worsening depression, he could put the case to bed with a clear conscience. And yet...

Petrosky refocused on Ron Boyle—the man's arms crossed again, jaw rigid. *Shifty bastard.* "Did you ever medicate him?"

"Oh, he was doing plenty of that on his own," Ron snapped. "I caught him drinking my beer once."

Beer? That was Gregory's big bout with deviance? "I don't mean beer. Anything prescribed by a psychiatrist that might have actually alleviated his depression?"

"He wasn't depressed," Adrian said and blinked—too slowly. For a moment, he wasn't sure she'd open her eyes back up. *Are we boring you?*

Petrosky raised an eyebrow. "I think most psychiatrists would disagree on that one."

"Obviously, he was sad," Ron said to Adrian. His voice was quieter now, though it maintained its hard, angry edge—a tone that almost sounded like blame. But who did he blame: himself, his wife, or Gregory? "Remember when he used to say stuff...that he felt different? That he wasn't himself anymore?"

"He was messing around," Adrian said, voice sharp but sleepy, the edges muddled like she had marbles in her mouth. But bright spots of pink rose in her cheeks. So she had emotions after all, even if there was a disconnect. She must have popped a pill to take the edge off.

Jackson lowered the notepad. "Did he make any statements to suggest he had thoughts of harming himself?"

Silence filled the room and pressed against Petrosky's rib cage until Ron sighed. And nodded.

"What did he say?" Jackson asked.

Ron frowned at his wife, who had her eyes locked on her knees. He kept his gaze on her and raised his voice: "He said, 'Little Greggie is dead.'"

*Well there's foreshadowing for you.*

"Yeah, because he was *angry*," Adrian said, and suddenly, her brow furrowed, as if she'd just recalled something critical. Her eyes cleared. "I...he didn't act depressed...there was no way we could have known. But he had to have been, I guess...since he did this." The woman had skipped right to acceptance. Unless ignoring her role in her son's death was her version of denial.

"He was just bad," Stevie said, leveling his gaze at Petrosky. *What the...* Petrosky waited for Mom or Dad to speak up, to show an ounce of sympathy for their eldest son, but Adrian just looked at her lap. Ron Boyle raised one beefy hand and massaged his neck. Somewhere, a clock chimed.

Not a single word of disagreement? These assholes were acting like it was a relief that their "bad" child was gone. His breathing was suddenly too loud. "With his alcohol use, his depression, and his history of *badness*," Petrosky said, the word bitter on his tongue, "you still believed it was okay to leave him home alone this week?"

Ron dropped his hand. "It was only a few days, and he said he had studying to do."

Petrosky narrowed his eyes at him, watching the little twitch at the corner of his lips. *Liar.* "It's the beginning of August, sir. Was he in summer school?"

Ron's jaw dropped, but it was Adrian who answered. "No summer school. But he…liked to learn things. He was good at science." She sniffed.

*Bullshit, bullshit, bullshit.* The hairs on the back of his neck vibrated furiously. "What about friends? Anyone he hung out with, who might have come over while you were gone?" Maybe a friend would be able to shed light on Gregory's final days.

Adrian and Ron both shook their heads again. Ron said, "He didn't have friends that he saw on a regular basis. No one ever came over. Anyone he knew from school…I wouldn't even be able to give you a name."

"Seems a little"—*lax*—"uninvolved for someone who lost their child once already."

"He was a teenager," Adrian said. "We couldn't…force him to tell us things."

"Did your son say anything to you before you left? Anything that might indicate his intentions?" *Maybe you just didn't want to deal with him being "upset" anymore.*

Adrian stared at Petrosky. "You think we would have… left him alone if we thought he was going to hurt himself?" But her voice was low, too calm, and she didn't look as devastated as she should have. As any normal person would.

Petrosky's face burned—he'd give anything to have his daughter back. The Boyles were royally fucked up, and Petrosky didn't trust fucked up when the deceased was a child, and the people who were supposed to care about him couldn't even muster a few sad tears after finding his shit-stained corpse swinging from the living room ceiling. He leveled his glare at Ron Boyle. "Passive avoidance, neglect—it's one way to get rid of a bad kid."

Ron Boyle shoved himself from the fireplace and charged, eyes spitting fire—there was the emotion. At the loss, or at the accusation? Jackson stepped between him and Petrosky, one hand raised. "Listen, Mr. Boyle, we're not trying to imply anything uncouth. But we need to know everything you can remember. These are routine questions so we can go back to our boss and tell her we investigated as well as we could before we closed the case. You don't want this popping back up in a few months because we didn't do our due diligence."

Ron's nostrils were still flaring, but he backed off Jackson. His shoulders relaxed. "Do what you have to. But if you ever so much as—"

"Point taken," Petrosky said, but he wasn't even a little sorry. Something was seriously wrong with this family. He backed toward the door. "I'll let Detective Jackson finish up, and we'll have the crime techs inform you when you can return to the house."

"How long will it take?" the boy—Stevie—asked. "All my video games are upstairs, and there's nothing half as cool here."

"We'll let you know," Petrosky said, his eyes on Stevie. *Seriously fucked up, just like his parents.* The boy had crossed his arms like his father and was staring daggers at Petrosky. Agitated—annoyed. And definitely not sad, not one bit. "Though you might have some clean-up work to do before you play video games, kid. Unless your parents want to scrub the living room on their own."

Adrian balked. Ron's face reddened. Petrosky turned on his heel and walked out into the foyer, glancing around for Kennedy. Maybe Kennedy would be more normal—maybe he could shed some light on whatever-the-hell this was. The homeowner was not in the plant-laden entryway, but Petrosky could hear his low voice from somewhere nearby—the kitchen. Jackson's voice murmured in the background, smoothing things over with the whacked-out family in the living room. He'd probably end up in the chief's office by the end of the day.

A boy about Gregory's age sat at the kitchen island, Damon Kennedy across from him in front of the sink, pouring something into a cup from a blue teapot. The boy's eyes were red—a friend of Gregory's? If so, he might know something about the circumstances surrounding his death, or at least whether Gregory had been unhappy, or unhappier, in recent weeks. Petrosky had enough to close the case as a suicide so long as the forensics checked out, but it would be easier to put suicide in the file if others corroborated the story. Especially since Little Greggie Boyle's parents seemed to care less about his death than they had about finding him when he was missing. All those press conferences back then, emotional pleas to bring their child home, and now, not a tear. So help him, if the forensics indicated anything amiss, he'd be back here with cuffs.

Petrosky knocked on the wall at the entrance to the kitchen, and the elder Kennedy nodded in Petrosky's direction. "Everything okay, Detective?"

"Just had a few questions if you have a minute."

Kennedy set the teapot back on the stove and gestured to the barstools. "Of course." He glanced at the hallway, where the voices in the living room rose and fell then rose again.

"Did you both know Gregory well?" Petrosky asked.

Kennedy shrugged. "Just from what his father told me."

Petrosky turned to the boy. "How about you, sir? Were you and Gregory close?"

The boy smiled, the tiniest, saddest little smile and said, "Not really. He spent most of his time in his house. I think he played games online and stuff." Online games? They'd have to look into that. Maybe he met the wrong person in an online world—at the very least, maybe someone there knew him better than his family seemed to.

The elder Kennedy cleared his throat. "He was a troubled boy, Detective. Malik stays out of trouble, doesn't like drama. Like his old man."

Petrosky kept his gaze on the child. "Did the other kids at school feel the same way about him?" Loneliness was a suicide trigger too.

Malik shrugged. "He didn't go to my school."

Kennedy cut in: "Malik goes to Sacred Heart, like most of the kids in the neighborhood. The Boyles attend the public school—Anderson."

If the other families in the neighborhood used private school…was it a status symbol, pretentious nonsense, or was there a reason? "Is that strange for the area?" Petrosky asked. "Is Anderson top-notch, or what?"

"No…I…" Kennedy stared into his teacup as if whatever floated there held the key to eternal life. Finally, he sighed. "They're having money problems, have been since a few years after Gregory disappeared. They'd been hiring private detectives and all that." He met Petrosky's eyes. "Not that I can blame them. If Malik disappeared, if something ever happened to him…" He shuddered, face suddenly haggard as if he were unable to imagine such horror, as if he knew it would break him. His dark hands shook around his teacup.

*There's the correct response.*

Malik reached across the island and touched his father's arm, and Kennedy patted the boy's fingers. Steadying himself. "Sorry. I just can't imagine." He cleared his throat. "Anyway, to answer your question, the Boyles used the public schools to avoid digging themselves deeper into debt. Can't hide it now, though."

"Why is that, sir?"

"Filing bankruptcy—their auto dealership is closing. Greg told me about it last week, asked if I knew any good attorneys."

Gregory had been helping his father get his bankruptcy in order? "Greg was in charge of his parents'—"

"Greg senior. Gregory's dad."

Hadn't the guy said his name was Ron?

As if sensing his confusion, Kennedy amended, "He goes by Ron for business stuff out in the community, his middle name, to match the dealership—it was his dad's place before it was his."

*Thud, thud, thud*—rubber-soled footsteps from the hallway. Petrosky turned to see Jackson enter the kitchen, her lips a tight line, eyes blazing like she wanted to punch him in the throat. He turned back to Kennedy.

"Is your wife around, Mr. Kennedy? It'd be great to speak to her, ask if she saw or heard anything unusual." Probably a moot point, but Petrosky couldn't shake the feeling that the Boyles were hiding something.

"My wife died five years ago," Kennedy said, and Petrosky refocused on his face. "It's just us here."

*Always the good ones who go young.* He swallowed hard. His mouth was too dry to speak.

Malik wiped his nose, and Kennedy passed the child a paper towel. "If you have any other questions, Detectives, feel free."

Petrosky nodded and finally cleared his throat. "Thank you, Mr. Kennedy." They were being dismissed, but they were done with the Boyles too—at least until the forensics came back. "We'll show ourselves out."

**3**

―――――――

THEY KNOCKED on the door of every neighbor who had a direct line of sight to the Boyle house—a dozen homeowners with wide eyes that glittered with something too close to excitement—but none had seen or heard anything strange. No noises overnight. No emotional disturbances or odd behavior from Gregory in recent days. One mentioned seeing a small truck at the front curb of the Boyle house as she arrived home from work four days prior, but she'd been unable to tell make or model—too dark outside to see well— and none of the neighbors' doorbell cams had caught it either. A truck at the curb didn't necessarily mean anything, of course. They'd have to ask the Boyles. But not today. They'd wait for forensics before they headed back to see those irritable pricks.

Jackson remained quiet at his side, professional and stalwart, but her energy pricked his skin like little zaps of electricity. She was angry at him. To her credit, she never let that interfere when they had a mission to accomplish; if she did, she'd probably spend every other day forgoing work just to kick Petrosky's ass.

By the time they finished canvassing the neighbors, the sun was blazing, their shadows dark puddles around their feet—lunchtime. Petrosky's stomach grumbled. From the sidewalk in front of the Boyles' house, a lone reporter—the one with blue eyeliner and the overly invasive mic—glanced his way.

Petrosky stepped into the road and paused at his Caprice's driver's door. "Let's stop at Rita's on the way back to the station. I need some—"

"Was that really necessary, what you did to the Boyles?" Jackson shot from the sidewalk; she'd parked her SUV closer to the house, like a fool. "They're suffering, this is the worst day of their lives and you…messed with them."

*There it is.* Good thing he'd decided to drive his own wheels instead of riding with Jackson today. His plan to pick up a new faucet for the neighbor girls was about to make his lunch hour much more pleasant.

Petrosky dropped the door handle and said over the top of the car: "Did you see them? Their child is dead, and they didn't even seem upset except to tell us they didn't want an autopsy—and any parent should want that exam done." He'd seen it hundreds of times, parents waiting on autopsy results as if it would help them sleep better, all of them desperate to know their child went as painlessly as possible. He'd been one of them, though Julie's results had done nothing to calm his worst fears. He met Jackson's eyes. "They just want to stick him in the ground so they can forget about it."

"They were plenty upset, and grief shows up in weird ways, as does depression; anger, agitat—"

"They were agitated that we were there, not because he was dead. It's fucking weird." Petrosky glanced past Jackson. The reporter was looking intently at them now—she took a step closer. Then another.

*Not today, lady.* Petrosky jerked open the car door. "See you back at the station, Jackson."

---

His faucet errand went smoothly—as did his quick stop at Rita's diner—and by the time he arrived back at the precinct, his nerves had settled. Maybe Jackson was right; maybe he'd been too harsh. He'd been a little edgy this week —"oversensitive," she called it—though he couldn't quite put his finger on why.

The bullpen was its usual zesty mix of ink, old files, frustration, and someone's microwaved burrito. Past the pillar that anchored the middle of the L-shaped room, he could see Decantor banging away on his keyboard, and Decantor's short Irish partner, Sloan, at an adjacent desk. But Jackson… she was at Petrosky's desk, albeit on the short edge. Probably because she knew it annoyed him, but maybe she was waiting for him so she could ream him out. Again.

He set the to-go coffees on the desktop, one in front of her. She glanced up, frowning, but took the coffee. "Everything go okay?" she asked.

He narrowed his eyes at her tight lips, the rigid set of her shoulders, the surprising softness of her gaze. Had she forgiven him? Or had something changed? He nodded, then grabbed his chair and gestured to the case file she had open on the desktop. "What've we got?"

"I was just taking another look at Gregory's old kidnapping case. You were…right. About something strange going on with the Boyles."

He raised an eyebrow. "Say that again."

"Don't get too excited. The way you treated the Boyles was absolutely wrong, but—"

"But I was right, you said I was right. This might be the best day of my—"

"Just shut up, you cantankerous bastard. And listen."

He did, sipping his coffee while she tapped the pages in front of them. "So, Gregory vanished after school one day, seven years ago—no witnesses to the abduction. Not a single lead. The police canvassed, put out his photo, but the case went cold. So the parents took matters into their own hands. They hired a private investigator, started having press conferences—they had the media's focus for six months, which is an awfully long time for something like this."

Petrosky nodded. These kidnapping cases usually lost media appeal in a few weeks unless there was something particularly scandalous about it. *If it bleeds, it leads.* "Journalists are a bunch of fickle bitches." *Especially Acharya.*

"They are. And once the articles stopped being printed, Gregory Boyle vanished into the database. The Boyles still had the private eye, though, and all the PI's information is in the file; he called in routinely from the looks of it, at least until they found Gregory wandering around the cemetery."

*Ah, the cemetery.* He'd almost forgotten that part. So much blood in that soil, and he didn't mean the corpses buried neatly beneath the headstones.

Jackson leaned closer, squinting at the tiny print in the margins of the case file. "Gregory couldn't remember his last name at first," she said, "but the birthmark on his upper thigh was a dead giveaway once they arrived at the hospital."

The hospital. So they'd done a full work-up. Petrosky reached for the file himself. Nothing about drugs in his system, so the kid's memory lapse was probably trauma-induced—or the result of brainwashing. "No suspects, no arrests, right?"

She shook her head. "But the kidnapping thing…it was weird." Jackson leaned over the desk toward him and pulled a few pages free. "He said he was yanked off the street by a man with a beard and taken to a warehouse, somewhere nearby because he wasn't in the car that long. The police showed him pictures of every viable warehouse within a forty-mile radius—nada. Gregory said the bearded man brought a bunch of food every morning, all his meals at once, but that he was alone the rest of the time."

Petrosky tried to imagine a seven-year-old kid sitting in a dark corner…for all of his waking hours. His stomach turned. "So, what did he do all day?"

"He said he sang. Kid had it in his head that he was going to be the next winner of *America's Got Talent,* but he can't carry a tune to save his life, according to the last detective on the case, anyway."

Petrosky squinted at the tiny writing. Detective Harris. The name sounded vaguely familiar, but he couldn't connect it to a face. "We'll go visit Harris, see what he remembers."

"No can do there."

"Shit, did he die? Why are all the people we need dead?"

"What?" Her eyes narrowed. "You mean Gregory? Who else is dead?"

"I...sorry, I don't know where that came from." He picked up his coffee cup, his hand shaking as he brought it to his lips. *What the hell is happening?* Was it his heart? His chest didn't hurt...not really. "So, why can't we talk to Harris?"

"Oh, we can talk, but we can't visit—guy retired to Hawaii, lucky bastard."

"That ain't lucky."

"Only because your Polish ass would be redder than a lobster in about five minutes."

"Exactly." He sent coffee down his gullet—acidic. Burning.

She frowned and leaned back in the seat. "And get this: there's one call from the PI on file six months ago. He stopped calling after Gregory came home, no calls for a year and a half, and then he suddenly picked up the phone to ask if we'd gotten any new leads. Sounds like he's still on the payroll, maybe looking for the kidnappers."

But Petrosky would still be looking, too, if it were his kid —or his case. Then again...he hadn't kept going when it was his child. He'd given up until Julie's killer murdered another woman and dragged him back into the fray against his will. Maybe, despite their inherent weirdness, the Boyles were better parents than he'd ever been.

And yet... He sipped at his coffee again, forcing it over the lump in his throat, the acid churning in his guts. "There's something wrong here, Jackson. I don't know exactly what it is, but I feel it."

Her eyes narrowed, thoughtful. "It's strange that the Boyles didn't bother disclosing their PI even if the kidnapping isn't the case we're actively investigating. I mean, they spent money they didn't have on the PI and not a dime on therapy for their child? And their other kid, Stevie—Jesus Christ, that kid's a psycho if I ever met one."

*Hell yeah he is.* Petrosky closed the case file. "Let's start a year ago when the parents say Gregory's attitude changed. We'll talk to his friends, the school. And the neighbor kid said he was alone a lot, probably playing online—I'm sure Scott will pick up his laptop from the house, grab anything else useful from Gregory's room." He didn't think they'd find laundry pods or paraphernalia from some random internet death-challenge, but you never knew. Petrosky'd heard stranger. And he'd definitely seen worse.

**4**

———

TWENTY MINUTES LATER, they were in Jackson's SUV headed toward Anderson, Petrosky sipping the dregs of his cold, bitter Rita's coffee. His notion that something was wrong with the Boyles grew heavier with every passing minute, weighting his flesh like concrete, making his headache throb.

"So what'd Harris have to say?" Jackson asked, fiddling with the GPS.

*Waste of a goddamn phone call.* "That asshole doesn't know shit. Said he took careful notes, put it all down, even his impressions of the family. Only thing he added was that something was off with the mother after Gregory came home—when he started the investigation up again. Like she'd lost her will to live during the time Gregory was gone. He thinks drug use." Petrosky sniffed. "I think something's wrong with the whole lot of them." He glanced out the window at the car beside them, a Chrysler convertible with the top down. The young metrosexual guy inside was driving with his knees, phone in his hands, typing with his thumbs.

*Jackass.* Petrosky scanned Jackson's floorboards—spotless. He could almost see fresh vacuum tracks. Jackson's eyes were on the road, focused on the traffic, on assholes like the guy beside them. Petrosky rolled down the window, squinted in the sideview—clear—and tossed his coffee cup at his neighbor's windshield.

The man swerved, narrowly close to Jackson's much larger Escalade, and fumbled the phone onto the floorboards by his feet. *That's what you get, dickhead.* He raised furious eyes and a finger to Petrosky, yelling something, but his words were sucked away by the wind on the highway and the whining of rubber on asphalt.

Petrosky raised his badge, hand halfway out the window, and waved. Then the window slid up of its own accord; Petrosky yanked his arms back inside to avoid losing them to the road. "Hey!"

Jackson released the power window button. "We had a deal, Petrosky. What if he'd crashed?"

Petrosky sniffed and slid his badge back into his pocket. "One less idiot in the gene pool."

"Honking only. Make them smear their lipstick, make them drop their cell, but you can't—"

"Okay, okay." Petrosky ran a hand over his jowly face. Had he shaved this morning? And the flesh on his face was tight, sensitive—just touching the stubble made his nerve endings sing. He'd been worried that something was wrong with the Boyle family. Maybe something was wrong with him.

*Good thing we're going to see a shrink.*

---

THE BUILDING WAS nice as far as schools went: one long line of rambling red brick, no windows along the front, double glass doors dead center like a dull, cycloptic eye. Maybe twenty cars in the lot—teachers and administrators getting ready for the upcoming school year. A few more days and the concrete turnaround would be a snarl of steel and frazzled parents trying to pick up little Johnny or Janey to sweep them off to their after-school activities.

The counselor's office was a converted classroom at the

back of the building, complete with windows facing a sunny playground, birds twittering on the sill. During the school year, it'd be the perfect place to watch for shady characters. Or to stalk little children for signs of unease so she could bring them into her shrink-y grasp.

But she sure didn't look like the stalking type. Nancy Holloway was short but large-boned, with a flowered top that reminded him of the sheets his ex-wife had put on their bed—like sleeping in the freaking garden. Light ginger hair with dark roots. She was elbow deep in a brown cardboard box when Jackson knocked on the door. "Mrs. Holloway?"

She smiled. Crooked front teeth just this side of yellow, thick lips, blue eyes so dark they were almost violet. Or were they actually violet? "Yes, that's me. Come on in and have a seat. Just getting things ready for Monday morning." She slid the now empty box to the floor beside the desk. From the looks of the room—a few photos, two notebooks, no knick-knacks—it was the only box she'd brought.

"You pack light," Petrosky said.

"I'm only here two days a week. The county has limited funding, so I have to travel a bit." She slipped behind the desk and into her chair with surprisingly lithe movements, like she'd been a trapeze artist in another life.

They sat across from her scarred walnut desk. "We'll get right to it, ma'am," Jackson said. "What can you tell us about Gregory Boyle?"

"Ah, Gregory." She sighed, glancing at the wall—at a photo of her and a rail-thin man with the face of a squirrel, both of them in bright flowered leis. She really loved flowers. "Is it true, what I heard on the news this morning?"

Petrosky leaned back in his seat. "Depends what you heard."

She frowned. "That he's...dead?"

Petrosky nodded.

She laid a hand on her ample bosom—if she'd been wearing pearls, she'd have been clutching the shit out of them. "Poor dear. And yes, I met him about two years ago, a few months after…you know. After he came home."

"Do you know why they sent Gregory to you instead of taking him to another professional?"

Her eyes narrowed. Definitely violet. Unnatural. People did weird things in the name of beauty. "Meaning?"

Petrosky raised a hand. "Nothing against you; I know you do good work here. But our files say that after he was returned home, he didn't see a shrink right away despite the hospital recommendation to do so—despite such a major trauma. They waited until the beginning of the school year specifically to send him to you."

Holloway assessed each of them in turn, gaze level—total shrink move. "I can't really say why they made that choice. I don't generally concern myself with why parents want one therapist over another; I just care that they're there. That the child is happy. His wellbeing is my only concern…*was* my only concern." Her lip trembled, but it stilled just as quickly.

Petrosky watched her fingers, one hand massaging the other—short fingers, but strong-looking. "And was Gregory happy, Mrs. Holloway?"

Her gaze rested on his face. "You know…he was happy, at least for that first year. Seemed to be adjusting so well to school, made great strides in all his classes."

Jackson cocked her head. "He integrated right into mainstream middle school classes?"

She pursed her lips. "Made very good grades, As and Bs, though he was a little slow with reading. That was often his main complaint, actually—that his English teacher was too hard on him, too demanding, that she should let him off the hook a little, that kind of thing."

*Huh.* As and Bs in regular classes seemed unusual for a kid who'd been locked up for five years without so much as a real conversation, let alone a book. Petrosky leaned closer and settled his elbows on his knees. "Did he ever tell you that he'd had a bit of a break from education? That he'd never had any schooling in the five years he was gone?" The case files said they'd asked Gregory about that—no schoolbooks, no reading materials of any kind, nothing. Were the reports wrong, or had Gregory lied about his captors and what they'd provided him? Or was the kid a genius?

She was already nodding. "Yes, no school, that's what he told me, but I'm not sure I believed it."

*Me neither, sister.* Petrosky waited for her to continue, and when she looked down at her hands, Jackson prompted her: "Ma'am? Why didn't you believe him?"

"Well…little things, really." She raised her head. "He said he hadn't read a single book in those five years, but he knew about *Romeo and Juliet*, something they don't cover in elementary school. He knew *The Grapes of Wrath* well enough to give a basic synopsis. And though his writing wasn't great, he was able to put an essay together pretty well, nothing at all like you'd expect from a kid who'd had no formal schooling since age seven. At seven, they're barely reading—definitely not writing comparative essays."

"Did you bring this up with the last detectives?" Harris had reopened the case when Gregory returned two years ago, but he hadn't gotten anywhere. The description—a bearded man—hadn't been enough to narrow the suspect pool, especially when they'd already looked at everyone at the school and those in the surrounding neighborhoods.

"I…no, actually I didn't. It was odd how easy it was for him to reintegrate, but I thought maybe he just didn't want to talk about his abductor—perhaps not give them any credit if they had educated him. I assumed we'd begin to work through those issues this year."

Jackson sniffed. "Seems like a long time to treat a kid without a breakthrough."

But Petrosky knew how hard it was to help someone, especially if the client was uncooperative. He wasn't sure how Dr. McCallum, the precinct shrink, had dealt with him all these years, but he was glad for it. Without the doc, Petrosky would surely be in a gutter somewhere…or worse.

"Healing is a process," Holloway said, bringing him back.

"When he first started coming, he had trouble remembering the most basic of things. He wasn't sure what the car that took him looked like, went back and forth on the kidnapper; sometimes he said the man had a red beard, sometimes black. I think he was torn between trying to forget so he could move on and voicing those memories as a way to purge them—admitting that it had even happened."

"Did he make any progress facing those issues—voicing them?" Or had the inability to forget his pain finally eaten Gregory alive?

She shook her head sadly. "Progress can be slow with trauma victims, especially if they're trying to forget a traumatic event. Even when he spoke of his time alone in the warehouse, singing, the details changed often—sometimes he sang one song, sometimes another. Confused. But..." Now her eyes clouded. "He really didn't have traditional symptoms of trauma, not what you'd expect from a child kept in captivity for five years."

The world quieted—even the subtle twittering of the birds vanished. Petrosky could hear the *thunk-thud* of his own heart.

"Do you think he wasn't kidnapped?" Jackson asked finally.

She balked. "No, of course, I don't think he was lying. I'm simply pointing out that his reaction didn't follow the expected patterns, and any of a million things could cause that."

Petrosky shifted in his seat. This was going nowhere. "You said he was happy for the first year after he came home...around age twelve to thirteen, right? What changed after that?"

"Well, that I can't say. But he came back from summer break last year looking...thinner. Down. And he no longer wanted to talk about his teachers. Instead, we talked about his family, his mother in particular. He said..." She averted her eyes, gaze locked on that flowery picture again. "He said he thought his mother didn't love him."

*Whoa.* Mrs. Boyle had definitely been acting strangely—dull and dry-eyed—but had she been actively neglectful? Uncaring? Or was it abuse? "Did he discuss any specific reasons for this feeling?"

"Not really. He was quite closed off about it, just spoke in generalities. I didn't have enough to be suspicious of wrongdoing. No indications of abuse or the like."

"Had he ever expressed this before? Any ongoing tension in the home since he returned?"

She shook her head. "Things at home seemed to be going well, actually, at least during that first year. He golfed with his father, ate family dinners. Some tension between him and his younger brother, but nothing too out of the ordinary. Name-calling, that kind of thing."

Ah, Stevie, the little psycho who'd been more worried about his video games than his dead brother. The kid seemed douchey, but it was unlikely he'd be able to drive Gregory to kill himself, and Stevie sure hadn't murdered him. *Murder?* Was Petrosky really thinking that? But he was, if only so they could rule it out.

"What about friends?" Jackson was asking. "Was he popular? All that publicity…" She shrugged.

"He didn't have anyone he connected with, not really. The only kids he ever talked to weren't running in a good crowd. He got into a few fistfights, suspended…twice, I believe. Nothing major, just schoolyard scuff-ups. I don't believe he had anyone he considered a friend."

Major trauma. Loneliness. Lack of social supports. A mother who "didn't love him." That was a recipe for depression if he'd ever heard one. "Sounds like he was acting out."

"I think the other children…they shied away from him. Like he was contagious or something." She dropped her gaze to her lap. "Children can be mean," she said to her hands.

*And bullying can kill.*

She sniffed and straightened once more. "But he lashed out at people who wanted to help him, too. Punched the school nurse clean out three weeks before summer break last year."

Petrosky's jaw dropped. *Punched her out?* The Boyles sure hadn't bothered to mention that; they'd just said Gregory was "bad." "Was he arrested?"

"No, she didn't want to press charges. He's always had a fear of needles."

"She was giving him a shot?" Jackson asked.

Holloway shrugged. Somewhere up the hall, a door slammed. It suddenly occurred to Petrosky how easy this was—too easy. No concerns about client confidentiality? Dr. McCallum would take his client's privacy to his own grave, whether those patients were dead or not.

He watched Holloway until she met his eyes, then said, "Do you think he was capable of suicide?"

Her gaze did not falter. "If you'd asked me three months ago, at the end of the last school year, I'd have said no. He didn't report any suicidal thoughts or ideations; he talked about plans for the future, wanted to be an architect. Said he wanted to build a house as huge as the warehouse where they kept him, but that he'd make it...beautiful." Her purple eyes filled—*purple like Gregory's dead tongue.* "No, he didn't want to die, not then."

But something had obviously changed.

**5**

---

"He was always a…tense kid."

They'd met the school nurse in her apartment three blocks from the school, the place as clean as you'd expect from someone with a degree in germs. A white sofa, stain-free but nowhere near as expensive as the one at the Kennedys' place, sat beside a white IKEA bookshelf stacked high with paperbacks. The romance novels were the only pop of color in the whole boring place. Even Janna Ogden herself sat primly at the kitchen bistro table, spine straight, legs crossed, golden blond hair cut cleanly just below her chin. But she had sparkling brown eyes that radiated warmth —like any good school nurse, he supposed.

"Always a tense kid?" Jackson asked now. "You knew him before the abduction?"

"Of course. I used to work over at the elementary school, but I transferred to the middle school when Yolanda—sorry, Mrs. Dunn—retired."

Petrosky glanced at Jackson as she pulled a notepad and a pen from her jacket. "Tell me about Little Greggie, before he got so big."

"Well…" Ogden squinted past them as if trying to remember, and maybe she was—he'd been taken seven years ago, and they were asking her to recall further back than that. "I

38

guess I remember more about him than most." She met Petrosky's gaze. "He was always sweet in that quiet kinda way. I worried about abuse briefly, when he was smaller, but there was no evidence of it—no bruises, nothing to indicate an actual problem, and some kids are just shy. I remember him mostly because of that awful fear of needles…all medical things, actually. Before he was…um…taken, he once scraped his knee at recess and showed up sobbing because he didn't want me to touch him with cotton." She frowned. "His mom said he used to have nightmares about it, of being sick—that was before the kidnapping, though."

They'd asked about current nightmares—Adrian Boyle had denied it. Was it likely that a boy prone to nightmares would suddenly cease to have them after a major trauma? And why would anyone hide that? A kid having bad dreams wasn't a sign of guilt, not on its own.

"What made you suspect abuse?" Jackson asked, handing the pen to Petrosky. He frowned at it, but took it when she furrowed her brow—*your turn.*

Ogden looked down for just longer than a blink, and when she raised her head again, her eyes were tight. "Well, when he got hurt, he was scared about his mother being angry; he said he worried she didn't love him enough to take care of him. Said he'd be better off running away and finding a new family."

Almost the same thing the school counselor had said— that Gregory believed his mother didn't love him. That was more current, but it seemed Gregory's parents had always been a little fucked up, even before the kidnapping. He wrote: "Boyles = dickwads," then turned back to Ogden. "And this was back when he was seven?"

She nodded and gave them a sad smile. "I'm sure you can see why he was hard to forget."

*Poor kid.* Petrosky wasn't sure what had happened in that house to make seven-year-old Gregory believe his parents didn't care, but psychological abuse was often worse than being hit. And with what he'd seen of the Boyles, he could believe Little Greggie had felt that kind of stress. Maybe he'd refused to tell his therapist or the police about his kidnappers because he was protecting them. Had he come to love them because they'd cared for him in a way his biological parents never had?

Ogden was shaking her head. "In hindsight, I'm not surprised he took off, even though I don't usually put a lot of stock in off-the-cuff remarks; kids say things like that all the time. I hate the way it ended up, but something was very wrong in that house."

*I knew it.* But...*took off?* "Wait, you think Gregory ran away?"

She frowned, brows furrowed. "Of course."

Petrosky and Jackson exchanged a glance, and Petrosky said: "But you never told anyone he might have run off of his own accord, correct?" He'd seen nothing like that in the file, and even if it were true, Gregory hadn't stayed gone on his own. Not at seven.

Her eyes widened. "I absolutely told you, or your department, anyway. That detective who came around right after he was taken...I'm sorry, I can't remember his name, but I'm sure I told him."

Petrosky wrote, "Detective Harris sucks" on the pad. If seven-year-old Gregory had run away, if he'd purposefully gone outside his standard walking route, the police should have expanded the search to a wider radius, and quickly. How far had they canvassed?

Ogden sighed. "We were all torn up about it. Every teacher in that school was a mess—watching every car that dared linger a little too long in the crosswalk, scoping out the joggers that used to run the track when classes were in session." She bit her lip, eyes glassy—genuine sadness. "This is just so awful. I can't believe he's...that he would do that."

"You're pretty forgiving," Jackson said.

She wiped her eyes with her fingertips. "I'm sorry?"

"He punched you in the face just last year, didn't he?"

She winced. "It sounds worse than it was. He was scared."

"I get nervous too when people try to stab me with things," Petrosky muttered. He drew a syringe with a "no smoking" sign over it.

Ogden's lips curled into a half-smile, but she shook her head. "It wasn't like that—there was a chicken pox outbreak three districts over, and we sent home requests for proof that the kids had had the vaccine. Most of the children have the vaccination records in their files, but his parents had an exemption form, and he never brought the paperwork back. All I did was call him down and tell him that it was a requirement for the district during the outbreak, and asked about the form—I didn't have a syringe, didn't even swab his arm."

Petrosky drew polka dots on the pad. "I guess he'd rather be itchy."

"Well, what he wanted wasn't exactly my priority, but I wasn't about to force it on him. I told him if he didn't get his form completed or get the shot somewhere, he'd have to stay home until he received it; or until the outbreak had passed."

He hadn't punched her because of a needle, but because she said he had to…stay home? "I bet he loved that." Petrosky raised his head from his notes.

"Well…yeah. Loved it so much, he punched me in the face, right?" She touched her cheekbone absentmindedly, her eyes on Petrosky's. "I came to with him standing over me, screaming. The only interaction I had with him after the kidnapping, and…" She shook her head. "That sweetness he had when he was small…I guess it had kinda vanished by the time he turned thirteen."

"What happened next? After he hit you?" Jackson asked. He glanced her way; she was frowning at his notepad. He slid it under the table.

"I think…" She bit her lip. "He just kinda walked out of the office. Of course, by then, the vice principal was in the hall—she'd heard the commotion. Greg pushed past her, knocked her down, but there were a few other teachers out, and they managed to stop him. Called his father."

"But you didn't press charges," Petrosky said, though he already knew the answer.

She pursed her lips. "He was just a kid, Detectives, and he'd been through so much." She shook her head. "At least he's in a better place now."

If you believed in the afterlife, maybe. All these worthless platitudes. But Petrosky knew what she meant: Gregory's suffering was over. Emotional pain was sometimes worse than feeling nothing at all.

Petrosky and Jackson said their goodbyes and headed down the apartment stairs and out into the lot. The heat had waned, the breeze redolent with fresh-cut grass and the Queen Anne's lace that grew in the culverts. The orange sun glared as they headed toward the freeway.

"Definitely something weird going on," Jackson muttered, knuckles tight on the wheel. "It sounds like Gregory went through a significant personality change in the last year. It might be the depression, all the acting out, but something had to have happened over last summer to trigger it." She shook her head. "It's so bizarre that with all the media attention this case got, not one station ever mentioned that he might have run away."

"Because they didn't know." Harris had managed to keep the press out of his case, just like Petrosky would have tried to. And this information probably wouldn't have helped anyhow; all running away would have meant was a wider initial search area—a larger radius where he might have found himself in the wrong place at the wrong time to be scooped up by that bearded man.

A horrid high-pitched sound shrieked into existence like a tornado siren, obliterating his thoughts with a vocal timbre that could shatter glass—loud, impossibly loud. Petrosky grimaced. "What the fuck is that?"

Jackson smiled—smug.

The sound came again. Not shrieking. Opera? And his pocket was vibrating. He fumbled his phone from his jacket and scowled at his partner. "Stop changing my goddamn ring tone."

"You have to learn how to fix it sometime."

But he hadn't learned when Morrison used to do it—it felt wrong to learn now. He snatched the cell to his ear. "Petrosky."

"Hey there!" Scott. Deep voice, though he was barely out of puberty. Okay, he was in his twenties, but still.

A horn blared through the phone, and Petrosky pulled it from his ear, looking at it as if he'd be able to see the offending car on the screen. "Where you at, Scott?"

"Driving back to the station, but this can't wait."

*He's been at the Boyle house all day?* Must have found something interesting. Petrosky glanced over and mouthed *Scott* when Jackson raised an eyebrow.

"No way the kid stepped off that chair or kicked it over himself," Scott was saying. "The abrasions along the underside of the rope and the wear on the beam are consistent with him being attached to the rope *before* it was pulled over that rafter."

The look on Petrosky's face must have given him away—Jackson frowned and said, "Shit," as he slipped the phone back into his pocket.

*Shit is right.* Gregory Boyle hadn't wanted to die last night. Someone had helped him.

---

## 6

THE RIDE back to the precinct was filled with uneasy silence, the sky so eerily pink, the light itself felt threatening, as if each sugary beam was poisonous. It made him crave cotton candy. And a cigarette, though he hadn't had one in over a year.

So who'd killed Little Greggie, the Reappearing Wonder Boy?

For now, all they knew was that Gregory had suffered well before he was kidnapped—he'd thought he'd lost his mother's love at seven, and his five-year captivity had done nothing to change that. And he'd talked about running away. Seven-year-olds might spout off when they were angry, but it wasn't as common for them to express the desire without provocation, especially in front of other adults. Now that they had a homicide investigation, they had to examine every possible suspect. The original kidnapper was one. But Mom and Dad weren't off-limits.

He sat at his desk, scouring the file. Gregory Ron Boyle, forty-five, owner of a soon-to-be-bankrupt auto dealership handed down by his father. DUI in his thirties, no other issues with the law. Adrian Boyle, forty-six, one psychiatric hospitalization three months after Gregory was abducted.

Might be the stress of missing her son, but there were probably other issues at play based on what they'd observed at the house. He could almost see that dull glassy look in her eyes, shocked but not necessarily sad; could hear the slow, halting way she spoke. Whether she'd started using in response to the kidnapping, or the drug use had been a predisposing factor to the family's unease, she'd been at it for some time; Harris had suspected drug use two years ago when he'd briefly reopened Gregory's kidnapping case. Even though Harris had found no leads on the kidnapping, there was plenty for Petrosky to review.

An envelope in the middle of the file held a dozen photos of Gregory taken at the hospital the night he was returned. Deep purple scars on his back, thick, like lines from a belt; small circles that might have been scars from cigarette burns on his armpit. Petrosky winced. The kidnappers had worked Gregory over, and he'd still kept whatever he knew about them to himself, denied any abuse at all. At least he wasn't in pain now.

*Yeah, keep telling yourself that.*

An hour in, he found a note at the bottom of a yellow piece of paper three sheets from the back, letters so small Petrosky had to take a photo with his phone and blow the image up to read it. Best use of technology to date.

*Nurse, Janna Ogden, claims Gregory discussed running away in years leading up to the kidnapping. Parents deny this.*

Well, of course the Boyles had denied it. Maybe they hadn't thought it relevant; Julie used to say all kinds of things when she was angry, though, with his work schedule, he'd heard about most of that second-hand. *Julie.* His chest constricted, and he pulled a hot, painful breath through his nose to inflate his rib cage. He sighed it out again.

They'd have to pay Adrian Boyle another visit—both the nurse and the school shrink had suspicions about Gregory's mother. And why had the Boyles refused services when Gregory was found? They'd even exempted him from vaccines. They had claimed fear of needles, but if your kid showed up lethargic, possibly drugged, nutritionally emaciated, scars all over his back, maybe just spent five years getting worked over by a sexual predator, you didn't balk at a needle stick because you hoped gonorrhea would go away on its own. Maybe you gave the kid a little nitrous first, a sedative, but you did what you needed to do to help your child.

Jackson leaned her hip against the edge of his desk. "Got hold of the PI."

"And?" Petrosky asked, closing the file. "He as big a dick as I'm assuming?"

"Bigger." She slid into the seat, the one she claimed as hers even though it was at his desk. "Mancebo says the only thing he ever really came up with, the only thing that made sense, was the kid running away and ending up off the beaten path. Too many cameras on the regular walk home and none of them caught a thing."

But...he was only seven when he was taken. "Who lets their seven-year-old walk home alone anyway?" Were they trying to get him abducted?

"Their house is only a few blocks from the school, straight shot. Dad worked, and Mom looks like she has some issues—addiction maybe. Hard to walk your kid home when the room is spinning."

Emotionally unavailable as well as physically. Petrosky imagined the scars on Gregory's body, the photos in the file —as much as the kid had wanted to leave when he was seven, what the kidnappers had done was worse than ignoring him.

"PI's weird, though," Jackson continued, wincing. "Passionate."

"What'd he do? Try to whisper sweet nothings in your ear?"

"Nah, he wants to keep his balls." Jackson winked, though he was damn sure she was serious. "Everything he said sounded…pressured. Not suspicious, not exactly, but worried. Like he has genuine concern for the family."

"That's his meal ticket, of course he'd be concerned."

"I guess he and Adrian go way back—high school sweethearts. Harris recorded dozens of calls from him right after Gregory vanished, half of them saying he thought Gregory was dead. When I asked Mancebo about it, he claimed it was a matter of statistics."

So the PI had thought the kid was dead, but he kept taking the Boyles' money—his ex-girlfriend's money. Kept sniffing around the case, calling the station all the time. That's what Petrosky'd do if he was a kidnapper—or a killer. "We'll put him on our list."

"Already did," Jackson said. "But he's alibied for the night of Gregory's murder. Got a group of poker buddies ready and willing to claim he was home playing all night and into the wee hours."

"What's his deal, then? Was he wringing them dry?"

"He says he was looking for the kidnapper. Sounds like he wanted to give the Boyles closure." She rolled her neck, stretching, her turquoise earrings catching the sun from the bullpen's window—turquoise…that was her favorite. Were they new? Jackson wasn't one to buy trinkets for herself. But before he could ask, maybe harass her about who had given her the gift, she squared her shoulders and said, "And get this: the PI said he talked to a few kids at the elementary school who said Gregory had problems before he vanished. At seven. Said he was crying a lot, even got sent down to see the school counselor a few times. He could see Gregory being depressed—hurting himself now."

But Gregory hadn't hurt himself, and confirmation of his depressive history made Petrosky uneasy. The parents had definitely held back—but so had Holloway. "You think the middle-school shrink knew about his earlier stint with therapy?"

"They could have been isolated incidents as opposed to regular sessions. The parents, even Gregory, might not have mentioned it when they set him up at the middle school after his return."

Petrosky shook his head and grunted. It was an ugly sound. "I know you're giving them the benefit of the doubt, but I don't like any of this." They'd both had cases where parents had hurt or killed their own children. Maybe the Boyles were just shit parents, maybe they hadn't killed their boy, but they should be cooperating with the investigation. If his classmates knew Gregory was having issues at age seven, Adrian and Ron Boyle most certainly had known. And they hadn't bothered to share it with the people trying to locate their child back then—hadn't shared it with the people investigating his death now.

Jackson's eyes had clouded. "I don't like it either. All that running away stuff… Gregory had to be really scared living there if he actually followed through. Kids are loyal to a fault, especially at seven."

Petrosky nodded. Kids clung to even the worst parents for survival in a world they couldn't navigate themselves. "So what would make seven-year-old Gregory Boyle actually leave?" he muttered, more to himself than to anyone else. But they had no proof that Gregory's threats had come to fruition. Maybe he really had been walking home from school when he was yanked off the street by a bearded man as he'd told authorities.

"Should we take another run at the parents tonight?" Jackson asked.

He was suddenly itching to get into the same room with the Boyles. They'd have to make the notification anyway—let them know their son's death was now a homicide investigation. But they didn't have to do it now. So far, only Scott knew the truth, and that kid kept everything close to the vest. He wouldn't leak it to the press, or to anyone else, before Petrosky and Jackson made it back to the Boyles' place.

"Let's wait a little." Let them sit with their weird detachment and omitted facts. And though Stevie did seem like a douchey turd-burglar of a kid, he wouldn't have been able to actually hurt Gregory, let alone string him up over the rafter —the older boy had at least fifty pounds on him. "We'll give them some time to get nervous."

"Yeah, they're not going to want to talk to you anyway, not anytime soon." Her earrings caught the overhead fluorescents. No hint of the sun against the metal now.

Outside, the world had lost its pink glow as it dipped behind the horizon, turning the sky a deathly ash gray. Corpse gray. His lungs were suddenly too small. He hadn't thought of the sky like that in quite some time—*corpse gray*— but there it was again, the black emptiness of things he'd lost, glaring at him from the encroaching dark.

He cleared his throat and forced out: "I wonder if the Boyles called to bitch about me yet."

"Probably." But her eyes were on his face. Watchful.

Petrosky tapped his pen against the file and turned back to the morose sky.

Shrieking—louder shrieking—coming from his front pocket. He glanced at the incoming number. Doctor McCallum, Ash Park PD's star psychiatrist; the man had helped drag Petrosky out of a few holes, even if most of his past treatment had been mandated. He raised the cell to his ear. "Hey, Doc. We already visited a shrink on this one, but we'll call when we're ready for a consult."

"Oh, this isn't about your case," McCallum said. "I just wanted to check on you this week."

His gut clenched. He glanced at Jackson, who had flipped open the case file and was pretending to study Harris's tiny scrawl. Petrosky swiveled his chair, his back to Jackson, facing the void outside the window. "And why is that?"

The line was silent so long, Petrosky thought he'd dropped the call.

"I understand that weeks like this, days that triggered you in the past…they are easy to forget. A trick of the mind as a form of avoidance. But the only way you'll be able to handle it, to finally let it go, is to face it head-on."

"There's nothing to face, Doc." But the tightness in his chest was more intense, wasn't it? Because now he knew what was wrong. His lungs burned, an aching, pulsing hole widening beneath his rib cage.

"I'm here if you need me, Ed."

Petrosky's jaw hardened. His knuckles ached around the cell. "I hear ya, Doc. I'll let you know." But he wouldn't.

**7**

———————

"WHERE THE HELL have you been, Petrosky?"

*Sitting on the bed. Staring at Julie's night-light. Running my fingers over the spot on the nightstand where I used to keep the Jack Daniels.* "Overslept." He listened to the clang of the stairwell door at his back and headed for his desk.

"Yeah, whatever, just come here." Jackson waved him over to her desk instead and tapped the open file on her desktop. "The Boyles signed releases, and so did Gregory, to share his therapy information." She rifled through the pages on her desk and came up with two sheets: medical release forms. "Remember when you were suspicious of Holloway, Gregory's school counselor? This is why she could tell us what we wanted to know."

He planted his fists on the desktop and squinted at the page. Gregory's sharp, messy scrawl adorned the bottom of the form in Jackson's hand; he'd signed away his privacy over a year ago, and not just to other physicians or insurance companies. The release looked like the shrink could tell damn near anyone about his progress. "Why would he do that?" Even under the best of circumstances, it was strange for a teenager to offer up his personal information. And Gregory had a shaky history with his folks and five years of no contact at all.

51

"They signed because of this." She thrust a new page in his direction, too colorful to be a release form unless it was for clown college—a screenshot from a social media post, *Hill Street Publishing* tagged below their names. "The Boyles are writing a book. They announced it via social media today, comes out in six months."

He straightened. They'd put out a book announcement the day after their child was found dead? "Tactful. If their other kid bites the dust, maybe they'll announce the movie rights are up for auction." Maybe that'd make it sting less. He rubbed at a sore spot above his breastbone and continued: "If they're announcing an upcoming release...it had to be in the planning phase for a while." Was that how books worked?

"Exactly." Jackson shook the paper. "A year almost to the day—social media post hinting at 'something exciting in the works' last September."

Last September. That was... "Right around the time Gregory started acting out."

She nodded. "Maybe he didn't like being put on display, or maybe he felt like he was a prop while they exploited his trauma for their own personal gain. And he was still messed up about the kidnapping, had to be."

But the timing of today's announcement was no accident. "They're trying to take advantage of Gregory's death in order to garner sympathy. And sales." *Those heartless fucks.*

"Right." She tucked the sheet back inside the file folder. "I'm sure the book's mostly done, but this might get them a television series deal."

"Or a punch to the kidney."

"Watch it, Petrosky."

"I'm just saying." He rubbed at his temples—his back ached, too, standing here like a tool beside Jackson's desk. He needed more coffee. Or a cigarette. *Both.* "So we have parents concerned with their own agenda—fame and fortune—even as they file for bankruptcy." His mind raced, a million thoughts colliding like droplets of whiskey in a shot glass. "File bankruptcy first, before the release, and any money they make after that can't be taken, right?" He pressed harder on his temples.

Jackson squinted. "I think so? I'm not an attorney, but—"

"And by now everyone's forgotten about Little Greggie. The Boyles need more publicity if they want the book to do well."

Now she frowned. "Wait, are you saying you think his parents killed him to increase book sales?"

"No, I don't think they're that stupid." Though, Gregory's parents did seem like a couple of conniving assholes. "It's just…it's very convenient, you know?" He released his temples and dropped his hands.

"It is. But they were out of town—easy enough to verify their alibi. And any halfway logical person would know we'd be looking extra hard at them for coming out with this book announcement before Gregory's body is even cold. So let's look at what else we know." Jackson was watching him, her expression strange—face still, almost sad. *She better be feeling sorry for Gregory and not for me.*

He shook the thought off. "We know Gregory had an unstable home environment both now and before he was taken. And…" He clasped his hands behind his back, frowning at the file still sitting on Jackson's desktop; at her Styrofoam cup, half full of coffee that looked more like ink. "I think we can assume that he didn't tell the whole truth about his captors. When I was reviewing the case file yesterday, I found photos of him from the hospital, taken the night he was returned. He was stick-thin and had quite a bit of scarring on his back and armpit—looks like ongoing abuse, not consistent with what he told authorities at the time, and definitely inconsistent with him being locked up with no human contact or violence. If he was isolated, he should barely have been communicating, let alone getting knocked around."

Petrosky paced, heading for the far wall of the room, where the windows belched hazy gray morning light onto the floor. From the corner of his eye, he saw Decantor glance his way from his own desk just beyond the pillar, his eyebrow raised. Guy had a thing for every pop star out there, especially the damn Kardashians, though he still wasn't sure if they were singers or not. Petrosky smiled, flipped him off, and turned on his heel, away from the window, back and forth, back and forth in front of Jackson's desk. "There's no way that kid was able to hop right back into school without some instruction…someone was teaching him. They educated him. It takes time to do that, patience, and for him to be protecting them—"

"He's loyal to them, despite whatever injuries they gave him. Or at least he was." Jackson frowned at the paperwork on her desktop. "Maybe whoever took him…maybe they came back for him. Hung him from that rafter to make sure he didn't tell anyone who they were. The original kidnapper is clearly predisposed to violence."

But they could have murdered him at any time—why now, two years after he'd come home? He raised a hand to his face; even his skin felt tired. "They could have picked him off years ago."

"Maybe they thought the book would lead police to them," Jackson said. "Figured without Gregory's identification, his testimony, it'd never stick."

But he'd never identified them before—never gave the police anything useful. Why now? *Why now?* He frowned at the floor, at his still-pacing sneakers, trying to imagine the type of person who'd abduct a kid, educate him, and care for him to the point that Gregory would refuse to disclose their identity. A person who'd then watch him move back home with his parents and wait two years to show up again and murder him. Petrosky'd seen a lot of kidnapping cases, a lot of child murder cases, but he'd never seen a perp so inconsistent. This guy had to be a maniac…unless there was more than one kidnapper. One who read books and let Gregory free in that cemetery, and one who beat him and came back later to finish him off? A male-female team might operate like that. Maybe the bearded man was the douchebag, and the woman cared for him, educated him. Or the other way around. But they could be overthinking this; perhaps the kidnapper had let him go because Gregory had simply aged past his usefulness. He was lucky; for many perps, children no longer held attraction once puberty hit, leading them to kill the kid to keep them quiet. And pedophiles often convinced children, and themselves, they had a real, loving relationship—perhaps Gregory had felt this attachment to his kidnapper, his abuser, and was so ashamed he'd refused to discuss it.

And still...why now? His hands were tight balls at his sides.

So many unanswered questions. But one thing was certain: Little Greggie's death was intentional. And whoever had killed him had done it very carefully to make it look like a suicide. That took time. Planning. This cold-blooded fuck had strung up a fourteen-year-old boy like it was nothing.

Petrosky stopped pacing, trying to relax his aching hands. "Let's go visit the Boyles again. I think it's time they answered some questions."

**8**

———————

THE BOYLES' living room was much as they'd left it yesterday, with one major difference—no body. Petrosky glanced at the ceiling, at the rafters, looking extra hard at the middle one where the rope had been. The wood there, so shiny yesterday, was now raw and gouged where Scott must have removed his forensic samples. If there was anything there to find, Scott would find it, no matter how deep he had to dig.

Ron Boyle had led them inside, then stood in front of the fireplace as he had at the Kennedys', arms crossed, again, shoulders square—taking up space—holding a water glass against his elbow like he might crush it in his fist. The floor in front of the couch was stained but not with shit now— lighter. The caustic odor of bleach still lingered despite the open windows. The nasty chair was gone, too, probably tossed in a dumpster or sitting in Scott's lab. Yet, despite those differences, if Petrosky squinted, he could still see Gregory's body. Limp. Swinging. His chest throbbed—slow, painful, hot.

"So, what is it this time?" Ron glowered.

Petrosky's sympathy vanished—what kind of person didn't want to help the police when the case was about their own child? *Someone guilty.* But even the most aggressive of guilty men knew how to tone it down when they were talking to the cops. He ignored Ron, opting to watch the man's wife—the woman Gregory had been so certain didn't love him.

Adrian Boyle sat alone on the couch, staring straight ahead, eyes glassy and dull as if she'd been shot up with dope. Harris was right, no way this was shock. Stevie was nowhere to be seen.

"We have some questions," Jackson said. Her voice seemed to come at Petrosky from a distance as he made his way across the room and sat on the couch a cushion away from Gregory's mother, leveling his gaze in her direction. She did not blink. Did she even know he was there?

"Mrs. Boyle?" he said.

She turned, slowly, slowly, eyes blank.

"Have you taken anything today, ma'am? Drugs?"

Ron's footsteps clapped nearer over the hardwoods as if they, too, were agitated—he stopped right below where Gregory had been hanging. "What's that got to do with—" Ron began, but Petrosky silenced him with a hand. "We have a few things to discuss, and it'd be better if she were sober."

She blinked.

"She's sober, she's just... The pills are from the doctor. Valium. She might have had a little wine today, too. Nothing wrong with that, especially under the circumstances."

Petrosky nodded—he knew more than he cared to admit about a liquid breakfast—but he kept his gaze on the missus. She blinked again, lethargic, as if her eyelids were too heavy. A little tranquilizer kept you sane; too much would make you numb. Among other things.

"How long have you been taking it?" Was it possible that her lack of tears, her bland expression, were side effects as opposed to active uncaring?

"About a year," Ron answered for her, a tightness in his voice under his agitation—worry. "Year and a half, maybe. She took something else right after the hospitalization, but that stuff didn't help."

Ah yes, the hospitalization a few months after Gregory's

disappearance; that had been in the file. But she'd started this medication regimen around the same time Gregory's depressive symptoms—his acting out—had begun; around the same time the book deal came through. *Interesting.* Not that psychological issues always took an expected course, but... "What made you start new medication last year, Mrs. Boyle?"

Adrian narrowed her eyes as if having trouble recalling. Or maybe she was trying to remember her life before losing a child, which was impossible; every memory from the moment your child breathed their last was tainted with the ache of grief. His heart squeezed, sharp, stabbing, and released.

"I just couldn't stop thinking about it," Adrian said now. "I felt so...guilty."

Was she talking about the kidnapping? What had changed in that last year?

"Guilty about what, ma'am?" Jackson's voice was soft and thick with empathy, another mother who'd lost her eldest son. "It wasn't your fault—not his kidnapping and not his death."

But they didn't know that, not for certain. *And she gets onto me for lying to suspects.* Was that what the Boyles were? Suspects?

Adrian licked her lips, but they remained dry. "I guess it wasn't anything major. I just...had trouble connecting once he came home. And he was doing the wrong things...he started taking money from my purse." Her words were coming faster now: forced, agitated. His shoulders tensed. Without the drugs, she'd probably be talking too fast to understand. "And he started hoarding food, too, taking entire boxes of snack cakes to his room and eating them all in one sitting. I didn't...like who he'd become."

Petrosky's chest burned, his lungs tight. Most parents who'd lost a kid would give anything to have them home again, and she'd squandered it because she couldn't accept that he'd changed in the five years he'd been missing. No wonder Gregory had been upset last year—he had to have felt that. The distance. The disdain. And he'd responded by acting out, punching nurses and the like, trying to get someone, anyone, to pay attention. To *care*.

Adrian sniffed again, but no tears welled in her eyes. "You must think I'm terrible."

*Yes, I do.* Petrosky leaned back against the arm of the couch. "Terrible is irrelevant. What's curious is the reports we got from the school and the detective who was initially assigned to the kidnapping case. You claim these issues started after Gregory came home, but they seem to think there were problems at home before he was abducted."

"Well…" Ron paused, and Petrosky drew his eyes from Adrian to the man standing before the couch. Ron's hairy bare feet stayed planted on the bleached hardwood, nothing between his flesh and whatever remnants of Gregory's shit still lingered on that floor. Petrosky suppressed a shudder. Ron sniffed. "There were a few issues, I guess, but nothing that out of the ordinary. Raising kids is hard." He shrugged, probably aiming at nonchalant—*kids, amirite?*—but his posture remained rigid, defiant.

"It's not so ordinary for your child to threaten to run away, not during times of calm with other adults," Petrosky said.

Ron's face reddened like a cartoon character. "He was *seven*. They all talk out of their asses!"

Petrosky agreed, but Adrian's face was what he was really interested in—emotionless. "Tell us about the book, Mrs. Boyle."

Adrian blinked. Petrosky glanced at her husband.

"Don't look at me; it wasn't my idea," Ron snapped. He looked down and abruptly stumbled back toward the fireplace as if suddenly realizing he was standing on the spot that had, until last night, been soaked in his child's fluids.

Adrian sighed. "I was just…trying to make things better… make the best of a horrible situation."

Jackson cocked her head. "Sounds like you were cashing in on your child's misfortune."

"I…*we* were doing no such thing."

"You exploited him before," Petrosky said, and Adrian stiffened. "Put him on display mere months after he got home."

"I didn't—"

"Signed away his right to privacy, even with his shrink." *Stripped away his only outlet for honesty, his only chance to work through what had happened to him.* If Petrosky had thought his own sessions were going to be public knowledge, he wouldn't have said shit. "What kind of thing is that to do to a teenager?"

Ron's jaw hardened, the water glass trembling in his fist, but he covered his emotions with a cough and a glare. Adrian's knuckles were white against her thighs. "We needed to give them the full story," she said. "The person who was writing the book—"

"We don't care about the author. You made a book announcement the day after your son died," Petrosky said quietly, his eyes never leaving her face. "In a homicide investigation that doesn't sit well."

Now Adrian's jaw dropped."Homici— You think he—" Her eyes widened. "You think he was murdered?"

Jackson stepped closer to the couch, carefully avoiding the bleached wood. "We know he was murdered. What we don't know is why."

Adrian stared at her husband, her breath coming too fast; Ron's jaw worked like he wasn't sure whether to cry or scream or bite them. But they'd had their chance—they'd had a chance with their child, and they'd exploited him, they'd blown it, and Jesus Christ, if he had just one more day with Julie—

"I'm hoping it wasn't one of you," Petrosky said, "or the kid you have left is going to grow up without you the same way Gregory did."

Ron's face crumpled. Adrian was shaking—more surprise and less guilt, he thought, but he'd been fooled before.

"It's not their fault!"

Jackson whirled around, but Petrosky didn't have to move to see the younger boy behind his partner. Stevie crouched on the carpeted steps halfway down the open staircase, his hands curled around the wooden balusters. How long had he been there? When he saw Petrosky looking, he leapt to his feet and careened down the remaining steps like a lanky skier who'd forgotten his equipment.

"It's all *Greg's* fault!" Stevie shouted, face as red as his father's. "He's a faker, that's what he is, a big fat faker and a jerk. He didn't even get taken, that fucking liar."

*Whoa.*

"Stevie, you shut your mouth," Ron snapped. "Don't talk about your brother like that."

But Petrosky was already standing, edging closer to the boy. "You think he faked the kidnapping? Why would he do that, son?" If it was true, it'd probably help with book sales—the more scandalous the story, the better.

"*Attention*." Stevie said it five octaves higher, sing-song, his eyes shining. "They all thought he was *so perfect*. He left, and they all talked about him. He came home, and it was *still* about him. About *Little Greggie*." He pointed a slim finger at his father. "You should hate him, too. I heard you through the walls. He made you and Mom fight all the time."

Usually, parents fought when they lost a child, not when they got him back. But grief ate adoration for breakfast, especially when looking into your wife's eyes—eyes just like your child's—hit you like a knife to the belly. Getting a child back couldn't repair the things that had been destroyed. It might help, but not everyone got a second chance, not with their kid, not with their spouse.

If Julie had lived, maybe his marriage to Linda would have stuck, too. He pushed the thought aside.

Ron had sweat on his upper lip. "Your mother and I fighting had nothing to do with Gregory—"

"It *did*. You said his name all the time! He should have just stayed gone, he—"

"Steven!"

"He deserved what he got!" Stevie screamed. "He's the one who ran away. I'm the one who stayed. I should get credit for that."

*Ran away.* There were those words again, and Stevie's eyes shone with certainty. But...he would have been five when Gregory disappeared. What did he remember with such clarity? "You're sure about that, Stevie? That he ran away?"

The boy's nostrils flared. "Of *course* I'm sure. He said he was going to go move in with his friend. I *saw him packing* before school."

Something crashed—Petrosky turned to see Ron staring dumbly at his son, mouth gaping like a fish, the remains of his water glass sparkling around his bare toes. "Go meet his... Why wouldn't you tell anyone that? Why didn't you—"

"I didn't want him here anymore." He crossed his scrawny arms—so many freckles, this kid. And the birthmark on his wrist looked so much like the one on Gregory's thigh that Petrosky's gaze drifted to the notched rafter again, then to the lighter floor in front of the couch. Which one of them had cleaned it? Mom? Dad? If he was a betting man—and he was—he'd guess Mom. She was just detached enough to pull it off without puking.

"I just wanted him to go away," Stevie said, pulling Petrosky from his thoughts.

"Go away to where, exactly?" Jackson asked.

Now Stevie's eyes clouded. "I...don't remember. Just that he was going to be with his friend."

But Gregory couldn't have gone to stay with another seven-year-old without their parents noticing. Looked like Little Greggie had an older friend. Had he been groomed? Had someone convinced him to run off? Someone had definitely helped him stay gone. Maybe they were dealing with a planned abduction, a series of steps between the abductor and the child before they finally snatched him up. But was it connected to Gregory's murder seven years later? But again, why now, two years after he came home? *Why now?*

Adrian was rocking on the couch, her hands wrapped around her upper arms. Ron hadn't moved from the halo of shattered glass around his feet. Still processing the fact that this was a homicide, or shocked at Stevie's accusation? Probably both.

"Did Greg ever walk home with anyone besides Stevie?" Petrosky asked. "Like a responsible grown-up? A babysitter?" At seven, most kids were still chasing butterflies into the street. Knowing he ran off to meet his abductor was all well and good, but they needed a name. A description. Anything.

Mom and Dad shook their heads. "No," Ron said. "I would have told the police. And he never mentioned having new friends...he didn't really have any friends, to be honest."

That made sense. Lonely kids were easier marks.

"What about connections on social media? Did he play online video games back before he was taken?" The neighbor had said he played online now, but had it started before he left? The internet was pedophile heaven.

"Nothing like that," Ron said. "He played recently, but he was fourteen. He didn't have a computer back before he... before he was kidnapped."

Adrian stopped rocking. "If I thought he'd run away, if I thought he knew the person who took him, I would have said. I can't believe...god. I just thought he was angry, threatening to run off. Stevie used to say it, too, sometimes, but he never..."

All eyes turned to Stevie.

"I always walked with him. There was no one else with us." When they all kept staring at him, he rolled his eyes. "I wasn't really going to run away; I just got mad."

Petrosky frowned. "If you always walked with Gregory, why weren't you walking with him on the day he was taken?"

"I was sick. I stayed home the day before, and I was going to stay home the next day too. And he packed his clothes. For after school, he said. I wasn't going to be there, so he was going to meet his friend. And then he was gone." He glowered at his mother, nostrils flaring, and whispered: "You all think it's my fault."

"Oh, Stevie, no." Adrian pushed herself from the couch and stumbled past Petrosky, then Jackson, to put an arm around Stevie. He flinched away from her. Not used to the affection? The boy crossed his arms, his eyes angry, dry.

Petrosky raised an eyebrow. "Do you know anything about this friend, Stevie?"

"He said they had a car, so he didn't have to walk much." He sniffed. And shrugged. "That's all. He never said anything else."

*Well, fuck.* And a car… He met Adrian's eyes, then turned to Ron once more. "Do either of you know someone with a dark-colored truck, probably a smaller pickup?"

Ron's brow furrowed. He shook his head. "Not that I can think of. But we do get lots of deliveries for the business, especially now that things are winding down. Boxes of close-out flyers, mailers, and the like."

A pickup wasn't a usual delivery vehicle, but they didn't have enough of a description to put out an APB. Why couldn't the witness have owned a car dealership like Ron Boyle? Then they'd probably know what the model was.

Jackson bent, her face at the boy's level. "I heard Gregory was sad in the weeks before he was taken," Jackson said. "Do you know why, Stevie?"

Steve shook his head, but Petrosky could guess—kidnappers, pedophiles, they could only groom so long before they lost control. The kidnapper might have told Gregory his parents were in trouble or that they'd be hurt if he didn't leave the house—even that his parents simply didn't love him. Perhaps that only the kidnapper would ever want him. By the time Gregory Boyle had left home, the kidnapper had gotten his hooks into the boy—Gregory would have followed him anywhere. He probably didn't feel like he had a choice.

## 9

DR. WOOLVERTON'S shifty eyes were five times too large behind his thick green glasses. Sharp nose. But the scalpel in his hand was sharper.

Woolverton's call had come in as Petrosky and Jackson left the Boyles', and they'd headed for the morgue without so much as stopping for food—much to Petrosky's chagrin. His stomach grumbled. Dr. Woolverton glanced at him with distaste as he set the blade on his equipment tray.

*Smarmy little twit.* But he wasn't really mad at Woolverton; he was just mad in general. And when he appraised Woolverton's face again, it wasn't distaste he saw there, not distaste for Petrosky anyway—hatred of the situation. Of what had been done to this boy.

Gregory Boyle's body had been cleaned, which was a small blessing, though a slight tinge of iron and musk remained beneath the stronger chemicals Woolverton used to do his work. On the table, the boy looked smaller than he had while swinging from the rafters, perhaps because he was no longer strung up by his neck, putting him head and shoulders and trunk above anyone standing below. Perhaps because if you ignored the bruising around his throat and the Y-shaped incision that bisected his chest and belly, he just looked pale. Asleep. Vulnerable, as he must have looked to the person who had groomed him and taken him. Maybe killed him.

Jackson nodded to Woolverton from her position near the bottom of the table, her gaze appropriately solemn—watchful. "What'd you find, Doctor?" She frowned as Petrosky's phone vibrated with a text message. *Not again.* He reached back and silenced it; the thing was ticklish, like a caterpillar on his ass.

Woolverton clasped his gloved hands in front of his crotch like he expected a swift kick to the dick and was taking evasive measures. "Your vic died between twelve and one. And your man, Scott...I was able to confirm his suspicions. Definitely homicide." Woolverton gestured to Gregory's neck, to the thick purple line where the rope had crushed his windpipe. "I'm sure you noticed the lack of defensive wounds—no scratching, no bruising outside of the single line around the throat."

Petrosky nodded, keeping his eyes off the boy's face. Yes, he had noticed. But murder victims often had defensive wounds elsewhere on the body—wounds from fighting against whoever was trying to put a noose around their neck. "Did you find other marks? Handprints, ligature?" He squinted at the boy's wrists—no sign that he'd been restrained at all.

Woolverton shook his head. "I did not. But I did find something else." He walked down toward the foot of the table, toward the boy's wine-colored toes—all that pooled blood—toward Jackson, who stepped back to give him room. Woolverton gingerly pried apart Gregory's second and third toe.

Petrosky and Jackson both edged closer and peered into the tiny crevice at a dot that might have been a freckle.

Jackson righted herself first. "Is that a needle mark?"

"Indeed," Woolverton said. "He had a heavy dose of tranquilizers in his system: Valium."

Petrosky glanced at Jackson, whose eyes had narrowed. Valium...that was what Adrian Boyle was taking, but Ron had mentioned the pill form—not injectable. "Are the drugs the cause of death?"

Woolverton released Gregory's toes, and the boy's foot settled back into place. A clue now, not a child. "Asphyxiation is still the cause of death, but from the amount of Valium in his system, he was unconscious before they hung him up. Probably didn't feel much of anything, if that's any consolation."

It should be, it should help to know that the boy hadn't suffered, but Petrosky's guts felt leaden and suddenly cold as if he'd swallowed a frozen cannonball. Something was wrong. *Yeah, like the dead kid on the table?* He focused his gaze on Woolverton, trying to tunnel his vision, trying to focus on the task at hand. "Wouldn't that hurt? Getting a needle stuck between your toes like that?"

Woolverton nodded. "Absolutely. And he fought, but not for more than a few seconds. It wouldn't have taken long for him to go limp, especially if he was asleep when they did it." The doc snaked his gloved fingers beneath Gregory's heel and lifted, just enough to gesture to the underside, near the Achilles tendon. "Hard to see with the staining here, but there were some superficial abrasions on the backs of his legs and along his buttocks, all hidden under the mess—the feces. He probably struggled, fell off the couch after he was dosed. Could also be that they dragged him a short distance to the place where they strung him up."

So he was drugged and dragged, and then someone tossed the rope over the rafter and watched the last of the life leak out of him. "That's a lot of work to fake a suicide when so many people kill themselves using drugs." And anyone would have believed he'd slugged back too many of his mother's pills—why bother hanging him? "Couldn't they have shoved some pills down his throat? Made it look like he'd overdosed?"

Woolverton replaced Greg's foot on the table and pulled a light blue sheet over his lower extremities. "Not without tipping us off. Even if I'd missed the needle mark—which I would not have—the pills wouldn't have had time to digest before he died. In order to have that amount of Valium in his blood, there would need to be evidence of more digested pills in his intestines."

Petrosky stepped back from the table, his eyes still on the place where the child's feet rested, inanimate, a tiny mountain range of bone beneath the sheet. "Was he dragged far? Rug burns, anything like that?" A larger male would have just carried the unconscious boy, but being dragged meant their killer was smaller in stature. Stevie's bony wrists flashed in his mind, then vanished. Their killer might be small but not *that* small.

"No rug or carpet burns—your forensic guy looked for fibers already. Wood trace only, and very minor abrasions, perhaps from being dragged off the couch to the floor. If I had to guess, I'd say he was resting on the couch when they dosed him." Woolverton picked up the corners of the sheet and drew it the rest of the way up Little Greggie's body, draping it over his face. The weight in Petrosky's belly lightened but stayed cold as Woolverton said: "However, that is not the main reason I called you down here."

Woolverton headed for the long counter that ran the back of the room, the thing covered with vials and bottles, and returned carrying a clipboard. "I could have called with the cause of death. This is what I needed you to see." He handed the paperwork across the table, over Gregory's shrouded blue form. Petrosky squinted over Jackson's shoulder at the tiny print. Two sets of gray bars glared back, both run through with little green and red bubbles like the glow of a multitude of streetlights over dark pavement. His heart stuttered and stalled.

"Holy shit," Jackson whispered.

Petrosky met the doctor's eyes. "You can't be serious."

"I definitely can be." Woolverton pointed at the top of the page, careful not to lean on the stainless steel table, on the boy, as if he did not want to invade Gregory's space. Petrosky liked him better for it. "The data on the top is from the missing children's database—the DNA from the time Gregory vanished." Petrosky stared at the first set of bars, the green bubbles, the red. "Below that is the DNA I collected from this boy." Woolverton moved his hand and pointed again.

These bars, the green and red bubbles...not the same configuration as the sample above it. Not even close. "What are you telling us, Woolverton? You're saying that this kid—"

"Is not Gregory Boyle." Woolverton pushed his glasses up his nose, shoulders back. Proud. And he should be. *How did no one else catch this?* And Gregory's parents—how the hell could they not know?

"This is insane," Jackson said, beating him to it. "I know my kid, the shape of his face, his toes, his fingers—if some other random child showed up, even after five years, I'd damn sure know it."

Woolverton was nodding. "It's crazy, but it's true. I ran our victim's DNA through the database, hoping to figure out who he was, but he's not in the system."

Jackson was still staring at the page. "Just...wow."

Woolverton smiled, but he didn't exactly look happy—the kind of smile you gave to a dog that puked in your shoes instead of on the more expensive rug. "Exactly what I said."

"You could have told us this over the phone, too," Petrosky said slowly. His stomach growled again—the icy cannonball gone—but no one acknowledged it.

Woolverton leveled his gaze at them. "I've never gotten to give news like this. I wanted to see your faces."

Jackson lowered the clipboard. "Like what you see?"

"Oh, yes."

*Fucking dork.* But one thing was still bothering Petrosky. Running the DNA wasn't automatic in a case where they believed they knew the identity of the victim. "What made you think to run the test in the first place?"

Woolverton nodded as if he'd been expecting the question. "Two things. First, he had a number of healed breaks—

someone hurt him terribly before he wound up with the Boyles. But I noted fusion of the acromion—"

"English, Doc."

"His bones were mature and fused in places they should not be in a still-growing child. This boy was at least eighteen. There were signs of chronic malnourishment, which would explain his smaller stature, but bones don't lie."

Eighteen? Petrosky tried to organize his swirling thoughts, but they clattered around behind his eyes, a headache taking root in his temples.

Jackson seemed to have no such trouble. "You said there were two things. What was the other?"

"The birthmark." Woolverton nodded sagely. "The original case file had photos of the boy, and some close-ups of the birthmark itself—that's what they used as an identifying mark when he returned home. I determined that this birthmark was almost the exact same size and shape as it was when he vanished."

Petrosky frowned. "Why would that be a problem?" Didn't all birthmarks stick around?

"Well, port-wine birthmarks, such as Gregory Boyle's, usually grow as the child ages. They also tend to thicken a bit and have an almost…crunchy feel later on in life. Like little stones under the skin. This one was completely flat, and the same size as it was at age seven despite the massive growth that occurs between seven and fourteen." His chest puffed up, bigger than Petrosky had ever seen it. "It's a tattoo and an *extremely* well-done one. The coloration was absolutely perfect, and he had a scar beneath part of it, too, which ran outside the borders of the birthmark. None of that, including the older, larger scar, was visible after the tattooist was done. Someone knew what they were doing."

*Jesus Christ.* Petrosky dropped his gaze back to the sheet, to the stranger hiding beneath it. Who the hell was he? He'd only arrived at the Boyles' two years ago, so someone might still be looking for him. Someone had to know who he was.

Petrosky dragged his eyes from the anonymous dead

child and nodded to the doctor, who had earned every bit of that title today. "Good catch, Dr. Woolverton."

The man raised his eyebrows and took his chart back from Jackson. "Coming from you, I feel like I've won the lottery." But he said it sarcastically. Petrosky liked him better for that too.

---

THE PARKING LOT wavered like a mirage, the dissipating heat of the afternoon waning into another sticky evening. Petrosky ran a hand down his face—scratchy. Within a week, he could have a nice little beard going if he wanted to be a goddamn hippie. "How the hell did we miss this? Eighteen?" But everyone had, even the PI. The parents.

*No, no way.* The Boyles had to know.

The world felt suddenly out of control—unhinged. Petrosky yanked open the SUV's door, suddenly wishing that he'd driven his Caprice to the morgue instead of leaving it in the precinct lot, that he could slide into the familiar reek of rancid french fry oil and old tobacco. "Funny how the Boyles conveniently refused basic medical care when he returned—almost like they knew a blood test would screw things up with their precious book deal." They'd claimed a fear of needles—*didn't want to traumatize the kid my ass.* It stank.

Jackson shrugged and wheeled them out of the lot. "We'll get to the bottom of it."

The sun cast bloody stains upon the other cars and turned the sky a dull, but somehow angry, orange. "So we have a murder and a still-missing kid." But most children kidnapped by non-family members were murdered within three hours of abduction. It was best not to lose sight of that.

His cell buzzed again—*oh shit.* He'd been so blindsided by what Woolverton had told them, he'd forgotten all about the earlier texts. Petrosky pulled his phone from his back pocket and glanced at it, sure there'd be some other bombshell about the case, but there wasn't. Two text messages. From his ex-wife.

He shoved the cell back into his pocket as if hiding it deep enough would also help smother his feelings. "So, where are we going to start with this kid? Old child protective service cases? Missing foster kids?" Had to be someone rather anonymous, maybe an orphan—his face had been plastered all over the news after he'd returned from his "kidnapping," and no one had stepped forward to dispute the claim that he was Gregory Boyle.

"Makes sense," Jackson said. "With the malnutrition and the old bone breaks Woolverton mentioned, it sounds like this kid had a shit home life. And he was older; he could have followed the case, figured he could sneak in there and take over Gregory's life."

Probably someone local, then, since he knew about the case at all—despite the media attention Little Greggie had gotten in Ash Park and the surrounding area, missing kids were a dime a dozen nationwide. Petrosky grunted. "What'd he do, see a missing person's story on Gregory and say, 'Hey, I want to get in with that family?'"

"If you don't have anyone who would miss you if you vanished, why not? From the outside, the Boyles at least look like they have money. And he was stealing from Mom, right?"

"Not enough to make the charade worth it. It's a lot of risk." Petrosky pictured the scars from the case file, the old wounds, the worst of which were hidden. Who knew what that kid had come from? He'd been manipulative, conniving, but maybe manipulation was all he'd ever known.

"Are the parents in on the imposter thing?" Jackson said.

"They have to be, right? Like you said, any parent would know their own child even after five years." But why keep that from the police? If there was any chance their child was still alive, they should have screamed from the rooftops that this kid was an imposter so they could reinvigorate the search for their boy. Unless…they already knew Gregory was dead.

*Who are you, kid?*

Pain throbbed behind his forehead. Petrosky peered through the windshield at the sky: A deep reddish-purple already, like the bruised throat of the boy they'd found hanging from the rafters at the Boyles' place. But he couldn't go home to sleep it off, not yet.

He had somewhere else he had to be.

**10**

———

"Thanks for coming."

Petrosky nodded and slipped into the booth across from Linda. If he squinted, his ex-wife looked almost the same as she had the day they'd married, except now she had more wrinkles around her hazel eyes, and her hair was streaked with delicate wisps of gray. And...she looked sadder. Maybe she'd been sad then too. "Hey, I have to eat, right?"

Not the best thing to say, he'd known it as it fell out of his mouth, but he'd never been good at saying the right thing—not to Linda, not to anyone.

She half-smiled. He glanced at his water; no lemon. *Thank god.* The staff at Rita's knew them by sight, which wasn't hard in these fluorescents—lights so bright he could have grilled a perp at any of the booths. But though Rita's wasn't much for mood lighting, the place made up for it in relaxed atmosphere and decent food. And the steady thrum of forks against dishes made lapses in the conversation bearable.

He picked up the menu.

"Oh, I ordered you the chicken sandwich already."

He raised his eyebrows at her over the top of the laminated page.

"I hope that's okay," Linda went on. "It's what you always get, so I figured you weren't going to change it tonight."

"Perfect," he said, sliding the menu back onto the tabletop. "Don't even have to talk. It's like you made dinner for me."

She smiled, but the corners of her eyes were tight. Her lip trembled as if she was exhausted from trying to hold the mask in place.

"What is it?" he said.

"Nothing, just been thinking a lot lately."

"About?"

"Us." She gestured at him and back to herself—or at their silverware?

"We eat here a lot, I guess. We can go somewhere else if you want to." But that weird coolness in his belly was back again, expanding, and the tingling reemerged at the base of his brain like a hundred chilled needles.

"Oh, no the place is fine, I just..." She swallowed hard, opened her mouth like she wanted to say something more, but closed it again as the waitress appeared. Sandy, who did not look like a Sandy at all—thick, as the kids would say, and pleasantly so, with wide hips and a wide mouth and dark shiny skin. No makeup.

"Evening, Detective. I've got your favorite." The chicken breast peeked from around the sides of a whole wheat bun, pepper flakes visible on the meat like little sprinkles of dirt. Salad on the side.

"Looks great." Petrosky nodded to the waitress as she set the plates down, but Linda's face remained drawn. He could feel her foot moving under the table, too—bouncing the way it did when she got nervous.

*Uh oh.* Was this the night she finally told him she wasn't going to meet him for dinner once a month? Maybe she was tired of taking the risk. Julie had died because he was a cop. His partner had died because of a case they were on—a case Petrosky had solved too late because he was busy hitting the bottle. At least Shannon lived out in Atlanta, where she couldn't wind up hurt because of him. Petrosky missed his partner's wife, and little Evie, too, but it was probably for the best.

He slid his plate closer and picked up his sandwich, busying himself by taking one bite, then another, but it was tasteless. Dry. He swallowed it down with his water and worked on his salad instead. *Dammit.* One of these days, he was going to order fries, pacemaker or not. What good was life if you never got to eat french fries?

Linda was pushing a tomato around on her plate—she hadn't eaten a thing. She caught him looking and raised her head. "Do you want to come over to the house on Friday night?" The words exploded from her lips, an entire sentence in one burst.

He forked up another bite of salad: crisp iceberg, bland without dressing. The chill in his guts was colder now. Harder. "I'm not sure. I'm on a big case right now, so things might blow up. Got a huge bombshell dropped on us today." He paused with the fork halfway to his lips, avoiding her eyes. "It's really interesting, actually, in a fucked-up way. We have a kidnapping victim, right? Shows up back at home five years after he went missing. Yesterday, he winds up dead—murdered. But it turns out he wasn't their real kid at all." He'd lowered his voice to make sure the other tables didn't hear, but Linda had been a social worker in Ash Park when they'd met, and she'd offered insight on a number of cases over the years—she always kept it quiet. "The whole case is crazy." He shoved the bite into his mouth, but his throat wasn't working right—it hurt to swallow.

Linda's jaw dropped. Then she shook her head. "I know you didn't forget, Ed, don't even pretend like you don't know what Friday is." She sniffed, and the needles in the back of his brain pricked more cruelly. "This year...it's harder than others, especially now that I'm getting older. Sometimes I think about the grandchildren we might have had, you know? Or I imagine what it would have been like to see her graduate high school."

*Fuck.* Friday. He knew the date, of course, and he'd known it was coming up, but he wasn't great at dates...or maybe he'd ignored this one on purpose. Ignored it, so he didn't have to watch it approaching like a tornado sliding nearer, inevitable and vicious, to destroy him. He set his fork down on the plate. He'd spent the morning staring at Julie's night-light, his tongue aching for a shot of anything that would numb that pain *just a little*. Being immersed in work had dulled the cravings, but now that burn on his tongue intensified, and the frigid ache in his guts spread through his abdomen and up into his jaw. *Goddammit.* This, losing Julie, was hard enough already without having to rehash it. Petrosky met Linda's eyes and tried to keep his voice level, but bile was rising in his lower esophagus—burning, bitter. "What are we going to do? Eat cake? Sing 'Happy Birthday'?"

"No, I…I thought maybe I'd make some coffee, look at her things? I think it's time to unpack them. Just to…remember. For one day."

What was he supposed to remember? That someone who knew him, who hated him, had decided to murder his daughter? Had slit her throat and lit her on fire? "I don't need to look at her things to remember my child is dead." His voice cracked on the last word. He pushed the sandwich away.

"Our child, Ed. *Our* child. And I'm not trying to remember that she's dead, I'm trying to remember that she was *alive*. That there was happiness. And that we did all we could—that in the time we had her, we loved her. I can't just ignore that she ever existed, and the fact that you seem to want to…" She sighed, but it was a disgusted sound. "I know what you're doing, why you're like this…but you should come over, Ed."

"I'll pass." He'd go to sleep early and pretend it had never happened. But it had happened. From the moment Julie came squalling into this world, his heart had been hers. And now she was gone, and the hole would always be there, and reliving every birthday, every smile, meant remembering the day he'd seen her dead with her throat slashed, the skin of her thighs, of her stomach blistered and stinking…

The ice in his guts melted. His insides burned like the fire that had charred his daughter's dead flesh. He'd talk to Linda again next week, after the fifteenth. No wonder they hadn't been able to stay married.

He tossed a twenty on the table with shaking hands.

---

PETROSKY LEFT the restaurant with his heart in his belly, and his chest still on fire. He shouldn't have been so…tactless. Linda was clearly in pain; of course, she was, and so was he. But he'd been okay—he'd been okay until that stupid dinner. Now, as he drove, though he kept trying to put Julie's birthday out of his mind, images of her face flashed in his brain, a whirring slideshow that grew faster and more frantic with every mile he got closer to his home.

Julie smiling, her dark hair flying, face kissed pink with sun.

He drove past a liquor store, lit up like a beacon of hope in the night. He tightened his fingers on the wheel. And put his foot on the gas.

Julie laughing, the way it always crescendoed into a higher pitch when she found you *really* amusing. Her eyes would shine when she told her own jokes, even if they didn't make sense. *Why did the chicken cross the road? To eat dinner!*

Bile rose in his throat. He was going to puke.

He took long, slow breaths through his nose, for once not enjoying the stink of fries and cigarettes from the old car's interior. Sometimes, the familiar was threatening, a gateway to pain. No, Linda didn't need him there with her to "celebrate" Julie's birthday. It was a cruel trick, looking at her things, remembering his baby girl, so happy, so full of *life*.

He'd seen her after it was over. After she'd suffered so horribly.

He stopped at a streetlight. Off to his right was a market, the front windows glittering with the reflection of the metal carts parked in front of the sliding doors. They'd have wine. *Stop, you've been sober over a year, tonight will not be the night.* Plus, wine was bullshit, just old, angry fruit. Petrosky smashed the gas pedal to the floor but squealed to a halt behind some asshole in a pickup truck stopped at the light in front of him.

He needed to get home. Home to his dog and a shower. Then television to force all this shit out of his brain.

The truck's taillights burned into his retinas, becoming other more deadly things—Julie's face, her pale, dead flesh, the gaping wound beneath her jawline, her mouth, her blue, cold lips, opening, smiling: *I love you, Daddy.*

He squeezed his eyes shut, opened them wide again. The taillights flipped off as the truck started forward. Petrosky took a deep breath and stared out the windshield, keeping his eyes on the glowing streetlights, the snake of white paint that marked the shoulder, the scrubby grass beyond. What he wouldn't give to have someone show up and tell him that they'd made a mistake about his daughter, that Julie was still alive, that someone else's child was the one he'd identified in the morgue. Was that what had happened? Had the Boyles been so desperate to believe their boy had come home that they didn't notice he was someone else entirely?

Maybe, even if it seemed like bullshit. But the cops had never found Gregory's body—the kid could still be alive. They'd need to reopen the investigation. While the statistics were against it, if there was even a chance... Was that cruel to do to the parents, to give them hope? Maybe it was better to let them accept Gregory was dead until they knew for sure.

He drove, buildings and trees racing past on either side of the car, the streetlights devolving into stop signs. The pickup turned off down a side street. No one else on the road.

Almost home.

The half-digested chicken sandwich danced in his gut. He laid a hand on his belly. The last liquor store appeared over the horizon—barred windows, two cars in the lot.

*No.*

No one would ever know.

*I can't.*

Julie's throat, the gaping muscle, the charred skin of her

thighs where the killer had lit her aflame. *My baby girl, he lit her on fucking fire.*

He wheeled the car into the lot in a scream of gravel and raw rubber. His tongue burned. His fingers twitched against the wheel. He faced the street, but he could still see the building in the rearview, the lights beckoning with the promise of blissful escape.

He should think about the case. He should think about anything else. He knew where this path ended: the metallic taste of his gun between his lips. His mouth felt like it had been stuffed with cotton.

*Go home.*

His knuckles were white on the steering wheel. His lungs had ceased to work, forcing him to take thin, wheezing breaths—even his legs ached, his eyes burning as if every muscle in his body was fighting against unconsciousness even as his brain craved it. A reprieve, no matter how short-lived.

*Call George.* Scott's father, and one of Petrosky's only friends, knew what it was to struggle, but he'd never been an addict. He'd somehow made it through Vietnam and a cancer diagnosis without wanting to numb it all. George was braver than Petrosky would ever be—it took far more courage to live sober.

*Maybe I'm tired of being strong. Maybe I don't want to fight anymore.*

He could call Jackson. She hadn't struggled with this, but she'd help him.

But Jackson had her own shit, and he wasn't about to burden her with his.

What about McCallum? Would the doc talk him down or would he tell the chief that Petrosky was losing his—

*Thunk, thunk, thunk.*

Petrosky jumped, hand moving for his hip, for the butt of his gun, but—no, just a knock. The window.

He rolled it down. A man in a Polo shirt stood outside the driver's door, a ponytail flung over his shoulder and a goofy grin on his face like he was holding a fluoride tray between his teeth and was desperate not to drop it. New worker at the liquor store? Had to be—a lot could change in a year.

"You okay, man? You've been out here a while."

Had he? It felt like he'd just pulled in. Petrosky swallowed hard. "Yeah. Just got a little lost."

"Need directions?"

*Not from you, you can't even find a decent barber.* "I've got it now, thanks." The man stepped away as Petrosky backed from the spot and hit the road again. Just a few more miles to his house and his dog and that goddamn night-light that still sometimes tried to rip his heart out.

**11**

AɴOTHER ᴅAY, another dollar, another shit cup of precinct coffee. But the bitter swill in his cup was insulation enough from his thoughts—he had a job to do. He focused on his footsteps, on Jackson's footsteps, on the weird garlic-hot-doggy smell in the precinct stairwell as they descended.

Evan Scott's basement office was conveniently right up the hall from evidence storage: a long room with a single forehead-height window on the far end; a shelf on the right filled with boxes of to-be-tested forensics; a long stainless table—three times the length of the ones in the morgue—down the middle; and computer screens everywhere else. Scott met Petrosky and Jackson at the door, wearing safety glasses and a smile on his broad face.

Petrosky was glad the kid had edged back into his first love instead of going the detective or the medical examiner route. Though what the kid had learned in his first couple years of med school would certainly help him in forensic science, Scott said that playing with the evidence—with the "bloody puzzle pieces"—was what got him out of bed in the morning. And kept him up late. And from the way the kid was grinning, he didn't mind being here on a Sunday either, not one bit.

Scott tossed the glasses on the table and gestured to the

bank of computers in the back left corner. "So, no trace from your suspect on the rope, though I did find powder consistent with latex gloves. And the back door seems to be how they got in—the Boyles claim they had to unlock the front door when they got home, but the back door was unlocked. No fingerprints outside of the family, though, not on the door or anywhere else."

Petrosky thought back to the layout of the house. The back door was near the middle of the yard, deep in shadow: Creep into the backyard, and you'd be protected from the prying eyes of any neighbor.

"I ran a few projections for you," Scott continued. "I was trying to get a height and weight for your assailant, but in this case…" He tapped a few keys, and a chart plinked onto the screen. "In order to pull him over the rafter, they wouldn't have had to be strong at all—the ligature and the rafter worked together as a rope and pulley system. Even a teenager could have done it, if he was strong enough to hoist the rope while he tied the knot at the banister to hold the body up."

Jackson sniffed, leaning closer to squint at the screen. "Or there were more than one of them."

"Well, yeah. Didn't find evidence of that, but it's not impossible." Scott tapped a few more keys, *clack-clack-clack.* "I spent a lot of time focused on the scuffs—the marks on the floor." Another screen popped up, an illustrated overhead view of the Boyles' living room complete with the couch and the upended chair. The floor was full of little numbers and sporadic red marks that looked like scratches.

Scott stepped aside just enough so Jackson and Petrosky could crowd in. This close up, Jackson's suit jacket smelled like bacon, just a little, but enough to make his mouth water. But she never cooked bacon at home. Lance hated the way it popped in the pan, would end up in the living room with his video game headset on, trying to calm down—autism was a bitch sometimes. Had she gone to breakfast with someone?

He glanced her way, but Jackson's eyes remained locked on Scott's computer screen.

"So this here is the couch." Scott pointed. "Then here are the places on the wood where there was residue from shoes with vulcanized soles." He touched a spot on the drawing just behind the couch, then tapped an area below where the body had been found. "The shoes had wide soles, but the marks weren't made by a heavy person—too faint. And there were fibers on the underside of the sofa. They hooked their toes under the couch, which suggests they needed to get leverage —that they were not strong enough to pull the body over the beam, and they didn't weigh enough to use their body weight to hoist him. Hell, they used the couch enough to both scrape their shoes on the underside, and move the couch itself from where it had been sitting." He paused, glancing at each of them in turn as if waiting for them to absorb what he'd said, then: "I think a bigger or stronger person would have stood beneath the beam and just pulled. But someone around your victim's weight, maybe as small as 120 pounds, would have similar patterns with both the strain on the rope and the scuff marks on the floor."

Petrosky blinked at the screen, then at Scott, whose eyes were glittering—the kid was practically frothing at the mouth.

"Out with it, Scott."

"Okay, okay. I just wanted to amp the suspense."

"Well, stop it," he snapped. Jesus, between Scott and Woolverton, he'd had enough theatrics. As if a dead kid wasn't enough drama. Jackson elbowed him anyway when Scott's grin faltered. Petrosky scowled at her, the kid tapped another key, and the image on the screen changed once more.

*Shoes?* Blue material on top, white soles, the shoe itself wider than usual and flatter than a sneaker.

"Meet your suspect's footwear. Like I said, they hooked their feet under the couch and leaned backward as they pulled. Once they got your victim where they wanted him, they walked back to the banister and tied the knot, and badly. I'm honestly surprised it held."

"So, not a sailor or a hangman, got it." Petrosky straightened and gestured to the screen. "You find enough fibers to help us identify these beyond general type?"

Scott grinned. "Of course. Navy shoes—the brand is Skate-Metal. Their skate shoes are wider, and the sole wraps up around the top of the toe for protection, secured with either stitching or foxing tape, of which this is the latter."

"You got all that from a few fibers?" Most shoes were made from similar materials; they were almost never able to identify a specific brand from a piece of cloth.

"The fibers aren't regular thread—they're woven from recycled plastics, and only one company makes them."

"Smaller company?" Jackson cut in. "Excellent. We'll see if we can get buyer lists from the local shops or from their home office, see which purchasers knew our vic."

"I wish," Scott said. "These shoes, in particular, are popular with the teenagers here; they're a local start-up, had a huge fundraiser at Anderson. They practically gave shoes away after a social media push—some viral stuff, made everyone think they were cool, or whatever. And they sponsored some skating competition, too, called it Metal—"

"Cut to the chase, Scott."

He nodded. "Half the kids in the area have a pair, but they're especially popular among boarders."

"Well, fuck."

"Yeah." Scott clicked off the screen. "I'll send you a printout of the findings, but from their use of the couch for leverage, the length of the scuffs which belong to a size six shoe, and the footwear itself...I think you're looking for a kid."

12

---

THE DOOR to Scott's office closed with a soft *ploomph* behind them, and Petrosky almost reached back to open and close it again with a proper slam. *Goddammit, goddammit.* What the hell was going on?

They hit the stairwell up to the first-floor interrogation rooms. "A killer kid, unconnected to the kidnapping? Unconnected to the imposter scheme?" Maybe the Boyles were cursed.

"The school counselor said he was running with a bad crowd, acting out," Jackson said to the stairs in front of her, voice muted by the sound of their steps. "He was fighting, even punched Nurse Ogden for the high crime of telling him he had to stay home if he wanted to be a human incubator for chicken pox. Maybe he was aggressive with his peers, too —pissed someone off one too many times."

Petrosky's lungs burned. The stairs required more effort today than yesterday, or was he just tired? He certainly wasn't about to consider alternatives. "Even the most twisted suburban badass would punch him in the face or bash him on social media—not kill him," he said. "And this took planning. Foresight. They brought the rope. They brought the syringe, filled with drugs that should have been hard for them to—"

"Kids are just as good at getting drugs as adults, Petrosky. Especially snotty rich kids—little shits with money and access to Mommy's Valium."

"Okay, you're right, but they used gloves, or Scott would have found DNA on the rope or somewhere else in the room." Their shoes on the metal treads echoed against the stairwell walls. "This was not an impulsive act or some accidental murder like you'd expect from a pissed-off teenager."

Jackson glanced back over her shoulder. "Our victim was older, too—at least eighteen, maybe even twenty, twenty-one? Might've gotten himself involved in something he shouldn't have, or he was killed because of something from his old life. And with all those injuries…he didn't just run *to* the Boyles. The plan itself was far too risky. He ran away from something else."

Petrosky gripped the railing harder, steadying himself. His legs felt heavy, like his shoes were made of stone. "So a murderous kid, or a woman if she borrowed her child's shoes," he practically wheezed. "Or a small man."

His cell buzzed. He glanced at it, declined the call, and peered back up at Jackson. She continued climbing—*only six more stairs, thank god*—but said nothing about his far-too-pressured breathing, his buzzing phone, or the fact that he'd figured out how to turn the horrible opera ringer off.

"Kid or a woman—either way, we don't even know who the victim used to be," she said now. "We just know where he ended up. We have no idea why anyone would want him dead." Jackson shoved open the door to the main floor and glanced at her watch. "I hope they're here already—we have too much to do to wait around."

They'd invited the Boyles to the station this time, sans Stevie. The kid didn't need to be privy to these conversations, and if Petrosky was being honest, something about that boy bothered him right down into his marrow. With what Scott had told them, maybe his feelings were justified. Not that he thought Stevie was the one who'd killed the guy —even if the nasty little mite had been in town, he was small for his age, less than 100 pounds soaking wet, and he didn't look particularly strong. He wouldn't have been able to hoist the victim up and tie the knot. Unless Stevie had a partner, he was out of the suspect pool, though they probably shouldn't rule out a pair of killers, even if Scott hadn't found evidence of that yet. If one rich sociopathic kid was bad, two feeding off one another was a recipe for disaster.

Jackson pushed into the interrogation room.

The Boyles were already seated on one side of the stainless table, Adrian Boyle staring straight ahead as she had been in days prior. Not shocking—unlikely that an addict would stop using after they found a body in their living room. Ron followed Jackson and Petrosky with his eyes as they slid into the chairs across from the couple.

The moment Petrosky's ass hit the seat, Ron snapped, "We've been waiting here for—"

"Gregory was not your child," Petrosky said. Jackson kicked him in the shin.

The man's eyes widened. "How dare you, of course he's our child, he—"

"We have DNA." *Rip that shit off like a bandage.*

Now Ron stilled. His lips parted, then closed again—shock. But Adrian… Sure, she looked dull and tired, as she had the first few times Petrosky had seen her, but her gaze remained steady. Even her fingers were relaxed, laced on the tabletop. Yeah, she'd known. "I have a feeling this isn't the first time you've considered this," he said.

Adrian swallowed hard and locked her gaze on her hands.

Ron growled, "You can't expect we'll just sit here and let you talk about him like that."

"Mrs. Boyle?" The silence stretched. Petrosky was opening his mouth to ask again when she whispered: "It was my last chance to have my boy home."

Ron reeled back in his chair so hard it rocked on its legs.

"What does that mean?" Jackson asked.

Adrian met her eyes. "Gregory's dead."

The room suddenly felt ten degrees colder, and Adrian's

body shuddered like someone had just run an ice cube down her spine. Ron's nostrils flared, but he was no longer looking at Petrosky—his gaze was locked on his wife. "Goddammit, Adrian, you—"

She whirled on him. "He's dead; he's been dead this whole time! You just don't want to accept it."

*I knew there was no way a mother just missed that she had the wrong kid.* Adrian was part of this charade. But why? It made no sense—unless she'd killed Gregory herself. What better cover than a replacement child? And then with the publicity, she could make more money off a book deal. He lowered his voice, eyes on her face. "Why do you believe Gregory's dead, Mrs. Boyle?"

"He's been dead since he left, since he vanished." She coughed and choked, and when Ron opened his mouth, she put up a hand and continued: "It's not like I gave up…like I was okay with it. I had a goddamn breakdown."

"Just a few months after Gregory was taken, right?" That was the only hospitalization he knew about. "Sounds like you lost hope pretty quickly." *Maybe you knew there was no hope to be had—maybe you know where he's buried.*

She nodded. "I tried to hope, but the statistics—it was obvious he wasn't coming back. A few hours after they're taken, they're dead, that's the norm."

Statistics? Come on. Parents hoped against insurmountable odds that their child might be the one who made it home. He stared at her. Adrian blinked back tears. So she wasn't emotionless after all—they'd just never discussed *her* child; only the stranger who'd infiltrated her home.

The Boyles had an alibi for this child's hanging death, Jackson had checked, but what had happened to Gregory? If this woman knew, he wanted her to admit it. "How can you be so sure that Gregory's dead?" he tried again.

"A mother knows." Adrian sniffed. "A mother knows." Ron was staring at her, but his lip was trembling. Anxiety?

Jackson leaned forward in her chair. "Adrian, if you knew, if you really knew this child wasn't yours, why not tell the police? Why let him come into your home, why let him stay there? That could have been very dangerous for your other son. Didn't you wonder why he was there? What he was after?"

Adrian blinked so slowly Petrosky thought she might pass out, but then she opened her eyes again and said, "Not everything has to be dark, Detective. At first, I thought he…that maybe he knew who did it…who took our boy. But in the end…I started to think he needed us as much as we needed him. And then the book deal came through and…he got… weird."

Jackson shook her head. "But if there was even a chance that Gregory was still out there—"

"There wasn't." She crossed her arms. "I needed to find a way to make things work with what was left, and that book… it was a way to help Stevie. A way for us to make something better come out of all the pain. And I tried to accept that boy…I did everything I was supposed to, I just…" She shook her head. "He wasn't a bad kid…he just wasn't *my* kid."

Petrosky wanted to leap to his feet, to grill her like a million other suspects he'd had in that chair over the years, but god help him, it felt like the truth. Her grief tugged at his heart and not at the hairs on the back of his neck like the guilty kind of grief did. And he understood the desperation that came with losing a child. McCallum had once argued that Petrosky'd replaced his own daughter with women he found on the street. The shrink was wrong—that shit had started way before Julie, for reasons he never, ever considered—but it wasn't outside the realm of normal. Or so McCallum said.

"Our… Greg…" Ron sputtered, his thick mustache vibrating. "This is *impossible*." He looked like he was having trouble breathing—shocked enough for both of them. "He liked the same foods as he used to. He watched baseball with me, and we talked about his little league team, from before. He—"

Adrian shook her head. "He didn't bring up those things, never said, 'Mom, do you remember when…' He just agreed with you and over time…it all became real for you." She looked at her lap. "Maybe real for him too."

"He asked for Frosty Ohs for breakfast his second day home," Ron said, but his voice was softer, more resigned. "Don't you remember how much he used to like them?"

Adrian put her hand on her husband's knee. "Every kid likes Frosty Ohs."

Ron gaped like he wanted to say more but couldn't find the words. Was he really that dense? Had he believed the boy in their house was their son? Maybe he'd been desperate enough to accept it. And even if he'd suspected, he had plenty to lose if the truth came out once the book deal was signed.

"I just don't… Why didn't you…" Ron squinted, then, as if reading Petrosky's mind: "This was about the book. All this time, you pretended because of that stupid book?"

Adrian dropped her hand. "I wanted something good to come out of this, Ron," she whispered. "And it didn't matter what I said. You didn't want to hear it."

Ron's shoulders sagged in defeat. He turned to Petrosky. "I…I believed him. He had…" He sat straighter, eyes brightening with hope. "What about his birthmark?"

"A tattoo," Jackson said.

"So he…he planned it?" Ron said. "All of it? How does a twelve-year-old go into a tattoo shop and—"

"He was older than he let on," Jackson said tightly, her voice low with regret, or maybe sorrow, but still steeped in suspicion. "At least eighteen when he died, likely older. He was probably an adult before he arrived at your house."

Ron massaged his chest, wincing.

Petrosky frowned. "You okay there?"

"I just…" He rubbed at a spot below his clavicle. "Yeah. I just can't believe this. Do you think… I mean, Stevie has been alone with him, I left him alone with this stranger—"

"Did Stevie always act like that?"

Adrian looked away. Ron swallowed hard. "I know he can be difficult, but he's always been jealous of Gregory."

That didn't bode well for Stevie; jealousy was all the

motive a little twit like him needed. Petrosky crossed his arms. "How did Gregory feel about the book?" *Fake Gregory.* He was an imposter, and it sounded like his behavior had changed around the time of the book announcement; he probably realized that the more publicity the case got, the more likely someone from his old life would find him.

"He was upset about it." Ron cleared his throat, cheeks reddening once more. "That's why Adrian and I...why we fought so much. I thought the book was hurting him. The publicity. He'd already been through so much...or I thought he had." He dropped his hand from his chest. "I guess now we know why he didn't want that damn book. He thought they'd come arrest him for lying." He spat the last word.

*You don't know the half of it.* With the abuse he'd suffered, Petrosky was damn sure the kid wanted nothing more than to stay hidden.

"Did Greg..." Jackson cleared her throat. "Did the boy like to skateboard?" *Ah, right, the skater shoes.*

Ron sniffed in a way that sounded more like a grunt. "What does that have to do with anything?"

"Just a question."

His fists clenched against his elbows—far too defensive for a question about hobbies, even if it was a stupid hobby. "No, not really. He hung out with a few people who were into it, but they weren't what I'd call friends."

"You made it sound like he was withdrawn—that he spent his time alone in his room," Jackson said gently, obviously trying to rein him in. A part of Petrosky wanted to see what happened if the man exploded.

"Well yeah, he did, almost always. Just every once in a while he would go out, maybe once a month or so. Said he was meeting some kids at the skate park."

"That would have been helpful information to have had earlier, Mr. Boyle." Petrosky leaned closer. "Tell us about these acquaintances of Gregory's who suddenly exist."

"I never met them—they never came to the house." Ron looked down, his jaw tightening. "I should have known better, but I thought he killed himself, I thought he… I mean, if I'd thought someone else hurt him, I would have mentioned those boys—bad news, all of them. I always knew he was with them when he missed curfew."

So, he'd been hanging out with anonymous bad-news skater punks? Who might have known he'd be alone in his very expensive house? Perhaps the homicide portion of this case wasn't so complicated after all, even if the hanging felt too elaborate for a few teenage boarders. "What makes you say they were bad news, Mr. Boyle?"

"Well, staying out late, like I said. He didn't tell me much else, but I was under the impression that those kids were at that park almost every day." He raised his palms as if to say, *isn't that enough?*

Adrian Boyle had gone stock-still, staring at the far wall, her only movement the twitching of her eyelids. Maybe thinking about the boy she'd lost. Maybe about the one who'd snuck into her home and ended up swinging from her ceiling. But either way, she was holding something back. Did she really think she'd sidestepped the question of why she believed Gregory was dead? *Statistics.* Petrosky wasn't buying it. "Mrs. Boyle?"

She sighed. "I think one of them was named…Christian."

Petrosky watched her with narrowed eyes. Waiting for her to blink—she didn't. *What else do you know, lady?* But she wasn't talking, not now, and the drugs in her system probably kept her cool enough to lie all afternoon.

The Boyles were not off the hook—if she wasn't going to tell them, he'd damn sure find out another way.

Jackson folded her hands on the tabletop. "How late did Gregory usually stay out with these skater kids?"

"Ten," Ron said, "sometimes even later. He was supposed to be back by seven, eight on the weekends."

Seemed like a pretty stiff curfew. But Ron wouldn't have wanted to risk losing his son again. Fat lot of good it had done.

# 13

---

JACKSON TOOK a deep swallow of her coffee and set the cup back in the cup holder. "I got our John Doe's photo sent out—hopefully, we'll get a hit."

"How did that happen so fast?" She'd only been upstairs for fifteen minutes—precisely the amount of time it had taken him to run to Rita's in the Escalade to snag their to-go cups.

"Well, Decantor offered to help out, fax the photo to some of the smaller precincts." She flicked a piece of lint off her collar.

Petrosky squinted at her: no earrings today, but she'd had those new turquoise ones the other day. And...the bacon. "Decantor's helping us with this?" he asked slowly. "Doesn't he have his own detective work to do?"

"There's something to be said for being nice, Petrosky." She kept her gaze on the windshield, her hands on the steering wheel.

"Are you guys doing it?"

"Doing what?"

"You know. The nasty." Outside, a lone bird flitted past, squalling as if fleeing some unseen threat. No cars beside them, not even another lane, just grass burned brittle by the end-of-summer sun.

She glanced at the GPS. "I thought he was fucking you."

"He wishes." He rolled down his window as Jackson swung into a parking lot and silenced the engine. Flowering bushes swayed on either side of the skate park's open wrought iron gates—everything so *clean,* down to the painted lines in the parking lot, still brilliantly white. Like they power-washed the whole damn place every day.

Petrosky grunted. "Pretty fancy for a bunch of kids who come here to headbang and smoke weed." They both watched a kid in a backward cap take off down the tallest concrete ramp, dead center in front of the gate, and zoom back up the other side of the steep U-shaped curve. He flew into the air and spun, grabbed the board, and then twisted his body around for the ride down. The board caught the top of the ramp. He tumbled with a cry, end over end to the bottom. *Ouch.*

Jackson winced and followed Petrosky out onto the pavement. "It's great exercise until they smash their faces on the ground, I guess."

"What'd you think I meant by headbang?"

She rolled her eyes as they crossed the gate's threshold. "I think those are our guys." She nodded toward a group of boys loitering near the back of the park beside a non-uniform concrete hole that looked like a giant empty swimming pool. Two of them held cigarettes between their fingers. Petrosky frowned, but his mouth watered.

A dark-haired kid with a faded blue T-shirt and a lip ring looked up as they stepped past the first set of ramps and within range of the group. Smoke curled around his nostrils. He nudged the bulky kid sitting beside him—north of 150 pounds in torn denim and a knit cap that made his blond hair flare out around his ears like the wings of a frizzy yellow bird.

Jackson pushed the hem of her jacket aside to reveal the badge on her belt. The two kids sitting on the ground rose, and then all of them turned like a single organism that reeked of tobacco, cheap weed, and some noxious perfumed body spray.

"Evening, gentlemen." How had the entire day gotten away from them? Petrosky put on his best shit-eating, "I'm not a scary cop at all," grin. "Which one of you is Christian?"

Four sets of eyes turned to the dark-haired one with the lip ring and the cigarette. He stepped up. "That's me."

Jackson nodded. "We're here about your friend, Gregory."

The smallest in the group raised his chin, a cig between his teeth. He had the gaunt cheeks of a chemo patient, but the little chub around his middle said he was about to go through a growth spurt. "Ohh, yeah." Voice like a nine-year-old girl. "Are you here to ask questions like that Johnny Depp looking guy?"

Jackson cocked her head and frowned. "What Johnny Depp guy?"

"I don't know—he didn't say his name, I guess. Just came in here yesterday and asked us a bunch of questions about Greg."

*Yesterday?* Petrosky waited for the boy to continue, but when the kid just scratched his belly, Petrosky prodded: "What kind of questions?"

The kid shrugged. "Just if we knew Gregory. If he had other friends."

"But we don't know jack shit," the big one said, frizzy yellow wings catching the waning sun. Beefy. He was older, too, at least sixteen, and no board, not like the others. Maybe he was too heavy to balance.

"Jack shit, eh?" Petrosky watched him, the defiant glitter in his irises. Was he hiding something, or did he just hate authority? "You don't know anything about a guy who used to hang out with you?"

Beef shrugged. The little one ground his cigarette out, and now Petrosky noticed the blue shoes, not dark enough to be navy, but close, and much like the ones Scott had shown them. Actually, they all had skating shoes like that—a telltale plasticky shine to the fabric—except for the bulky guy who was wearing sandals that showcased his hairy toes. They'd have Scott test everyone's shoes, just in case.

Christian dragged on his cig again. They weren't even worried about talking to the cops—rich boys didn't ever think they were going to get in trouble. Usually, they were right.

But not today. "Where were you on Friday night?"

Beef's nostrils flared, uncertainty creeping into his gaze. The others frowned.

Jackson stepped closer. "Come on, guys, we're just trying to narrow down our list of suspects."

"Suspects?" Beef scratched his fuzzy yellow head. "For what?"

"Yeah, we didn't do nothing." Christian.

"Maybe nothing. Or maybe you broke into Greg's house while he was resting," Petrosky said. Someone had gone in with a syringe while the vic was asleep—no way he'd have let them shoot drugs between his toes if he was lucid.

Furrowed brows. Narrowed eyes. "Why would we break into his house?" the smallest one said finally. "We didn't even want to hang out with him here."

"Yeah, he didn't like anybody I don't think," Christian said, lip ring glittering. "And nobody liked him back." Beef nodded as did one of the others—dark hair, dark eyes, a bruise on one cheekbone.

"Then why'd you let him hang out with you?"

"Man, we didn't," the smallest said. "He just used to come up here. And sometimes we were here at the same time."

So Imposter-Greg lied to Ron about coming here to see these kids? He didn't see a reason for Ron to lie—Ron surely knew they'd be verifying his statement. "You boys ever see him with anyone else?"

Christian pursed his lips. They all shook their heads, all except…Beef.

"No," the little one squeaked. "I never saw anyone with him. He used to just sit in the corner. Didn't wave or nothin'."

"Can you think of anyone who'd want to hurt him?" *Like*

*one of you?* Shrugs all around, what appeared to be genuine confusion, not that they'd say if it was one of them—he'd check their alibis. But if their victim wasn't here to spend time with these boys, he could have been meeting someone else. Petrosky scanned the park. Thick bushes and wrought iron all the way around to keep the skate park hidden, keep the neighborhood looking nicer. The only reason they'd been able to see the boys at all was that the front gates had been open, and these boys had happened to be hanging out near the center of the park, in full view of the lot. Anyone sitting along the front wall, behind the greenery, would be invisible to passersby.

Jackson must have been thinking the same because she asked: "Where'd he usually sit?"

Lip Ring—Christian—pointed, and Petrosky followed his finger. Tables crouched in the deep shade of the massive oak in the front right corner. Petrosky hadn't even noticed the seating until now. Between the hedges and the fencing and the tree, it was the perfect spot for someone trying to hide.

"And you're sure you never saw him with anyone?"

"Naw, man, he was always alone," the dark-haired, bruised-cheeked one said.

Christian: "He really wasn't friendly. Seriously."

Petrosky dragged his gaze over the lot of them. "Not like you fellows, huh?"

The small one shrugged but smiled. The others narrowed their eyes, more…suspicious. Beef was chewing on his cheek.

Petrosky addressed him. "What about you? You see him with someone over there?"

"Well… I did once or twice, yeah." He scratched at his fluffy hair again. "Some guy. It was a little later, after these guys took off—like nine or whatever."

"What'd the man look like?"

Beef frowned. "It's dark over there, and I wasn't really paying attention. I think he might have had on a blue T-shirt."

*Very goddamn helpful, kid.* "How tall?"

Beef shrugged. His friends were all staring at him, eyes wide. Because he was telling their secret, or because he'd never told them?

"White? Black?" Jackson prodded, a hint of irritation in her voice.

"I dunno, I was pretty stoned." His jaw dropped. "I mean, no, I mean, I was tired."

He couldn't even tell race? This kid was useless. "Come on, kid. Give us something. A hat, sunglasses, any physical description at—"

"He had a beard. Dark, kinda bushy."

A bushy beard? That was the way their imposter had described the kidnapper—though he'd never been abducted. Petrosky glanced around once more; even the kid who'd bit it on the ramp was gone. No one else in the park. No wonder they liked coming here. "What time do you guys usually leave?"

Christian looked at the sky. "Around eight in the summer. Have to be back before sunset if I'm skating because the boards don't have lights." They all nodded agreement. All except Beef.

And Imposter-Greg had been out until ten, at least once a month.

## 14

<hr>

Petrosky waited until they were on the highway to grumble: "We'll verify alibis, but I don't think those punks have the patience to plan anything further out than buying their next pack of cigarettes." One of them would have let it slip. A look, a twitch, *something*. They were barely edgy about being questioned; not one of them seemed shifty enough to be a murderer. Petrosky ran a hand over his chin—scratchier than yesterday, sharper. *Julie used to love the beard.* He dropped his hand.

"The killer had to know the layout of the house, too," Jackson said, grabbing her coffee so aggressively he edged against his door, trying to avoid the wayward drops that erupted from the hole in the plastic lid. "Ron said none of the skaters ever came to the house, but our killer knew about the rafters in particular. Most houses these days don't have a great spot to string up a body."

He made a fist against the car door. His head throbbed, dull and achy.

"Who do you think our vic was meeting at that skate park?" Jackson asked.

"We just have to look for a bearded but otherwise nondescript fellow of indeterminate race who wears T-shirts sometimes." The street whizzed past through the passenger window, the sky edging into pink once more—another day gone. Another day and they were no closer to finding Gregory Boyle or his kidnapper. Or the imposter's killer. Were they the same person? But that was impossible to tell—yet.

Petrosky cleared his throat. "If our vic was meeting someone, I'd guess it'd be whoever helped him vanish from his old life and insert himself into the Boyles' home."

Jackson slipped her coffee cup back into the console and turned her eyes to Petrosky. "What makes you think he had help at all?"

"Maybe not help exactly," Petrosky said, shaking his head. "But his face was all over the papers, the television—it was this big heartwarming reunion that got enough press for a publishing house to pick it up. If our vic's real parents were alive, or even an old friend, a single acquaintance…someone would have seen the stories. Someone had to recognize him." He finished the dregs of his coffee and pressed his fingers to his temples. His brain felt mushy, soft. Dull. "About a year ago was when things really started going downhill, right? Around the time the announcement, about the book came out. What if our vic wasn't nervous because he was worried someone might find him and turn him in…what if he got nervous because they had?"

Jackson tapped her fingers on the steering wheel—*rat-a-tat-tat-a-tat-tat-tat-tat*—and his heart responded in kind, throbbing almost as painfully as his brain. "Makes sense. And he was pretty banged up, a definite history of abuse either at home or in foster care. If I'm an abusive parent, maybe I don't care that my kid vanished initially—he was an adult anyway, or close to it."

Petrosky dropped his hands from his aching head. "But then they see him on television or read about the upcoming book deal and—"

"They see an opportunity to get a little something back."

*Blackmail?* It was a stretch, maybe, but he'd seen crazier. He squinted at the orange-maroon clouds, low in the sky as if the burden of blocking the dying light was too much. "And he was stealing from the Boyles," he said. "Could be petty theft, but maybe he was trying to pay someone off. With the family being on the news, they probably assumed he'd be making big money. It could be a friend, another relative…even a skater-shoe wearing brother. Anyone who knows his dirty little secret."

"Right." She eased them off the highway, the tires whining a sad song of rubber and pock-marked asphalt. "And we have to assume that he lied about pretty much everything. We've been looking for a man with a beard, but this boy was never kidnapped. Everything he said was a lie right out of the gate. And that tattoo…"

Petrosky nodded. Woolverton had said it was exceptionally well-done, something not every artist could pull off. If they could find the tattooist, they might be able to narrow down where John Doe came from. His phone buzzed. This time, he turned it off without even looking.

"You need to get that?"

"Nope." Shannon knew Julie's birthday was coming up, had to or she wouldn't be blowing up his phone now—she hadn't called him in months.

Jackson frowned at him, suspicious, but turned away and shrugged. "The tattoo, then. Can't be too many artists who do pieces like that. It was just a birthmark, but skin tone and scar repair aren't easy to get right."

He narrowed his eyes at her. "You know a lot about tattoos. You have a secret tat somewhere, Jackson?"

"Wouldn't you like to know."

He sniffed. "Fine. I'll ask Decantor."

She rolled her eyes at the darkening sky. But for the second time that day, she didn't deny it.

***

JACKSON DROPPED him off at his front door, but he didn't linger there; he headed across the lawn toward the neighbor's place. The dull ache in his chest had softened during the drive home, but now it brightened, throbbing in time to his footsteps.

He rubbed at the sore spot above his breastbone, almost the same place Ron Boyle had been touching earlier. Was that where everyone carried the pain of a dead child? At least his headache had eased.

Billie opened the door before he'd climbed the porch steps, and his Great Dane bounded out, practically knocking him back down the stairs. Billie laughed, blue eyes glittering, her dyed hair silver in the porch light. "I always know the moment you get home. This sweet boy has a special bark for his daddy."

He scratched the big dog's ears; his hands suddenly wet with slobber. "You miss me, Duke?" But his heart wasn't in it. His chest was killing him. He straightened anyway. "How's the faucet working out?"

"Everything's great here. And I'm going to take care of the lawn in the morning after I finish my coursework." Billie was a year into her bachelor's degree; she wanted to be a social worker, just like his ex-wife. Pain bloomed behind his rib cage. He swallowed hard, his useless sandpapery tongue catching on the roof of his mouth.

Jane walked into the foyer and smiled over Billie's shoulder. "Is that Ed?" Jane was the newcomer to the group, just a few months off the streets, but already she looked healthier. The purple T-shirt he'd given her wasn't sagging as much as it had been, and her ash-blond hair was curly, shining—no more frizz. Was she wearing makeup?

"You have dinner plans?" Jane asked. "Candice should be home from work any minute. I made tacos." Work—it was the main reason he let Jackson drive him around instead of taking his own car. The girls usually needed it more.

Petrosky scratched Duke's head again, his stomach rumbling. Shit, had he even eaten lunch? But hungry or not, he didn't want to eat with anyone else. He was certain the girls could read his grief stamped like a KEEP OUT sign on his forehead.

*What are you going to do? Go sit on your bed and stare at Julie's night-light? Try to imagine what she'd be like if she were here?* Would she be married, have kids? Would she be a social worker like Linda too?

Duke nudged his leg. He'd stopped scratching the dog—his hand was on his breastbone again.

"Eddie?" Jane stepped around Billie and onto the porch, brow furrowed. "Is it your heart?" She'd been pre-med once; he remembered that…he thought. But his brain was suddenly fuzzy, too fuzzy to pick out individual ideas. Tired, he was tired. Of fighting. Of his whole goddamn life.

He shook his head and dropped his hand. "No, I'm fine. And tacos sound great. Can I bring anything?"

"Just yourself." Billie smiled. "I'll set another place."

**15**

———

Jackson dropped the phone into the cup holder and said to the windshield: "Acharya's on board. He'll call a few other national publications and put the story out online today, see if someone recognizes our John Doe. Say's it's weird enough it might go viral."

Petrosky glanced out the Escalade's window—brick buildings, power lines, a weird little jewelry boutique that looked like it also sold fishing lures. "How's giving it a cold going to help us, Jackson?"

"No, you old bastard, viral means..." She sighed. "Never mind." She flipped the blinker—*tick, tick, tick.*

*Time to find out who our victim was.* Only a few tattooists in the metro Detroit area specialized in the type of natural flesh detail they needed, someone who could replicate a port-wine birthmark so closely that even his own father couldn't tell the difference. While they weren't positive the tattoo work had been done nearby, their dead guy was likely to be local since he knew about Gregory. And while a less adept artist could have inked their victim's birthmark, Woolverton had said the piece was very well done—tricky with that scar. Hopefully, one of the tattooists they visited today could put the word out even if they hadn't done the piece themselves. Sometimes talking to the right people was all it took.

The first tattoo shop they went to was still closed, but not empty—a phone call and a flash of the badge at the door got them admittance from the owner who lived in the apartment upstairs. He promised to show around the picture of their imitation Greg but assured them the boy hadn't been inked there, especially if he was even a week underage. Two other shops yielded similar results; tattooists with apparent integrity and a business model to match. No one recognized their victim.

The fourth and last stop on the list was Ink On, a tattoo shop that worked closely with reconstructive surgeons in the area. This guy's services were far more expensive than most of the others—the last place a kid would look to get a tat on the sly—but the artist was renowned, connected. He should know of anyone else who did that kind of work.

A hand-carved wooden sign in the front window said YES, WE ARE OPEN with a dragon etched into the wood beneath, flames bursting from between its teeth. *Flames.* Julie's burned, dead flesh flashed in Petrosky's brain, and he shoved the image aside so violently he almost jerked with the force of it.

"Nice place," Jackson said.

He blinked. The room buzzed, and it took him a moment to realize the sound was coming from the room itself and not from inside his fucked-up head.

Unlike the other parlors they'd seen that morning, Ink On had no posters on the walls featuring colorful designs of cartoons, or flowers, or MOM in a giant heart. The walls were a light minty green; everything scrubbed as clean as a physician's office. Three love seats sat against the long front wall of the space, separated by carved wooden end tables topped with leather-bound books. The rest of the room was taken up by a series of eight booths with red leather tattoo chairs, all empty, and one door, dead center on the back wall.

The buzzing continued, a long, low drone.

Jackson knocked at the door.

The forty-something man who opened it had brilliantly

blue spiked hair, but no tattoos at all that Petrosky could see save for a tribal circle on his inner forearm. Starched green shirt, khaki pants—he could have been working at a hipster office supply store if not for the purple gloves he had clenched in one fist. In the room behind him, a brown-haired woman with gray river rocks for eyes reclined in a black leather chair. Pink silk robe. She appraised them calmly, curiously.

The man grinned, revealing fine lines at the corners of his mouth. "I've got a few appointments open later, man, just have to finish up with Molly here. Want to come back?" His voice was low, kind, but there was something off about his... mouth?

"This your place?"

"It is." His smile fell. "You're not here for a tattoo, are you."

"No, we aren't," Jackson said, flashing her badge. "Your name, sir?"

"Shae McCartney."

Was something wrong with his tongue? Petrosky raised an eyebrow. "You're about as Irish as they come, aren't ya?"

"So my mother tells me."

He gestured to the guy's hair. "She still speaks to you?"

Shae laughed, revealing the inside of his mouth, and there *was* something wrong, something... His tongue. It was split down the middle like a butterflied shrimp. "She thinks the world is better with a little color." He glanced back at his client, who nodded to him—*go ahead.* "What can I do for you?"

"Have you ever seen this boy?" Jackson pulled a photo of their victim from the folder and turned it so the man could see—one of the pictures they'd gotten from the Boyles' place, taken when the kid was still alive.

He squinted at it. His eyes widened. "Yeah! Corey, I think? It's been a while, though, a couple years at least." His brow furrowed, crinkling the skin of his forehead. "He in trouble?"

"He's dead," Jackson said.

Shae's jaw dropped, exposing that sliced monstrosity of a

tongue. "I…how can I help?" His eyes darted back and forth, Petrosky to Jackson, and back again.

Petrosky waited until the man held his gaze. "We're trying to figure out who he is, Shae. You got a last name?"

He shook his head, mouth open like he was ready to say something else, but the woman was already climbing to her feet, cinching the robe at her waist. "Oh! He's that boy from the news! The one who was kidnapped, right? And then killed himself?"

*Ah, yes.* But that old story was about to get turned on its head.

Petrosky crossed his arms as Shae's gaze darted from Molly to Petrosky and back as if waiting for someone to explain. "You been living under a rock, Mr. McCartney?"

"No, but I don't watch the news. It's depressing."

"He's kinda famous for it," Molly said quickly as if Petrosky might bash him for not listening to journalists. "It's a running joke on his social media pages."

That explained why Corey had chosen Shae McCartney to do his tat, expensive or not—any other artist would have outed him the moment they saw the story on television. The kid had done his research. "This boy used a fake tattoo to weasel his way into the home of a kidnapped child. A tattoo you gave him."

The woman behind McCartney stiffened.

"Are you generally in the habit of tattooing underage boys, Mr. McCartney?" They didn't know he was underage—Woolverton said he was *at least* eighteen when he'd died, and a kid that malnourished could have had a lot of permanent growth deficits—but Petrosky was tired of screwing around.

Shae's face went from frozen to baffled. "Absolutely not. He had a valid driver's license."

"How can you be sure it was valid? You have a way to tell if it was a fake?"

He shook his head, blue hair a spiky, immovable helmet. "It wasn't fake, but even if it had been, he was with his mother—a parent's permission is all I need."

His mother? The woman who'd given him all those bruises? Had she put him up to it, thinking she'd be able to cash in, then killed him when it didn't pan out?

"We're going to need a description." And this man might be able to do one better. "You're a good artist, aren't you, Mr. McCartney?"

He straightened, proud. "I am, sir. But I only saw her from a distance. She was outside, had a cap on, and lots of makeup—she was applying it when I peeked out. I remember she had dark hair, but outside of that..." He shrugged.

"Height? Weight?"

"Maybe...between five-three to five-six? No idea on the weight. I mean, she was sitting on the bench out there." He gestured to the glass entrance. Petrosky took a step backward and squinted; the bench was visible at the side of the lot, but no way he'd be able to tell details from here. And if she was sitting, height and weight would be even harder to determine.

"Dark hair, that's the only thing I'm really certain of," Shae went on, his hand tight around the gloves clenched at his navel. "And it's been...years. I don't think I'd trust my memory to give you an accurate picture, no matter how much I want to."

Wait...she hadn't been inside with Corey, then. How did he know they were together? "Did you ever actually see them speak?"

Shae frowned. "Well, I guess not. But people don't usually sit out there unless they're waiting for me to finish working on their friend or whatever—lots of folks want to be here for support, but they get skeeved out by needles."

*Needles.* But...no, the needle phobia wasn't relevant here, they already knew their guy didn't have a phobia—that was the real Gregory. But sitting on a bench didn't make you related to someone. "I still don't understand why you thought—"

"I told him he looked young, and he pointed, said his

mom was there, but that he was legal. And then he gave me the driver's license—the license was real, so I let it go."

So no way to tell if they were actually together, but they'd look into it. "What'd he say about the work you did? The birthmark? I can't imagine that's a usual request."

"That's why I remember him." Shae squinted. "I think he said his father had the same mark. That his dad died, and he missed him. A kind of…memorial tattoo." His knuckles were white around the gloves. "If he was underage; if he lied—"

"We're not trying to jam you up, Mr. McCartney. You did the best you could, not like you were obligated to ask for a birth certificate." Petrosky sniffed. "You keep records of the people you tattoo?"

Shae nodded. " I run a legitimate business here, got copies of driver's licenses and consent forms from everyone I work on."

Petrosky could have hugged him.

"We're going to need to see those files," Jackson said.

Shae glanced at his client again, then back to them. "Sure. I don't keep them all here—past years are in storage—but I'm happy to scan and email you over whatever you need. I'll look through them all tonight—got a break in my schedule around five. Do you know what month he might have been here? I can't remember that part."

"Sometime before April second, two years back." When he was found in the cemetery. "Outside of that…" Petrosky shook his head.

Shae eyed the kid's picture as Jackson slipped it back into the folder. "I'm really sorry I didn't know to call you."

Molly had climbed back onto the leather recliner. McCartney snapped on a fresh pair of gloves and picked up his tattoo gun. A low droning buzzzzzzed through the air and Molly tensed—just a little. She loosened the knot on the silk robe, but Shae paused and glanced back at them. "If there's anything else I can do…"

"We'll let you know," Petrosky said.

Jackson set her card on the edge of the recliner, by Molly's feet. "Email's on the back."

"That poor kid," Shae muttered. Molly untied the robe but held it together in front of her chest. What was she getting? Angel wings? The initials of a child? New areoles? Petrosky had a tattoo of Julie on his shoulder, but it had since been torn apart by a bullet. Ruined like his little girl. Appropriate. His chest constricted along with his lungs, but he pulled himself together in time to hear Shae say: "All this, all this work I do...I just want to make people happy." His voice cracked. "To think I helped cause something awful..." He took a breath, straightened his shoulders, and tested the needle again, preparing to go back to work.

Like all of them had to.

## 16

"Unbelievable. I mean, if that was really his mother, which I guess we can't verify."

The afternoon sun glared off the bumpers of the cars around them, reflecting an agitated yellow back into his eyeballs like it was trying to stab him in the brain. This kid—he'd planned it well. Smart. He'd only had one chance to do the ink right, and what better person than a man who would never recognize him?

"But someone had to pay for it," Jackson said. "The kid was scrawny as hell—a kid without money for food probably wasn't willing to shell out extra dough for perfection on a tattoo that may or may not secure his spot in the Boyle household."

A car pulled beside theirs—young woman, hands at two and ten like the driver's manual said, seat belt on, rear-facing infant in the car seat in the back, kicking their legs, face red. Screaming bloody murder. Mom kept driving. Eyes on the road, knuckles white.

"So we might have this kid's mother in on it here…and a male suspect seen with our vic at the park." Though it was possible the mystery park-goer seen with Gregory meant no harm, just an old friend or family member who didn't want to lose touch, they needed to find him—to rule him out. "But why is he dead? If he was telling the truth, and that woman was his mother…shit, if she was helping him get in with the Boyles for financial gain, she wouldn't hurt him. And no way it's a coincidence, that this imposter scheme is unconnected to the killing."

"So maybe financial gain was never the reason. Maybe Mom and Dad, or whoever those two were, were working different sides." Jackson squinted through the windshield. "Maybe…maybe this was about hiding, hence why Corey got so upset about the book. Maybe Mom wanted a better life for him. I know that's a long shot, but if someone in the house was abusing him, a father, stepfather maybe…"

She had a point. Domestic violence situations often required victims to run far away from their partners, and women were most at risk of death when they tried to leave. So had she been trying to protect Corey? But… "If you're trying to hide your child, you don't place him in a high-profile family. The father, the boyfriend, he could have seen the kid anytime he turned on the news, and then the kid's cover's blown."

"Well…yeah. And his cover did get blown, right? He was murdered. Maybe she was desperate, but didn't think it all the way through." She sighed. "There's a lot that makes no sense."

The mother in the car beside them pulled one hand from the wheel and wiped her eyes. If only he could tell her it got easier. But sometimes it got worse.

Petrosky turned away toward Jackson. "The PI you talked to…you think he's still working this?" He had let Jackson take the reins on that PI asshat, hadn't wanted to deal with him at all, but now…

Jackson shook her head. "He was on the initial kidnapping, but he didn't know anything about our murder."

"But the kids said there was a guy at the skate park yesterday asking questions. The one who looked like Johnny Depp. Whoever was there poking around wasn't one of ours." Petrosky pulled out his phone and punched in the PI's name, then turned the cell to Jackson. "Dark hair, dark eyes...does he look like Johnny Depp to you?"

. She shook her head. "Maybe in that pirate movie, but... not really. And he looks a lot younger in this photo than he is —maybe he got more Johnny as he aged."

*Or maybe those skater punks don't actually know who Johnny Depp is.* "Did he mention going to the skate park when you talked to him?" Had to be him, right?

Jackson frowned.

"Seriously, he works a case for five years, the kid comes back, then two years later the kid ends up dead? If I were the PI, I'd be poking around on it, connected or not."

"Right." Her eyes widened. "And Adrian believed her son was dead, but she kept Mancebo on the payroll. That's weird too. I understand he was her friend from high school, and I understand wanting the killer caught, but she was in debt up to her eyeballs already. For a mom willing to let a strange kid live in her house in the hopes they'd make enough off a book deal to help them financially...it just doesn't mesh for her to keep paying the PI." Unless there was something shady happening that they weren't privy to yet. And Adrian seemed pretty certain of her child's demise—had Mancebo found something that neither had shared with the police?

Jackson tap, tap, tapped on the wheel. "Won't hurt to swing by his office. Worst case, he has nothing more to tell us."

He sighed. "I fucking hate PIs."

"You hate everyone."

"It's part of my charm."

---

THE PI DID NOT LOOK like Johnny Depp. He was a Don-Juan-looking dickhead with an easy smile and deep bedroom eyes that appraised Jackson in a way that made Petrosky want to punch him in the jaw. The man straightened the lapels of his green and gold Hawaiian shirt. A gold watch studded with what were probably cubic zirconias glittered from his left wrist, ostentatious and just as useless. Petrosky frowned down at the black and red University of Georgia T-shirt Shannon had sent him last year—half-hidden under his black suit jacket—and commenced glaring at Julian Mancebo, PI extraordinaire.

Jackson eased herself into the white modern chair beside Petrosky. "In a perfect world, we wouldn't be working against each other, Mr. Mancebo."

"I didn't say we were. But the last detectives on this case…" Mancebo's voice was that of a pandering politician—middle of the road, with just enough passion under the surface to rile the crowd when he started yelling about the price of pharmaceuticals…or whatever those assholes argued about these days. "Two years ago, I get a call saying the kid is back. Cops run in here, asking to see my files, telling me they need to take everything I have."

Petrosky nodded approvingly. That was why they already had his notes on file—the ones he'd shared, anyhow.

Mancebo kept his eyes on Jackson. "I'd called every time I had something significant on the kidnapping, either the mother or the authorities. Nothing panned out—all they stole from me were notes they'd already been informed about."

*Stole.* Mancebo hated the cops as much as Petrosky hated PIs.

Jackson crossed her legs—maybe she could feel Mancebo's stare like the prickle of a spiny weed against her flesh. "And since then? Have you learned anything new recently?"

*Perhaps about our homicide?*

"Well, since then…there have been some complications." He stood abruptly, so quickly that Petrosky jolted upright, but the man headed for the white file cabinets in the back. White chairs, white cabinets, white walls. Only the desk was wood, a dark walnut that made it appear larger in the otherwise bright room. Probably a conscious decision: making himself look bigger, more important. Not everyone could be a real cop.

Mancebo slid the second drawer open. "The publishing house…they threatened to sue me about a year ago."

"For trying to find Gregory Boyle's kidnapper?" Jackson said.

He returned to his chair with a folder, Hawaiian shirt fluttering back into place—was that silk? What kind of self-respecting man wore silk? "Adrian said that she thought the publishers were moving too quickly, that they knew things they shouldn't. Let's just say I was looking into their own a little too closely, and they did not appreciate it."

Huh. Adrian hadn't mentioned the publisher. Or the PI. And…Mancebo was staring at a spot on Petrosky's forehead, avoiding his gaze. This wasn't about the publishers, and he knew it. He was feeding them a line because he had something else he didn't want them to know.

"But you stayed on the case even after Gregory came home," Jackson said. "Why? Weren't you hired to find the child?"

Mancebo's face hardened. "For five years, I looked. After he came home, I looked for the kidnapper, a man you never caught, as she asked. I'm still doing what she asks."

"So you had a lot of contact with the boy, then? After he came back?" He would have been talking to Corey, not Gregory, but maybe the imposter had said something he hadn't told anyone else.

Mancebo pursed his lips. "No. Adrian didn't want to upset him. And I don't want to upset her."

"Upset her?" Petrosky grimaced. "You think if you pissed her off, she'd cut off your paycheck?" She surely would if he admitted defeat.

Mancebo leaned back in his seat, slick black hair shining in the overheads. His face was a mask.

The hairs on the back of Petrosky's neck vibrated furiously. "Mr. Mancebo, I get the distinct impression you're not telling us something."

"I've told you what I know."

*Liar.* "You told us what you want us to know. What we don't know is why Adrian kept you on the payroll. And why she was so convinced her child was dead nearly from the day he disappeared."

No wrinkles appeared on the PI's forehead, not even a subtle tightening of the lips. He'd said he looked for Gregory for five years, but Petrosky had just casually dropped that Adrian believed Gregory was dead from the day he was taken. No reaction?

But maybe that made sense. If you *knew* your child was dead, maybe you let another boy live with you—*It was my last chance to have my boy back.* If you didn't have proof, you looked for that kid until your last breath. She didn't just suspect based on statistics—she knew. *She knew.* And so did the fuckhead sitting across from them.

When Mancebo remained silent, Petrosky said, "The child is dead now, though. It's over. And yet you're still working."

Mancebo sniffed. "Nothing has changed."

Jackson glanced Petrosky's way, then back to Mancebo. "The boy was found hanging in the living room, Mr. Mancebo. How can that not change anything?"

Now Mancebo's eye twitched—guilt, dishonesty, the tell of a man with something critical to hide. Mancebo knew their victim was an imposter, too, Petrosky was certain of it.

"How long have you known the boy living in Adrian Boyle's house was not her child?"

Mancebo licked his lips. "Even if I suspected, that's not illegal."

"You did more than suspect, Mr. Mancebo. Working for Adrian Boyle, your old flame, you wouldn't have just let that slide."

He leaned closer, gaze locked on Jackson as if confiding his darkest secret. "I ran a test over a year ago. Took his toothbrush." The PI smiled, but there was a fierceness in his eyes. A challenge. "So yes, nothing has changed, not for me. I will still look for Gregory's killer, as she asked me to."

"You mean Gregory's kidnapper." *Or Gregory himself.* The kid wasn't in the morgue like their imposter...that they knew of.

Mancebo sat back in the chair, crossed his arms, and steadied his gaze.

Petrosky's fists clenched. "Gregory could still be out there, Mancebo. Being held by his abductors, waiting for someone to show up and save him. If you knew the boy at the Boyle house wasn't Gregory, you had an obligation to tell us. To give Gregory a chance."

The silence stretched so long Petrosky thought Mancebo was getting ready to kick them out—*Try it, asshole*—but then he sighed. "Gregory is dead. He's been dead since he was taken." He opened the file on his desk and flipped a few pages. Too calm, like they were discussing brunch. Petrosky could barely breathe with the rage constricting his chest

Mancebo tapped a page, eye twitching harder now. "Two streets up from the route Gregory usually took home, there was blood on the sidewalk, near the curb—a few drops, but still enough. And I called your detectives about it at the time."

Petrosky's fists ached.

"You have any proof that it was Gregory's?" Jackson said.

"Yes. I had it tested when the police did nothing."

But Harris would have done something had he known about the blood—Gregory's blood. "The kidnapper could have injured him getting into the car, something superficial —that doesn't mean he's dead. So what else you got?" Petrosky snapped. "Because you know as well as I do, that you wouldn't be sitting there so goddamn certain of his death if you didn't have better than a little blood on a curb."

Mancebo's nostrils flared. "Your detectives...they dismissed me. Years and years on this, and they ignored me." His voice was rising. "One laughed right in my face when I asked to be included in the investigation."

"This is about your ego? You were slighted, so fuck the police and fuck Gregory?"

Mancebo's eyes narrowed, teeth bared.

How much trouble would he get in for punching this jackwad in the jaw? He lowered his voice, his rage concentrating into a hard ball of fire behind his Adam's apple. "I'm done messing around. We're going to find out eventually. And if we find out on our own, without your help, I'll make sure you go away for impeding a police investigation."

Mancebo met Petrosky's gaze with steel, nostrils still flaring, jaw working. But finally, he nodded. "The blood on the curb was where you might place a trash can. When *your* men did not show, I took the liberty of going to the dump."

"Say what now?" But the thought of this guy in his silky floral print scrounging around in a steaming pile of garbage made Petrosky feel a little better. Until he remembered that the man had been looking for a child's corpse.

"There are three landfills in the area," Mancebo continued, "but only one utilized by the company that picks up the trash along the route where I saw the blood. That's where I found Gregory's backpack."

Not his body. His backpack. Petrosky forced his fists to relax before he punched the asshole in the gut. "His backpack? You found—"

"His name was stenciled on the side of it. There is no mistaking the bag, though it was in very rough shape. But a kidnapper would not throw away a child's prized possession. You do that when the child has also been disposed of. When you need to cover your tracks."

"You a shrink, Mancebo?"

The man opened his smug mouth to respond, but Jackson was already raising her hands in a what-the-hell gesture. "Alive or dead, why wouldn't you turn that over? We could have—"

"There was no DNA from anyone who might have harmed him—I had tests run to confirm that no additional

DNA was on the pack, ruled out his parents and his teacher, even his brother."

*What in the ever-loving—*

"Who ran these tests?" Jackson demanded.

"A forensic company out in Lansing—they do exquisite work. The reports will hold up in court, always have before."

Jackson shook her head, mouth agape as if she were trying to think of something else to say, but it was too late to do anything about this. Petrosky had half a mind to arrest this sack of shit right now, but he might come in handy later. Plus… "A backpack doesn't necessarily mean he's dead, Mancebo, blood or not."

Mancebo's eye twitched again. He averted his gaze.

*Goddammit.* Petrosky leaned closer. "We're dealing with a homicide case, the death of a teenager. If you also have a child homicide, we need to know before someone else gets hurt. You okay with another kid's blood on your hands?" And two dead kids made it all the more likely that the cases were connected.

Mancebo swallowed hard. "There were clothes—a torn shirt and his shoes. In the bag." He finally dragged his gaze back to Petrosky. "That's where the blood came from. So much blood it soaked right through the bottom. A child losing that much blood…no way he survived it."

*Bloody clothes.* "How do you feel about obstruction of justice, Mancebo?"

"I shared my suspicions. I called the tip line, asked them to send cadaver dogs out to the landfill, but they did not."

Petrosky had seen that note: *caller says to send dogs to the dump.* But there had been twelve more calls just like it requesting dogs to other random parts of the city. The ones they'd researched turned up a jilted dick-bag trying to harass his ex-wife, a fourteen-year-old crank caller, and one seemingly legit ask leading to a field with a dead raccoon.

Petrosky shot to his feet and slammed his fists on the man's desk. "You didn't tell them you had a reason!" Rage heated Petrosky's guts, broiling his belly. "You wanted to suck that family dry when you knew their kid was dead in the goddamn dump." And now, he'd just be bones. Bones beneath a mountain of trash.

"I did my job." Mancebo returned Petrosky's gaze, even, calm as a psychopath. *Maybe he killed Gregory himself.*

"Yeah, you did your job, all right, you did your job for Adrian and..." He narrowed his eyes at Mancebo. "You told her. You're the reason she had a breakdown three months after he vanished. You told her you found the pack soaked in her son's blood, that he was gone."

Mancebo's jaw clenched. But he nodded.

"Where's the bag now, genius?"

"I have it in storage here." Mancebo turned back to Jackson, whose eyes were spitting fire.

*Punch him. Punch him in the head.* Petrosky eased back into his seat. *No, don't give him the satisfaction of filing a lawsuit.* But wiping that stupid smile off his face would surely be worth a night in jail.

"And you told no one?" Jackson said, her voice far calmer than Petrosky felt. "Not only about the bag, or the goddamn shirt, but about this new kid not being the Boyles' real child?"

Mancebo pursed his lips.

*You stupid shit.* "Adrian already told us, asshole, just spit it out before I get tired of chatting and perp walk you out of here."

Mancebo met Petrosky's eyes. "Adrian asked for discretion because of the book. I wanted to help Stevie, wanted to help her. I wanted something good to come out of this." He shrugged. "I cannot imagine losing my child once, let alone twice. What she has been through...it is abhorrent." An emotion flitted across Mancebo's face and vanished—pain. Real sorrow. And...he kept calling her Adrian. Not Mrs. Boyle, or "my client." Adrian.

"You seem to have an awful keen sense of what Mrs. Boyle needs." Petrosky glanced at the man's naked ring finger. "You sleeping with her?"

"That is not your concern."

*Well, that's just great.* And come to think of it...they went way back, all the way to high school. Little Greggie had dark hair, dark eyes—like this guy. "Was Gregory your child?" Shit, maybe Mancebo really did take him, kidnapped his own damn son—at least then there was a chance, albeit a tiny one, that he was still alive despite the backpack. Maybe Mancebo had faked that shit to throw them off. Petrosky swallowed the heat that was rising in his throat.

"No, Gregory was not my son." Mancebo shook his head, his gaze steady. He seemed genuine, but surely he'd know lying wouldn't work—a DNA test and they'd know the truth.

"What else have you kept from the Ash Park PD?" Jackson asked.

Mancebo opened his mouth, surely ready to lie his ass off, and Petrosky snapped, "We don't want to give her false hope any more than you do. We just want to find Gregory Boyle, dead or alive, and we need to know who killed the boy who's been calling your girlfriend Momma for the last two years."

Mancebo stared, sighed, and addressed Jackson. "I just talked to the kids at the skate park, that's all—they didn't know anything." *So much for Johnny Depp—damn kids.*

Gooseflesh crawled along Petrosky's arms and down his back. "You're in possession of a backpack belonging to a kidnapped child, and you're sleeping with his mother while wringing her bank accounts dry. Seems pretty suspicious to me." He wanted to believe this guy had done it, wanted to snatch him up and drag him down to the precinct and lock him in a cell, but...it didn't feel right. What reason would Mancebo have to kill the kid? Why hurt a woman he seemed to care about? Jealousy?

Mancebo's jaw dropped, but his eyes cleared—resigned. He pulled his file closer. "I have told the police most of the information here. But..." He flipped a few pages and pulled out a sheet of lined notebook paper—a crappy drawing of a blue car.

"What the hell is that?" Jackson asked.

"From back when Gregory was taken. I called into the tip

line and told them they needed to be looking for an older model blue sedan."

Petrosky wracked his brain, trying to recall ever seeing an investigation into cars, but came up blank. Then again, he did remember the huge stack of papers that had come from the tip line—had they dismissed it? Or had they looked into it and never gotten anywhere?

Jackson took the picture and frowned at it. "Where did you get the sketch?"

"A kid at the playground, three blocks from Gregory Boyle's school."

*Oh shit.* They had an eyewitness? "You've got to be kidding me, Mancebo."

"Your people didn't think it was vital because the witness was only twelve—but that is old enough for her to know what she saw. She was sitting with her older brother on the bench in front of the park three blocks from the school, waiting for her mother to pick her up. She said she saw Gregory talking to someone in a blue car."

"How long before he vanished?"

"The day before."

Stevie had mentioned that Greg was planning to run off —that he'd known the day before. Was this how Greg and the kidnapper had planned his abduction? Had they been making plans for the following day? "She was sure it was Gregory?"

He nodded. "She described his backpack in detail, and there was another child in the backseat—she said the other boy rolled down the window and winked at her." It might be true, but asking again would be utterly useless—fresh witness statements were questionable, and interrogating a child seven years after she might have seen a blue car? It'd be as helpful as that shitty picture she'd drawn.

"The brother see anything?" Jackson asked.

He shook his head. "He said no. And neither saw the driver. But I think the driver was talking to Gregory because they intended to take him."

"You and me both, hoss, but what you've got is thin." Even if Mancebo was right, there was no way to run down a nondescript blue car from seven years back, and they had no idea on the specific make and model—a blue sedan would get thousands of hits. Far too many to be of use to them.

"This other boy in the backseat, though…she said he looked like Gregory." Mancebo's eyes shone almost hopefully. "And like your victim."

"Our…" But that made no sense. "Wait…are you saying you think our murder vic, Corey, was the boy in the backseat? That he was part of the original plan to kidnap—"

"I am saying that this vehicle, the one seen with Gregory before he vanished, had another boy inside it. And I don't like that—maybe your kidnapper has done it before."

Though Petrosky wouldn't say it aloud, he agreed—he'd seen other similar cases where children had been used to lure new victims. Donald Jarvis Ponce was one of the most notorious: four girls over six years, and he'd bring his old kidnapping victim with him to find a new one when he got bored. It was always the last trip they ever took.

Petrosky stood. They'd take the DNA reports and the backpack, and anything else this motherfucker had that might help their case. Two murders—probably. Two dead children. There had to be a connection here. And maybe later they'd come back and lock Mancebo in a cell for fun.

**17**

---

Jackson's fingers tapped on the steering wheel, a beat that throbbed in time to the pulsing of blood in Petrosky's brain. Almost to the precinct. How long had he been staring out the window?

"I want that shithead in cuffs when this is over," she muttered.

Petrosky did, too, but his rage had cooled—inside, he felt hollow, spent. "Do you think Gregory's dead?"

Her face hardened, her lips a line etched in stone. "Yeah. Bloody clothes, a bloody bag—especially that amount of blood from a seven-year-old? Doesn't bode well for survival. But he was groomed first...lured out to wherever they took him. That's a lot of work just to kill him right off."

"Maybe he fought." Often, abductors used violence because they were desperate to take the kid, even if they hadn't planned to cause them harm. Then again, it depended on what the kidnapper was planning to do with him. Pedophiles often felt a deep love for children, convinced themselves that the child wanted them—they were often horrified by the thought that their actions were harmful. But sadists, psychopaths...they didn't have that concern. Narcissists, too, had far less empathy than the average pedophile. There were plenty of abductors who relished the pain of others—and psychopathic pedophiles, well… Gregory would never have had a chance.

The sun glowered, well past the halfway mark—in a few hours, that bloody red would return, signaling another day that they'd failed. He peeked into the backseat at the box containing the shrink-wrapped backpack. "Fuck Mancebo," he said.

"He'll get time—you can't hide a bloody shirt from the cops. But I don't think he hurt Gregory. Or Corey. I'm not seeing motive—his meal ticket's gone now." Jackson wheeled into the lot and jammed the car into park.

"He's still trying to earn his keep, figure out who killed Corey."

"We'll have to beat him to the perp then, won't we?"

Petrosky frowned at the building. Frowned as he crossed the lot after Jackson. He was still frowning when the blast of super-cooled air hit him in the face. As much as he hated the PI, he didn't think the guy was responsible for Gregory's disappearance either. If he was, he wouldn't have kept the shirt at his office, and he definitely wouldn't have told them about it. And while it was possible he'd found out Corey wasn't the Boyles' real child and had blackmailed the kid, he seemed dedicated to Adrian Boyle. Mancebo was a dick, but Petrosky didn't think he'd torment a kid, not when he was willing to go to jail to keep the mother's secrets. Plus, the PI was too big to be their killer; he wouldn't have needed to hook his toes under that couch to get leverage.

The stairwell still smelled like hot dogs.

"So, what if this witness was right about the blue car?" The sound of Jackson's feet on the stairway thrummed in time to her words. "What if there was another child in the car who looked like Gregory?"

He followed her, knees creaking louder than their feet on the steps. "It could have been Corey, but I'm not feeling it— no reason to take a different kid, then put yours in his place five years down the line. Maybe the kidnapper has a biolog- ical child, though, or there's another victim." His chest ached, his lungs too tight—from the exertion? He looked longingly at the precinct door half a flight up and pressed on, his heavy breath mingling with the echo of their footfalls.

She paused at the door to the bullpen, hand on the knob. "Whoever did this…they knew what they were doing. Stevie said Gregory was meeting an older *friend*. Gregory talked to them in that car the day before he was taken, then went home and packed a bag, knowing he wouldn't have Stevie with him the next day. He didn't plan all that at seven, not alone."

And it had been executed perfectly—until Gregory had been injured, bled out all over his clothes, bled enough that it had soaked clear through his backpack. That much blood… the kidnapper had sliced something important, and arteries didn't repair themselves. But no one had taken him to the hospital; the hospitals had been on high alert during the kidnapping investigation. No way the kid had walked away from that.

Petrosky followed Jackson into the bullpen and collapsed at his desk, then waited while she dragged her seat over; someone had taken the chair that usually sat across from his. Decantor? But the big man only had one chair at his desk, and his ass was in it. When Jackson was settled, he said, "So maybe the kidnapper…maybe there were other children before Gregory."

Jackson rested her elbows on the desk, suddenly looking as tired as he felt. "We'll have to look more closely at any kidnappings that might be related."

"They'd have found that before, though." The last detectives on the case had already searched for related kidnappings, and the thought of looking through a pile of other missing and probably dead children was more than his heart could take at this moment. And it probably wouldn't help them anyway. "Hopefully, tracking down this Corey, figuring out who he was, will give us something. He had to have been reasonably certain that Gregory wasn't coming back, and even more sure that they wouldn't make him take a blood test—shit, he had to know about the needle phobia, right? One test is all it would have taken to out him."

"Yeah. And that needle thing wasn't made public," Jackson said. "So it's most likely that our kidnapper knew both Gregory *and* Corey. Gregory's older friend could have been feeding Corey information before he headed for the Boyles' house—maybe the kid in the backseat was the older friend. There has to be some connection here, even if I can't see it."

Petrosky rubbed his still-smarting knee. So many unknowns, all of them leading to another rabbit hole. "I hate Mancebo."

Jackson sighed. "I know. But he definitely isn't Greg's father. When they put Gregory into the database, they took samples from the parents too. And Greg and Ron have the same birthmark. Didn't you see it on Ron's arm?"

No, he hadn't. He should have—that was his job, to notice things. What else was he missing? "I'll have Scott double-check, just to be sure."

"Fine, whatever helps you sleep at night." She narrowed her eyes at him. "You *are* sleeping, right?"

"I'm fine."

"You don't look fine."

*Drop it.* "The dog snores."

"Is that why you're wearing the same shirt you had on yesterday, complete with a coffee stain?"

He eyed the dark splotch on the red letters just above his paunch, his ribs tightening. "The dog drools, and I'm a little behind on my laundry. You should have seen my other choices." He kept his voice even, but his face was hot. *Why is she looking at me like that?*

She leaned across the desk and lowered her voice. "Listen, Petrosky, if you're having a hard time; if you need help—"

"Jesus Christ, let it go!" he said, far too loud. The bullpen quieted. Across the way, Decantor rose from his seat.

Jackson stared at Petrosky. Worried.

"Your boyfriend's coming," Petrosky grunted.

She looked over her shoulder as the bigger man stepped up beside her. "Everything okay here?"

"Just dandy," Petrosky snapped, then lower, "Mind your own business, you J-Lo-loving fuck."

"You don't seem fine."

Was there a goddamn echo in here? "I'm constipated."

Decantor glanced at Jackson, then headed back to his seat, tossing Petrosky a backward glance over his shoulder as he slid back into his chair. Petrosky rubbed his aching chest. His skin was on fire, hot and tingling.

"If you're really okay, I'll drop it."

*No. No, I'm absolutely not okay.* "Just a little indigestion. I think I need to cut the oatmeal and eat more donuts. I didn't have this problem with eclairs."

"No, you had a heart attack with eclairs."

"Rub it in a little deeper, why don't you?" He forced a smile.

She did not look convinced.

**18**

———

Shae McCartney's email came an hour after they got back to the precinct, complete with a picture of the signed tattoo consent forms and a driver's license for one eighteen-year-old Corey Gagnon. No mistaking that picture. This was the child—the young man—who had pretended for two years to be Gregory Boyle. And that wasn't the most significant shock.

Corey Gagnon's ID was Canadian—the kid was a damn Canuck. It would be hard enough to track a kid down in Ash Park or the surrounding metropolis, but adding another country into the mix? *Goddammit.* Petrosky pulled his keyboard closer and snatched up the phone.

For three hours, he researched and called and tried like hell not to snap at the Canadian officials who were having too much trouble pronouncing their vowels to worry about his bullshit. Everything looked legit—the photo was definitely the boy in the morgue, and the name and birthdate information matched up with the Canadian social insurance number for Corey Gagnon. The location where the driver's license was issued was minutes from Corey's last known address.

"Nicest people in the world," Jackson said, collapsing into the seat beside him with a stack of papers and a cup of coffee

—it'd be his fourth. But instead of pushing the cup his way, she sipped at it, then set it beside her files.

He eyeballed his own cold, down-to-the-burned-dregs cup and said, "I talked to the precinct near Corey's last known address, the one from his license—that was the one the report went through when he didn't show up to school. Those cops sound happy just being there."

"So it was the school that reported Corey missing? He was eighteen—why would they care?"

"Corey was a senior with a known history of abuse; when he didn't show up for a week, with no call-ins and no one answering his home phone, the principal called the Mounties. But because he was already eighteen, there was nothing they could really do, especially since everyone assumed he'd finally run off. Which it turns out…he had."

"Another runaway, huh? I'm sensing a pattern. But check this out." She slid a folder toward him. "Mother, Rosalie Gagnon, died March fifth at Fountainview Medical Center in Windsor. Drug overdose. But Corey was with her at the hospital that night. That was the last time anyone up there saw him, so far as the police can ascertain."

Petrosky squinted at the tiny blurred dates on the death certificate. "About a month before he showed up claiming to be the Boyles' child."

"Exactly. Which means his mother was dead *before* he got that tattoo—if the woman outside McCartney's shop was there with him, she wasn't his mom. But it's possible they were never together at all, that Corey just pointed to someone when he got a raised eyebrow about how young he looked."

But he wouldn't have had to tell Shae McCartney that the woman was his mother—he was legal. Why say it if it wasn't true? Petrosky cleared his throat. "Corey wasn't the other boy in the blue car Mancebo's witness saw—he was in school that day." Another dead end. "Father in the picture?"

"Real father was never around, but he did live with a stepfather." Jackson slipped a few stapled sheets from the folder, the headers glaring blue: Children's Aid Society. Photos of Corey on page two. And three. Five. Purple bruises around his rib cage from what looked like a fist or a boot to the kidney, bleeding stripes down his back, and on the last sheet a very different looking Corey with blue and black beneath both eyes and blood on his teeth.

"Was he in protective custody up there?"

She shook her head and grabbed her coffee cup off his desk. He squinted at a wayward drip on the desktop as she said, "He was never taken away at all."

"The hell?"

Jackson set the cup back down and took a sheet from the folder: another driver's license. Corey's stepfather was a white man, early forties, with a bushy beard and the cold dead eyes of a rattlesnake. Skinny through the arms, maybe small enough to need to use a couch as leverage, but Lowell Fournier did not appear to be the type of man who'd wear skater shoes, and he was too tall to have a size six foot… probably. Petrosky went to hand the photo back but paused, squinting. The beard…he looked like the suspect sketches they'd put out after they thought Gregory Boyle had returned. Was this the man Corey had described to authorities when they found him in the cemetery? The man from the skate park?

"Here's the deal," Jackson said. "Corey denied abuse every time, told authorities he got beat up walking home from school, and they believed it—there were numerous verified reports of violent behavior at the school itself, expulsions for fighting and the like. Even the marks on his back got written up as him being thrown against a fence. And the investigations didn't turn up wrongdoing on the part of the mother or her husband either. The house was clean, no evidence of drugs despite Mom's checkered history, and this stepfather figure…from the reports, it sounds like he was sober, at least when they came to interview him. But get this." She tapped the page so hard it had to hurt her finger. *Thunk, thunk, thunk.* "The name he gave, and his United States license—

stolen. Not his. All the information he gave them was false, right down to the social security number. Children's Aid copied his license and took down his social, but they didn't look for a death certificate. The real Lowell Fournier died twenty years ago in Boston."

"Ol' Lowell sounds like a shyster." And probably a sociopath. Petrosky ran a hand over his bristly face and pushed the keyboard aside so hard the phone came off the cradle and clattered onto the desk. He stared at it. Jackson stared at it. She reached over and put it back on the hook.

"A shyster for sure. I gave his photo to your journalist friend, Acharya, but facial recognition pinged in Vermont for related crimes before I even got off the phone. Social security fraud, taking payouts after people died, stealing disability payments—the list goes on. Hopefully, someone will recognize him and tell us where he is."

They might. But had he killed Corey? Would he have taken Gregory? And why? Kidnapping and murdering a stranger's kid was a far cry from social security fraud. Maybe he'd intended to ask for ransom. Or maybe replacing Gregory with Corey was just another long con for a guy who loved to cause pain, but why would Corey agree? Petrosky sighed. "There was a huge alert out on this guy two years back—not the name, but we had a similar sketch. Corey accused him of kidnapping, in so many words." Which meant Corey and Fournier probably weren't in it together.

"Yeah, but if this guy was in Canada..." She shrugged.

"Moose-fucking bastard," Petrosky muttered. "Okay, so Corey's mother...she dies at Fountainview Hospital, and—*Bam!*—Corey decides impersonating Gregory is his ticket out? Someone had to tell him about Gregory in the first place, at least help him across the border. I doubt he paid for the passport fees himself."

"Maybe, maybe not. But he probably used a real passport as opposed to a fake one, which will tell us when he crossed—he used a real license at the tattoo shop. No one would bat an eye if he said he was coming down to see if our poutine was better than theirs."

"Which it definitely is not." Petrosky sniffed. "Fries with gravy are always better over the border." He peeked into her coffee cup—empty. *Dammit.*

"It might not matter how he crossed—that part wouldn't have been hard, and once he got here, he figured he'd get a job, run a con, whatever. He didn't have much to lose. But since he knew about the needle phobia...maybe he got mixed up with the kidnapper once he got here."

"So the kidnapper goes after him...or this guy does." Petrosky glared at the photo—Lowell Fournier. Who named their kid Lowell? And with his history of social security fraud, Fournier was probably living under another assumed now. "Corey could have made something up when they asked who took him, could have told us he didn't remember, but he described this guy to a T, except for the variable beard color. Maybe Corey thought the guy'd be after him eventually— maybe he was right."

"But if they actually caught Fournier, they'd have realized who Corey really was, that he wasn't the Boyles' child—that's risky for Corey too."

They lapsed into silence.

He leaned back in his chair, the springs squealing like an angry pig. "Anyone seen this clown since the night Corey's mother died?"

Jackson was looking at him strangely—had his voice cracked? She shook her head. "According to the authorities, he vanished right after Rosalie died, just like Corey. He was her medical emergency contact; they called to ask about arrangements for the body, assuming a funeral home would be taking her, and nada."

"He vanished? After her drug overdose?" Usually, people ran when they did something wrong; maybe he thought he'd get in trouble for having the drugs in the house, but—

"Heroin overdose is the official cause, but she had a skull fracture, too, and some older bruising around the throat. They thought she'd hit her head when she passed out, which isn't uncommon in OD cases, but I'm betting Fournier roughed her up. It's possible this guy thought he'd hurt her worse than he had and took off to avoid prosecution—it was a fluke she was drugged up enough to kill her, making her other injuries secondary. If we can find him, we might be able to use that to squeeze him."

Petrosky swallowed, his throat arid yet somehow acidic, like the fumes leftover after some caustic chemistry experiment. The bruises on Corey's face flashed in his brain—the kid's bloody teeth. "Psychos like this...I could see him figuring out what Corey was up to and coming after Corey, blackmailing him—and Corey paying Fournier for his silence." They'd have to bring Fournier's photo to the skater kids, see if Beef recognized him as the man in the park.

His eyes blurred. He blinked hard, trying to clear the fuzziness from his vision, but it stuck.

"You okay, Petrosky?"

*No.* "Yes." He squinted again at the bearded brute in the image. A guy like this would know his way around a needle if the kid's mother was a heroin addict. But those little skater shoes.

Jackson drummed her fingers on the files. "If this was the guy Corey was meeting at the skate park, I could see blackmail being on the table. But why bother paying? Just to avoid getting in trouble for impersonating Gregory? Corey was of age—he could have left the Boyles' place if he needed to get away, gone out, gotten a job, gone back to Canada even. Why deal with Fournier?"

"Maybe he didn't feel equipped to do that, or felt like it was hopeless." At twenty years old, his math skills were on par with a fourteen-year-old's, but he was even lower than that in reading comprehension. "If I were him, I'd figure I could repeat school, graduate, and actually go to college... start a better life, one that wouldn't have been available before. I sure wouldn't want to give that up."

Jackson's drumming fingers stilled. "The ultimate scholarship."

Petrosky nodded. But if this was true, Corey's motivations, and his death, weren't connected to Gregory's disappearance, which meant they were no closer to finding Gregory Boyle's killer—if the kid was dead as Mancebo thought. Maybe he'd just been badly injured. But the backpack, the blood soaked straight through…no, someone had murdered Little Greggie and dumped him in the trash.

His chest tightened. "We got a set of fingerprints on this fuckstick?" There hadn't been prints inside the Boyle house —whoever had killed Corey had worn gloves and seemed quite a bit more careful than a man who liked to beat teenagers and his wife for shits and giggles. But if Fournier had ever been fingerprinted, they could at least look at his history, maybe figure out known associates. And someone should have his real name.

"Nope. He never got popped when he was living as Fournier, or anywhere that I can gather. Even Rosalie Gagnon's death was an overdose, so they didn't look at the house—the only reason I knew about Rosalie's injuries is from the ME up there. We have no prints for comparison."

"Maybe we don't need old fingerprints." Petrosky squinted at the wall. "Let's go take a look through the box of stuff Scott pulled from Corey's room at the Boyles'."

"Are you okay, Petrosky?"

"I'm fine, why—"

"It's just…you think Fournier went through Corey's stuff? It doesn't make sense."

"I wouldn't put it past him. Guy's a thief by trade."

"He's an identity thief by trade, I guess, but Scott already dusted up there, you know that. Every print on Gregory's… Corey's stuff is legit, and the guy wore gloves to murder Corey—not like he'd peel them off to go rummaging through his things."

She was right. Petrosky rubbed his aching temples, trying to clear the bleariness from his brain. "So…let's say Fournier is the guy our skater punks saw with Corey at the park—how did Corey know when to meet him? Did they have a set day and time, or was Fournier contacting him somehow?" Scott had run the kid's cell, looked at the house phone, too—no numbers were unaccounted for.

"Maybe Fournier met him in person. Or gave Corey a note that he tossed out after he'd read it."

Petrosky snorted. "Passed him a note? What is this, fifth grade? Corey was on the computer a lot; they could have chatted there." But... He sat straighter. "Someone did see a car out there, right? One of the neighbors saw a darker truck at the curb."

Jackson flipped a few sheets and tapped her notes. "Mailboxes, that was his thing. That was how he used to get the social security checks from dead men, the reason the Vermont police ended up with a photo; someone's doorbell camera caught him rifling through their mail. And sticking a letter in the Boyles' mailbox would be effective, Petrosky. He could hide his face, his body—he wouldn't even have to get out of the truck."

And no one had run fingerprints on the mailbox. "I wonder if there would still be any prints."

"I'm sure the mail carrier will be psyched about giving his prints to rule him out. But it's worth a shot."

Petrosky reached for his cell. "I'll call Scott, see if he can head over there before Stevie's bedtime."

**19**

———————

"THREE THINGS," Scott said before Petrosky even said hello. Scott's voice had an air of superiority, as well it should, but tonight it grated on Petrosky's nerves. Even the subtle breeze from the much-needed precinct air conditioner was suddenly making him want to throw the damn thing across the room for the high crime of cooling his neck.

"One: I just finished looking at the stuff you got from the PI. There's trace on that shirt from the backpack, the one Gregory was wearing, when he was kidnapped—I found a drop or two of blood from someone else besides Gregory Boyle, but almost all of it is Gregory's."

But... was this good or bad? Was the blood from their killer? "You get a match on it?"

"Only a partial profile. The samples were too degraded." Too degraded because it had been seven goddamn years. *Fucking Mancebo.* They were definitely going to arrest his ass.

Scott continued: "I'm more worried about the condition of the shirt itself—sharp cuts on it, like knife wounds concentrated around the collar. Someone stabbed him, Petrosky—right around the neck area. Cut his throat. A seven-year-old kid. What kind of monster..."

Scott's voice faded in his ears as he imagined Gregory Boyle, seven, trying to fend off an adult wielding a blade, the kid crying, screaming, throat open—and then it was Julie, throat slit end to end like a gaping smile on her pale neck, the scent of burning flesh in his nostrils. There was no air. He wheezed.

"You okay?"

He pulled the phone from his ear, coughed and licked his lips, and forced out: "What else?"Scott hesitated a beat, then went on: "Two: Gregory was Ron Boyle's child, not Mancebo's—the results were already in the system. No way they're wrong unless someone hacked it, which is pretty much impossible."

"And three?" He inhaled deeply, forcing his lungs to inflate. Another dead end. Was there even worse news Scott had saved for last?

"No matches on any of the skater kids' shoes. I took Stevie Boyle's shoes, too, just in case. His parents were none too happy to see me again."

His heart was a bass drum against his rib cage. "Maybe you should have reminded them that they would still be living in a goddamn hotel if you didn't have the fastest swabs in the west."

Scott laughed. "You know, I tried that, but I can't pull off the western talk. Too nerdy for spurs."

"Never too nerdy, Scott." His chest relaxed. "But, you'll have to turn on the charm again—need another favor." Petrosky filled him in on the mailbox idea.

"Okay, I'll stop there in a few and bring everything back here before heading home."

Petrosky glanced at the windows but saw only the bullpen reflected back to him from the blackness. What time was it? And the line had gone quiet. Petrosky was about to hang up when the boy cleared his throat. "My dad has been asking about you. You free this week?"

Petrosky's eye twitched, Julie's face flashing and vanishing. No, not free this week. "This case is taking a lot out of me, Scott, but I'll head over to see your pop once it winds down."

"Maybe you can just take a break for an hour? You guys can order dinner or something."

Dinner? George Scott was into pork rinds and a ball game, not idle chitchat and Chinese take-out. It was one of Petrosky's favorite things about him. Petrosky glanced at his partner, who was steadfastly pretending to read a case file at her own desk. "Jackson put you up to this?" She did not react to her name. Definitely suspicious.

"Jackson? No, my dad just...you know how he is. He wants to see you, but he's too proud to call. And he can't get around as easily on his own. But I can take him down by your place if you want. Even tonight. You're going home soon, right?"

*Nope.* "I don't have time this week, Scott. Let him know I'll head his way by the end of the month, okay?"

Hopefully in a couple weeks, he'd be able to eat a pork rind without smelling his daughter's charred dead flesh.

But he doubted it.

---

PETROSKY HEADED for home with a heaviness in his gut. Linda had called three times in the last two hours—he'd sent them all to voicemail.

Maybe he was a dick. Maybe he had to be. True, all Linda wanted was companionship, some understanding, someone to tell her it was going to be okay. But he'd rather be an asshole than a liar.

The first liquor store passed in a fog, the glass, even the black window bars reflecting the glowing neon sign. His mouth watered as he ripped a pack of cigarettes from the glovebox. He'd never told anyone they were there—he'd quit after all—but tonight...he'd never been more glad the girls hadn't found them.

The click of the lighter was like music, and the acrid burn on the first inhale felt less like smoke and more like the hot breath of a lover. Delicious. Distracting—but not enough.

His hands were shaking on the wheel by the time he stopped at the light a mile from the last liquor store. Just a few minutes from home. What could it hurt? Not like whiskey could make him feel worse than he did already.

*Sure it can. I don't have a gun between my teeth yet.*

The light changed. He dragged on the smoke, trying to ignore the tightness in his chest, the achy way his throat itched after so long without tobacco. The easy way his brain relaxed into the pleasant haze of nicotine. *If I can just sleep, I can do better tomorrow.* Just a little nip, the slightest bit to numb the edges—if he drank enough, he could lie to Linda, and at least one of them might have some peace. That was the decent thing to do.

The last liquor store approached, bright, glowing, red and blue and green. It might as well have had a target on it.

He slammed on the brakes, knuckles tight against the wheel, tires shrieking against the asphalt as he swerved into the parking lot.

**20**

---

"WAKE UP, you old bastard. Customs and Border Protection got back to us: no record of Corey ever crossing the border, so either he used a fake passport, or he came over in someone's trunk."

"You woke me up to tell me that?" he grumbled.

"Nope. I woke you up to tell you that the fingerprints Scott pulled off the mailbox popped in the system."

Petrosky pulled the phone away from his ear, stifled a yawn, and dragged his feet from the living room couch to the floor, narrowly missing Duke's head. He'd given up on the bedroom around three—all through the wee hours, Julie's night-light had blinked at him, shuddering into his field of vision even after he closed his eyes, reminding him of what he'd lost. That it was his fault. But he still hadn't been able to unplug it.

He glanced at the bottle of Jack on the coffee table. *Still full.* But it had a weight to it beyond the sixty ounces of liquor; he could feel it on his skin, a low, insistent vibration that made the whole room heavier.

"Did you hear what I said?"

"Yeah, yeah, hang on." Petrosky shoved himself to standing, unsteady, every muscle aching, skin smarting around the waistband of his jeans. He headed for the laundry room. "So

142

Scott found usable prints. Kid's a rock star." His tongue was covered in cottony fuzz.

"Yup. The biggest issue was trying to rule out all the random prints—took hours. What he got was a little degraded, but he stopped once he had one good index from a man who looks just like our suspect."

"So, where's our guy now?" Petrosky rummaged through the clean laundry basket for—*there*. He yanked a faded black T-shirt over his head and peered around for a jacket or a sweatshirt. *Whatever.* "Don't tell me—he's serving life without parole in some penitentiary and couldn't possibly be our killer."

"Nope. Our guy, real name Jemond Roux, got picked up on Friday down in Toledo for speeding—doing twenty over heading south on the same day we found Corey swinging from the Boyles' ceiling."

Petrosky paused in his clothing search. "Busted for speeding, eh? Must have been in a pretty big hurry."

"He sure was: reckless endangerment. But his prints were what fucked him. He's wanted in Maryland for social security fraud, too; pulled his prints off a P.O. Box where he was collecting a dead man's disability checks. He must have been traveling down into the US for his scams while he was living with Rosalie and Corey up in Canada—Maryland DA thinks he's got him on a dozen counts there, figures Roux will be serving fifteen if they convict."

Petrosky snatched a blue blazer from the back of the laundry room door and shrugged into it. "Let's go talk to that goat-blowing piece of shit." Toledo was only an hour away, and they had evidence linking Roux to their victim, and to the crime scene. This man who had fractured Rosalie Gagnon's skull, who had probably beaten Corey within inches of his life—the poor kid was probably scared of this bastard until the day someone finished him off.

THE RIDE DOWN to Toledo took fifty-six minutes, and another hour to deal with the detectives who were working the fraud case, two hardened ladies with buns and suits who probably didn't use lipstick for anything unless they were testing it for DNA. By the time Ohio's finest finished grilling Petrosky and Jackson, he was even more drained than he'd been the night before.

But he woke up as they entered interrogation.

The moment Petrosky set his eyes on Jemond Roux, the hairs on the back of his neck stood up, bristling with the cold, nervous energy he always felt around someone who didn't give a shit whether the people near him lived or died. Dense black beard, as Corey had said, the shoulders of a lumberjack, greasy shaved head that shone in the overheads —nothing like the far thinner and far hairier guy from the driver's license photo, except for his dead eyes. Roux was a stone-cold psychopath. But the man knew he was cornered, and the detectives who were surely watching even now from beyond the two-way mirror already had a confession and a deal from the Maryland DA. A lot can happen in fifty-six minutes.

Roux leaned back in his chair, arms crossed—pretty smug for a guy who already knew he was going to jail. "So I've taken social security numbers from a few people, you got me. What more do you want?"

Petrosky smiled in a way he hoped looked predatory. "I want to know if you sold a social security number to Corey Gagnon."

He wrinkled his nose as if he'd smelled something bad. "Now, *that* is not on my rap sheet."

"I just want to know whether you did it, Roux. I don't care about charging you for it." *Because you're going down for murder one.*

"My lawyers say it's a very bad idea to cop to things you didn't do." His voice was slick as an oiled trash bag.

"It's a worse idea to lie to the police," Jackson said. And they knew the guy hadn't called a lawyer—he was betting on his own intelligence to get him out of this, which was a terrible idea. For him, anyway.

Petrosky resisted the urge to glance at the two-way mirror. He could almost feel the detectives' eyes boring into his face, and if this asshole asked for his lawyer now... Petrosky's fists clenched, and he hid his hands beneath the table.

"Let's reboot, Mr. Roux." Jackson smiled, but it wasn't friendly—it was her lie-to-me-and-I'll-fuck-you-up smile. "We know you were living with Corey up in Canada. We know you vanished after his mother died. Maybe you remember her? Rosalie Gagnon?"

He squinted, though his eyes glittered with recognition. "Sounds familiar, but I might need a little refreshing."

*Faker.*

Jackson pulled two sheets from her folder: Corey staring from his driver's license photo, and another of Rosalie Gagnon's license that the Mounties had faxed down to them—frizzy dishwater hair, acne scars, hollow brown eyes. Jackson laid them side by side on the wooden tabletop.

Roux glanced at the pictures, but when he raised his head, he kept his gaze on Petrosky. "I haven't seen her in years." A twitch tightened the corner of his lip.

"You mean since the day you killed her," Petrosky said.

"Oh, you almost got me." Roux licked his teeth like a vampire trying to decide if they were sharp enough to cut flesh. "I wasn't even there that night. You can ask anyone."

Jackson shook her head. "You're a piece of shit, Roux, but we're not here about Rosalie. We're here about Gregory."

Roux squinted. "Gregory? Who's Gregory?"

"Isn't this Gregory Boyle?" Jackson pulled a third photo from the file—Corey dead on a slab in Woolverton's office. She slid it across the table. "You knew him before he changed his name. You know a lot of people before they start messing around with their identities, don't you?"

Roux barely glanced at the picture. "Someone killed that

little shit?" He frowned, but his eyes did not change—no remorse, and more critically, no surprise.

"Someone did," Jackson said, her voice low—dangerous. "Maybe someone in this room, what do you think?"

"No way." He shook his head. "I mean, I didn't like the little asshole, but I wouldn't hurt him."

But he had hurt him. Maybe they should whip out the images of Corey's bruised flesh. His broken nose. "You were in an awfully big hurry to get away from Michigan the night he died."

"I wasn't trying to get away from anything. I was headed down to see my girl."

Jackson: "What's her name?"

"Candy."

Petrosky snorted. "I think I know her sister. Cinnamon, but with an *S*, right?"

Roux's face was molded in stone, unmoving but for the dangerous gleam in his eyes. Petrosky stared him down.

"Got a phone number for Candy?" Jackson said, her pen poised above the case file.

"Nah." Roux was glaring at Jackson—he wasn't going to tell her shit. Was he a racist, or a misogynist, or did he just hate cops? Either way, Petrosky wanted to put a sneaker in his ass.

Jackson set the pen on the table and leaned back in her seat, watching him calmly. "Address?"

"I know what her place looks like."

"And where might her place be, exactly?"

"Tennessee. Out in the mountains." He winked at Jackson. *Winked.* "Don't even think it's got a mailbox for an address."

"Convenient for you."

Petrosky sniffed. This was going nowhere, and it wasn't like Candy, if she existed, was in cahoots with this jackass. Probably. "When was the last time you saw Corey?"

"Two years ago. A few days before he ran away."

"Wrong answer, Roux." Petrosky pulled a sheet from the

file and slid it across the table along with a photo of the Boyles' mailbox—now sitting on Scott's examination table.

Roux licked his lips nervously, like an anteater testing the ground for dinner.

"Guess whose prints are all over the mailbox of the house Corey was staying at the last two years?"

He shrugged, but his eyes had a more bitter fierceness to them now—defense mode. *Just where I want you, dickhead.*

"We also have a few people who can place you at the skate park where you met with Corey." This one was a stretch—they weren't entirely sure it was him from Beef's lame description, and they hadn't had time to go back and ask yet. But from the way Roux's jaw tightened up, Petrosky'd guessed right. "So now, instead of going down for fraud, you're going up for murder one."

Roux chuckled, but it was forced. "You can't prove anything. And this is harassment."

Harassment? Was that why he hadn't called his lawyer, figured he'd try to con a judge into believing his confession was coerced? But Petrosky knew better than to worry about that—the ladies outside were surely taping them.

"You're wrong, Roux. On both counts. Even if you think you were careful here, you weren't perfect, as the fingerprints all over the goddamn mailbox ought to remind you." But their killer…he was cautious, wasn't he? Petrosky pushed the thought aside. "We talked to the medical examiner up in Canada, too. You know what they told us? That Rosalie's skull was cracked in two places along with her hyoid bone—probably had your fingers around her throat, eh?" That wasn't true either—yes, she'd had bruising around the neck, but no broken bones outside of the skull fracture. Her injuries wouldn't have killed her, which was why there was no investigation, not without a witness who could accuse him—they'd never have gotten a conviction. But this guy hadn't stuck around to find out if she was okay. He probably didn't know the damage he'd caused. Or didn't care.

Roux crossed his arms.

*Think you can stare me down?* Petrosky met his gaze. "You know they can match a handprint by the size and shape of the bruises?"

Roux's mouth spasmed again along with the corners of his eyes, tiny movements, but definitely there—trying to decide whether he believed Petrosky? He shouldn't—it was mostly bullshit—but Petrosky was a better liar than Roux was. Even if he couldn't, or wouldn't, lie to Linda.

*Time to bring it home.* "Even more telling are the witness statements from the neighbors in Rosalie's apartment building. You want to take a guess at what they said?"

Roux's nostrils flared, his mouth a single bloodless line—too tight now to twitch.

Petrosky smiled. "The Canucks want you back, Roux. They're looking to put you on trial up there the moment you finish serving your time here. You won't even be able to count your years in Maryland as time served. You'll serve whatever bullshit deal you got in Maryland plus whatever they pin on you in Vermont, and then you'll go home to be locked up for the rest of your natural life with that mandatory twenty-five year shit the Canadians do."

Roux swallowed hard.

"That is unless I make a phone call." Petrosky leaned closer to the man over the table, the wood far warmer than the stainless steel at the Ash Park precinct—or maybe it was his blood, burning in his veins, boiling hotter the nearer he got to the vicious fuck across from him. "I'm trying to solve Corey's murder. Help me do that, and maybe we can convince the Canadians that Rosalie was an accident, see if you can get some leniency. Maybe up there, they'd actually believe you, gentle bastards that they are."

Roux licked his lips, eyes grazing Petrosky's face, then Jackson's. Finally, he sighed and let his arms drop to the sides of his chair. "Fine, okay. I left him a note on Wednesday, and we were supposed to meet at the park the night he died, but he never showed."

That explained why there were prints left to salvage at all. "Did you go over to see what happened to him?"

Roux shook his head. "I'm not an idiot."

"Not sold on that, Roux."

"Why would I go there? I'd risk someone seeing me. And when I heard what happened on the news, I took off—wanted to put as much distance between me and him as I could."

"Because you figured you'd be a suspect," Jackson said.

Roux shrugged. On this, at least, he seemed genuine.

"When was the first time you met with Corey?" Petrosky asked.

"About…a year ago, I think. Left him a message, met him up at the park." That fit with the timeline—when Corey had started acting out.

"And why did you arrange this meeting?"

"I took care of that boy his whole life." Roux chuckled—bland, humorless. "His mother wasn't worth a damn, always out of her mind on dope, didn't even *feed* him. The only reason he was alive was because of me." He sniffed and crossed his arms again. "I saw him on the news, those folks crying over him, hugging him… I figured he had a cushy gig here, ought to repay the favor."

"So a little blackmail, then?" Not far from the social security scheme the asshole was going away for.

Roux's face did not change. "I just reminded him it was important to help your old man. Even if he couldn't shell out more than a couple hundred here and there, he'd be rolling in money soon enough once that book came out."

A hundred here or there—that was why he was stealing money from Adrian's purse.

"But you weren't really his father, were you?" Jackson said.

"I was as close as he had."

Jackson leaned forward in her chair, elbows on the table, eyes locked on Roux. "Does that mean you were entitled to knock him around? Break his ribs?"

He wrinkled his nose. "Ain't illegal, spanking a kid. And god knows that boy needed it."

"I think we'll let you and your lawyer worry about that, Mr. Roux." Jackson's voice had gone dangerously quiet—she was probably trying just as hard as Petrosky not to kick this asshole in the balls. "You have an alibi for Thursday night to Friday morning? Around midnight?"

He frowned. "I was out drinking." But his skin had gone waxy.

"Anyone who can corroborate that story?"

"Well…I had a lady companion."

"We'll need her name and contact information," Jackson said.

"We never got around to…the niceties. But we met at a bar over on the west side. The Clumsy Stag."

Petrosky knew it—hole-in-the-wall tavern if ever there was one. They could check security cams and talk to the bartender, but Petrosky had a feeling that if this shmuck had killed Corey, he would have coughed up an alibi faster than he could say "I'm a fucking dickwad." But that wasn't the only reason. Roux fancied himself a businessman. And dead folks couldn't pay blackmail. Plus, the shoes—size six. This lumberjack looking prick was nowhere near that, and he definitely wouldn't need a couch for leverage to hoist Corey's body.

Jackson shook her head. "You need to do better than that, Roux."

"That's where I was! I can't just lie to you, can I?"

"The best alibi is telling us who else might have done it," Petrosky said. "You knew Corey better than anyone—knew his real history. Who else might have had it out for him?"

"Maybe the kid who was supposed to be living there. Why don't you ask him?"

The world stopped. "Are you talking about Gregory Boyle?"

"Yeah, that kid. Maybe he was mad Corey snuck in there and was living the life he was supposed to have. If I was that kid, I'd be pissed as hell that someone took over my family."

If Gregory was pissed, it was because his flesh had been eaten by rats at the trash dump. But Roux clearly didn't know that. "Gregory didn't need to be jealous, Roux. He could have come home anytime."

Roux shrugged.

"Do you know anything about Gregory Boyle?" Jackson prodded.

Roux shook his head. "I have enough shit to worry about. But Corey knew a lot about that kid. He said someone told him all about the kid he was pretending to be, that they helped him make everything look perfect—I guess they knew Gregory real well. Corey stayed with them down here for a bit before he moved in with that family, but I don't know where."

So someone *had* helped him. And it wasn't Corey's biological mother, trying to keep her kid safe—she'd died before he left Canada. Who else was there? Who else could possibly have a stake in sending an imposter into the Boyle house? The kidnapper would clearly know Gregory, but why send Corey in his place when his mere presence would draw unwanted attention to an otherwise cold case? "You ever see this mystery person? The one who helped Corey get in with the Boyles?"

"Nah."

"Man? Woman?"

"Never said." Roux shrugged. "He just said someone helped him and not to worry about it. Which I didn't, so long as he was paying me." On this, Petrosky believed him. Fraud wasn't the same as abduction, and Gregory had been groomed, coerced into running away, not kicked in the ribs until he agreed. Roux was not schooled in the art of finesse.

Roux narrowed his eyes. "Can I go back to my cell now? I'm getting tired, and I think I've given you more than enough to pay my way into a better arrangement." He smiled. *Smug bastard.* He hadn't been arrested before—lucky for him

—but unluckily, he didn't know the rules of engagement like most seasoned offenders.

"One more thing, Roux." Petrosky stood, and Jackson shoved her chair out beside him. "Do you know what the penalty is for collaborating in a scheme like the one Corey was part of? Tricking the family all those years, causing us to stop looking for the real Gregory Boyle?"

Roux's grin faltered. He straightened, nostrils flaring. "Hey, where are you going? You promised me a deal!"

Petrosky glanced back with his hand on the door. "I said it'd help you if I made a phone call. I didn't say I would. It'll be a cold day in hell before they let you out." Too bad shithead hadn't gotten a thing in writing, nor had he called his attorney—he was just narcissistic enough to believe he was smarter than the cops. And Petrosky would do everything in his power to make sure that Roux never saw daylight again.

**21**

———

"Damn, I really wanted it to be him." Jackson slammed a palm against the steering wheel hard enough to make Petrosky wince. *So did I.* They'd check his alibi, but the only way for Roux to get paid was to keep Corey alive, and Corey had even more at stake than Roux if he outed the man—not like Corey was going to turn him in.

"But what he said; Corey learning about Gregory from someone else…" Petrosky could think of only one reason to try something so crazy—so desperate. "What if whoever took Gregory needed everyone to stop looking, so they decided to put someone in Gregory's place? Our case was cold, but Mancebo was still out there poking around. Maybe the kidnapper got nervous or was tired of waiting to get caught." After all, it wasn't just a kidnapping—Gregory had been stabbed in the neck, bled out. "They're trying to skate on homicide."

Jackson pulled one hand from the steering wheel and shook it, presumably to ease the stinging in her palm. "So you think the kidnapper lives in Canada, maybe knew Corey up there—enough to see he needed out? And his mother's death was the perfect opportunity to pull the trigger on their plan."

"Maybe, but the kidnapper spent time in Michigan, also,

to groom Gregory into running off." He frowned at the curb, the concrete whizzing by in a streak of dirty gray. "Maybe they went to Canada specifically to locate a replacement. Our police files don't overlap—neither does our news, not really. It'd be safer to get an imposter kid from out of state and out of the country is a thousand times better if you want to make sure your secret stays safe."

"Yeah, until Roux showed up asking for a handout."

The curb had given way to the highway's equally dreary block walls—even the sun was hazy today, a dingy yellow tinting the bumpers like a jaundiced plastic film. "And once Roux was in the picture, they figured their cover was blown. They could either hope to god Roux wouldn't spout off— which is a terrible bet—or get rid of the evidence. Get rid of Corey. Maybe they'd have gotten rid of Roux, too, if they'd been able to find him. His slew of fake names might be the only reason he's still breathing." *Damn shame.*

She nodded, thoughtful. "But this is assuming the kidnapper was still in contact with Corey. That they somehow found out Roux was blackmailing him." Jackson's fingers tapped on the wheel—*tap, tap, tap, tap, tap.* The whiz of the tires on the asphalt grated on Petrosky's eardrums. He pulled a cigarette from his pack.

"No goddamn way you're doing that in here." She frowned. "Since when are you smoking again?"

"Since always."

"Stop fucking around, Petrosky."

"Fine. But you look like you need one more than I do." He nodded to her tapping fingers but replaced the cigarette in his pack, the dry tobacco itching in his nostrils. She shot daggers at him.

He swallowed hard. "We don't know if the kidnapper knew about Roux," he said. "Could have been Corey's instability that made them anxious to off him." But something about that wasn't sitting right. "Killing the kid, though…that calls more attention to everything."

"All the more reason to be careful—they took great pains to make it look like a suicide." *Tap, tap, tap, tap, tap.*

And maybe killing Corey was part of the plan all along—he was the last loose end. Except for Mancebo. The kidnapper must not know Adrian and Mancebo were aware Corey wasn't a Boyle. And really, if it hadn't been for Woolverton, the world would have assumed Gregory Boyle was in his family's plot. No reason to search the trash dump or anywhere else.

Jackson stared at the road, fingers working overtime on the wheel. "Do you remember what Stevie said? About Gregory running away to stay with a friend?" *Tap, tap, tap, tap, tap.*

Petrosky nodded. That's why they'd thought he had been taken by someone he knew—someone who'd gotten close to him.

Silence filled the car and tightened around Petrosky's ribs. Jackson's tapping hands stilled. "What if….what if this is like the Ponce case? Do you remember that? I think it was Decantor's."

Petrosky eyed the dashboard. He'd thought the same the other day, and the fact that Jackson, too, had felt the similarity niggled at the base of his spine and sent gooseflesh up his back. The Ponce case was a horrific exercise in brutality. The kidnapper had groomed young girls, one at a time, then kidnapped them and locked them up in his house. Every time a victim outgrew her usefulness, or started to bore him, Ponce strangled her and buried the body in the hard-packed dirt of his basement floor. But not before he took each girl on one final outing—to meet her replacement.

"You're thinking the boy in the backseat…"

Jackson shrugged. "I don't know what to think. Gregory's blood all over that shirt, his bag—maybe he fought, and they had to dispose of him before they'd planned. But you don't just bring another kid to a kidnapping, or to meet a future victim, without a reason."

He nodded. Whether the other boy had been in the backseat of that car as bait or to restrain Gregory, he had a purpose to the kidnapper. But who was the other child? Another kidnapping victim? "The original detectives looked at other kidnappings in the area. If only they'd found some."

"Well, yeah. But I think it's a good bet. There's a level of planning here that makes it feel like it wasn't the first time. But maybe it wasn't labeled that way, as a kidnapping—the detectives on the Boyle case only looked at kidnappings, but they didn't know Gregory ran away."

"So, we'll look at runaways." The droning of the tires drowned out the rest of his thoughts, except his nagging need for a smoke. He clutched the door handle and leaned back against the seat.

She nodded slowly, eyes still on the road. "We should chat with Dr. McCallum, Petrosky. We could use a psychologist's input on this."

He shook his head. "We already talked to the school shrink. And we know enough about kidnappers, Jackson, we see this shit all the time."

She narrowed her eyes at him—suspicious? But she appeared to think better of arguing because she said, "Even still, all we know is generalities." She raised one finger. "The kidnapper is most likely to be male." Another finger. "More than three-quarters of kidnapping victims are dead within three hours." She lowered her hand. "This isn't a ransom case, so there are other motivations—could be a pedophile situation for Gregory, then a clean-up-the-loose-ends situation for Corey if we're right about them being connected."

"We don't have enough for McCallum to help. He's great at speculation but—"

"What do you think we're doing? Speculating, making educated guesses, it's what we do, and what he does—and he's got more education than your sorry ass. And since when do you not want to—"

"Fair enough, I'm a speculator." His smile made his face hurt. He didn't want to see McCallum. He didn't want the doc to see him like this, sniffing dry tobacco to get a fix, eyes still bleary from a night spent staring at a bottle. The doc had a way of seeing right through Petrosky's bullshit, and McCallum would insist he stay to chat after the profile—maybe even pull him off the street until he "got himself under control." *Forget that.* Petrosky already had Jackson breathing down his neck. And Scott. Linda. Even Shannon was trying to, but it was harder for her from Atlanta. And going to a therapy session or a goddamn AA meeting wasn't going to make Julie any less dead.

"I've got a guy," Petrosky said.

Her eyebrows hit her hairline. "Besides McCallum?"

"McCallum's busy this week. Vacation."

She frowned.

"Just trust me, okay?"

She met his eyes. And nodded.

---

THE VIDEO WAS HAZY, but Petrosky could still see the ice in the man's gaze, the glint of white on his teeth like a frothing predator before a kill. Which was exactly what Ponce was. Just looking at the guy made the tiny hairs between Petrosky's shoulder blades stand at attention, and he was only watching a screen.

Decantor, years younger but just as burly, sat at the stainless table across from the killer, shoulders rigid, big hands steady—no easy smiles or cracks about the Kardashians were going to happen in that room. Just bad cop meanness.

The cuffs on Ponce's wrists sparkled in the white-hot fluorescents. Ponce was tiny next to Decantor's bulk, with wavy ash-blond hair, the long, thin face of an elf, and twitchy little hands that had done so much damage. A man no woman would look twice at in a bar—common of pedophiles. Shit, maybe they really did have a small man, a guy who'd decided he'd take what he wanted from children since no woman would want him. Children who'd be unable to fight him off. Decantor opened the file in front of him and laid the photos on the tabletop. In one, dirt spilled around shy white bones and a moldered piece of clothing, the skull a yellowed shell. Another showed more dirt, more bone, the hem of a pink dress with white flowers still intact. Decantor kept his eyes on Ponce.

Usually, perps looked away from the evidence if only to avoid suspicion, but Ponce gazed at the photos with naked interest, lips peeling up at the corners, gaze brightening in a way it had not thus far. Decantor laid the last glossy image on the stainless tabletop. All the girls they knew about, all in various stages of decomposition, all pulled from the hard-packed dirt beneath Ponce's cellar floor. Mostly bones, but the last child, the oldest, the freshest, was a mess of shiny bloated flesh and the gaping wounds of a leper.

"Lovely, aren't they?" Ponce's voice was silky, smooth, like a lounge singer or a pastor at Sunday mass. It would have been easy to get those poor kids to trust him.

Bile rose in Petrosky's throat.

"Hard to tell now, Ponce. But they certainly were lovely in life." Now Decantor pulled out new photos: school pictures full of smiling, happy faces, all with long brown hair, big blue eyes, pink lips. *Julie's lips, her blue, dead lips.* Any of these girls could have been her sister.

"So glad you agree." Ponce smiled, the lights glinting off his sharp teeth. "A parent loves to hear that."

"Did you know their parents? Because I do. I've met them all."

The man's smile faltered, and when he spoke again, his voice was higher—tight. "I was their father. They all needed a father."

"Yeah, very fatherly." Decantor touched the photo of the dead girl with the gaping wounds, skin sloughing from her bones like discarded chicken fat. Ponce followed his finger, then raised his own hand, cuffs rattling against the table, and touched the image, stroking her cheek. How many times had he done that to her cold skin before he put her in the ground?

"The places they came from...those men didn't deserve to have these girls."

*Didn't deserve to have these girls.* Petrosky's heart clenched. He hadn't deserved his daughter—hadn't deserved anything good that had come his way. And now he had nothing left.

"Did they tell you how much they loved you while you were strangling them to death? Did they croak it out while you were tightening that belt around their throats?"

Ponce blinked. "They were suffering. I helped them let go as peacefully as I could." Voice low once more—the voice of a man who fiercely believed what he was saying, believed it with such conviction that he need not raise his voice a single decibel. And the way he spoke, that soft, calm, determined timbre, was so much like that of the man who'd killed Petrosky's own daughter that his heart seized.

"You could have sent them home."

"Girls need their father. Otherwise, the world is too frightening." And that....it was motive. Motive for Ponce then, and for their killer now. Both Gregory and Corey came from homes where they had at least felt unloved. Was that how the kidnapper was choosing them? Predators were great at spotting vulnerable kids. They could smell it like perfume, a salty-sweet yearning for acceptance made heavy with the musk of desperation.

"You did take them out into the world, though," Decantor said. "But you didn't take them to the mall or to the movies. You took them to meet your next victim. That's how you got each new one into the car, right?"

Petrosky leaned forward, squinting at the television screen—the boy Mancebo's witness had seen in that blue car. Was that why that child was there? For Ponce, having another girl with him made each new kidnapping victim let their guard down. He didn't even have to groom them; Ponce had no connection to his new victims before the day he pulled them off the street.

Ponce lowered his gaze to the images once more and touched the flowered hem of the dress, then traced what looked like a dirty femur, the cuffs sliding against the tabletop like the frantic warning from an angry rattlesnake. *Shhhht-shhht-shhht.* "That's a private matter between a father and his daughter."

"What'd you do, tell them you'd let them go if they got you a new victim?"

Ponce's head snapped back up, but his eyes remained cool, his fingers on the photo. "They weren't victims. They wanted to help me."

This delusional fuckhead, he really believed what he was saying: that those girls wanted him to be happy after they were gone. That, they wanted to help him choose their own replacement. But whatever he'd told those girls was irrelevant—there were plenty of ways to convince a child to help you. All you had to do was lie.

"Tell me about the burial site," Decantor said, just as low as Ponce, but far more agitated, as if he were one step from grabbing the man by the throat. Maybe he was.

"I was going to bury them outside again, but I couldn't stand the thought of that, couldn't imagine them being out in the cold without anyone to love them. Without me."

"What do you mean 'again,' Ponce? Where are the other bodies?"

But Ponce wasn't going to tell him. He had never told anyone. How many more fathers were out there waiting for their daughters to come home? Maybe it was better not to know. Not to see their bones. Not to see the way this asshole stroked the image of their corpse.

"Ponce!" Decantor slammed his hands on the table and leaned across, his nose almost touching Ponce's forehead, probably smelling the man's musky breath, his prison-issued shampoo, the salty, vinegary tang of his sweat. When Decantor spoke again, his voice was soft and more threatening than Petrosky had ever heard it. "You are going to tell me what you did with those girls, or I will take my frustration out on your pasty murderous ass."

Ponce smiled.

The tape went black.

**22**

———

"HAVE YOU BEEN HERE ALL NIGHT?"

Petrosky glanced up at Jackson with bleary eyes. "Yeah, I couldn't sleep." *The bottle on the coffee table was talking to me even here, trying to call me home.* But he knew what would have happened if he went.

Jackson frowned at his half-full Styrofoam cup, a dozen soggy cigarette butts floating in the last of yesterday's coffee…or the first of this morning's. He'd lost track. She set a paper Rita's cup on his desk. "Guess you'll be needing this." She glanced at his shirt, winced, and dropped into the chair across from him. He was considering what the look meant when she said, "Now fill me in."

"Fill you in? All you need to know is that this is going to be impossible." After watching Decantor interview Satan Reincarnate, he'd spent the night in hell, slogging through years of data, with approximately 1.6 million kids listed as runaways each year. Even after he narrowed for males with dark hair, he'd still had hundreds of thousands of runaways every year to rule out. And there were more kidnapping victims in this case; there had to be more—he could feel it like an eel writhing in his guts. Their kidnapper wasn't happy with one stolen kid any more than Ponce had been.

"I pulled child murders, too," he said, "trying to find

connections, but I think we're better off assuming that Gregory was hurt because he didn't cooperate. Grooming a kid for months just to kill them a few hours later doesn't feel right. Not that I think our perp is letting any of the kids live, but…a planner, right? Not someone who'd normally leave blood on a curb." He snatched up his coffee. Hot and acidic on his tongue, but he barely tasted it.

"That reminds me: I called the chief about getting some cadaver dogs down to the dump," she said, watching him. "We'll see how that pans out—to search a place that size, we'll need a lot of personnel, so it'll be two weeks on the inside to put it together. But at least the brass knows about Mancebo, knows what we're dealing with. They'll charge him, but I told the chief you'd probably want to cuff him yourself for withholding evidence."

He shrugged. "I don't care who does it so long as he gets what's coming to him."

"Wait…really?" She paused, index finger tapping the side of her to-go cup. The silence stretched, then: "Get anywhere with your new shrink contact?"

"Oh, he was busy last night, but I'll get in this week." Petrosky ran a hand down his face, catching his callouses on his sandpapery chin—softer now that the hair was long enough to lie down against his flesh. His white lie about the shrink didn't matter—they had more pressing things to do than chat with a psychologist anyway. "If we believe Mancebo's witness, about the similar-looking child in the backseat of the car with Gregory, we already know the kidnapper has a type."

"Or kidnappers."

"What?" When she raised an eyebrow, he amended, "Of course, it could be more than one person. A male-female team, even two men or two women." But at least one of them had to be a woman, a teenager, or a small man—a man like Ponce. The latter scared him most, but less than five percent of kidnappers were women, and women almost always took infants, usually trying to convince a boyfriend to stay because she'd given birth to their child, that kind of shit. He blinked. He wished he could believe it was a woman—it'd up the chance that any other victims might be found alive. Either way, male or female or both, their best chance to close the case was if the suspects had done it before. The Canadians should have more on Corey soon, but as of now, Gregory's case was seven years old and cold as hell. "I already looked at the four years before and after Gregory Boyle's disappearance," he said. "I started with a five-mile radius. Runaway seven-year-olds like Gregory are less common, so I started there, and I cross-referenced every case, looking for similarities. Almost all of them came home on their own or were found with a family member." And the ones who hadn't come home were found dead within weeks—none of them hidden, none in the trash. "Only two are still missing, but they don't fit the physical profile of Gregory Boyle or the boy in the car." He slugged back more coffee—still hot, burning down his gullet—and when the bitter liquid hit the oily bile in his guts, he straightened lest it come back up.

Jackson was staring at the desktop. "Petrosky?"

He blinked, trying to focus his eyes—the bleariness cleared a touch, but not enough. The world was still hazy, like a dream stubbornly clinging to his consciousness. "What?"

"We're looking for cases of children of a similar age, thinking the kidnapper has a specific type. But what if they don't?"

"You mean they just like the boys young?" But the kid in the car and Gregory Boyle, both of them fit a certain profile —same age, dark hair, all that. Coincidence was just a word people used when they couldn't figure out the connection. And there had to be a connection here, had to be.

Her eyes gleamed. "Same age. But not necessarily both kidnapped at seven. Remember what we were talking about yesterday?"

"We talked about a lot of things yester—"

"About Ponce."

He glanced at the computer screen, half certain he'd see Ponce's face staring back, blue eyes glittering over the top of a pile of photos—pictures of the girls he'd murdered. "Yeah, I remember."

"It was bothering me, so I talked to Decantor about the case last night. Four girls, all taken at different ages, progressing years, which is why they didn't connect it initially: first, he took a four-year-old, the next year, a five-year-old, two years later, an eight, but she looked younger. The eight-year-old lasted the longest; he didn't take another kid until he kidnapped a ten-year-old three-and-a-half years later, but she only lasted six months."

Petrosky's gut was churning, hot and oily and sick. He'd watched that video of Ponce because he was thinking about the replacement angle, that the other child in the car might have been part of a "new victim" ritual—that his body was also out there somewhere. But Ponce had needed help because he was a creepy dude who didn't bother grooming anyone; their kidnapper wouldn't need help restraining a seven-year-old, not after grooming him to run off.

Still…there had to be a reason, even if it was just loosening Gregory up. Building trust.

Petrosky cleared his throat. "You're thinking this kidnapper is following Ponce's pattern? Progressing ages?"

"I don't think that's what this is," Jackson said. "Gregory's attack was probably spur-of-the-moment, Corey's more planned, but both were brutal—not about adoration, not with the killings. Even the Ponce case had elements of remorse: those burials were highly ritualized. He put flowers on the abduction sites, for fuck's sake. That was how Decantor caught him."

His fingers burned—he glanced down at the coffee still clutched in his hand, the wax on the outside of the cup indented, crinkled around his thumb. As calm and collected as that baby killer had been during the interview, Ponce had cried at his trial, talking about how he missed those girls— his victims. Remorse hadn't kept that bastard from killing.

And it wouldn't stop their perp either. "What the fuck are they after?"

She shook her head. "Hell if I know. But we need to look at kids of other ages since we haven't made progress sticking with seven. I'm thinking that the boy in the car was another victim—we just don't know when he was taken. He could be the kidnapper's own child, but we don't have a way to track that; not like we can interrogate all parents whose children were born in the three years on either side of Gregory Boyle."

Petrosky nodded, but his chest was hot. He should have considered this before. And even if the kidnapper wasn't using progressing ages as Ponce had, opening up the search to more ages should have been next on his list. Maybe he should just hang it up already—retire. Stay at home with the dog.

And that fucking night-light.

And a pack of smokes.

*And my bottle of Jack.*

"Petrosky?"

He finished the rest of the coffee in three long swallows and slammed the empty cup down like a shot glass—wishing it was a shot glass. "Our kidnapper might still be nearby if they were watching Corey, especially if they knew Roux was after him." And someone had fed Corey all that information about Gregory Boyle. He shook his head. Most would have run off, but their kidnapper had far too much riding on Corey's acting ability to just leave town, and now that Corey was dead...

Jackson was still watching him, brow furrowed.

Petrosky pulled the keyboard closer. "Let's get to it."

---

"GOT A FEW POTENTIALS, but none of them are perfect." Jackson laid out her images on the desktop, yellow sticky notes attached to the lower right-hand corner of each. Four little boys, all with dark hair and big brown eyes, three smiling, one frowning in his school photo as if he knew that this picture was his last, and he was pissed about it.

Petrosky laid five pictures on the desk next to hers. No sticky notes for him—he'd scribbled his data on the backs of the portraits. "Looks like we're spanning runaways ages five to nine?" The oldest he'd found was eight.

She tapped the frowning child. "This one's ten, but he looks young like Corey did. And all within a ten-mile radius."

Still a tiny search area, but he felt the closeness of this kidnapper—*killer*—in his bones.

"None of these kids got a second glance from the detectives on the Boyle case?"

"Nope. They focused on more overt kidnappings, though all of these were listed with the missing and exploited children." Jackson leaned across the desktop, squinting at the images. "I have two others, confirmed deceased, but I pulled their pics anyway, because…"

Because Gregory was almost certainly dead, too, like Corey. He sighed. This case was putting his brain through the wringer. A suicide-turned-murder, a kidnapped-and-presumed-dead, an abused child looking for a new family, a career thief with a penchant for blackmail—a PI with a love connection to one victim's mother. Where would it end? And which pieces mattered to find their perp?

They studied the nine runaway child cases at the frenetic pace reserved for horse jockeys and meth addicts and cops chasing down a suspect. He read through press releases, reviewed leads on each case no matter how tiny, scanned tips that had been called into the station. And then…the calls to the families. He hated himself more with every number he dialed.

"Mrs. Beckett? This is Detective Petrosky from the Ash Park Police Department. I'm calling in regards to—"

"Did you find him?" Her voice was so excited that it stabbed him right in the chest, his heart brightening with her pain. "Did you find my Raymond?"

And every time he had to listen to their spirits deflate. He'd lost Julie, but he knew where she was. Would it have been worse to never know? To imagine her still suffering at the hands of a monster? God knows he'd seen that enough times in his career—cages and chains, imprisonment. Torture. Death was better.

Death was always better.

He'd just hung up after the last call when Jackson slid back into her seat—at the corner of his desk this time, the wooden top almost completely covered in papers and file folders and empty coffee cups. She laid her papers beside his. Two of their possible victims had been found dead, out in the open, so not likely to be connected to their current case. And one had returned home—six years old, and he'd hidden in the neighbor's shed for three days after breaking a vase. Petrosky leaned back in the seat, his back groaning in protest. "Still have three of mine I can't rule out, but there've been no new developments—nothing to suggest we have the same perpetrator. No evidence they were groomed ahead of time. Good families, too, none of the weirdness like the Boyles, or abuse like what Corey endured."

"Same," Jackson said. "Lots of possibles, no new data. Except for him." She opened her case file to one of the youngest snapshots: Kingsley Stinton, taken two years before Gregory Boyle at…five years old? "This kid was listed as a runaway?" He brushed at the picture—a tiny line marred the photo over the kid's ear. The mark did not budge. Some clumsy asshole had probably folded it or drawn on it with an errant pen.

"Technically, he's listed as a missing person, but this kid left a note and everything." When Petrosky raised an eyebrow, she continued: "Told his friends, his teacher, anyone who would listen that he was going to run off. Also got two calls to Child Protective Services about him, so definitely a kid vulnerable to a super-nice kidnapper. But the CPS calls never amounted to anything. No abuse confirmed, just…weird."

"Weird?"

"I guess the family's into role-playing or something. Stuck in the past. Fucked up, but not illegal." She shrugged. "Anyway, there was a parent-teacher conference about the runaway threats scheduled for the night after he left. And..." She tossed her legal pad on the desk. "When I called just now, his older brother Roman said they got a call last year from someone claiming to have seen Kingsley. Dad thought it was a prank, so he didn't bother to call it in."

*What a dumbass.* "That's no reason to keep it to himself." Any parent would have given their right eye to get a call saying their child was okay—at least alive. They'd have called it in no matter how much of a long shot it was. And that weird detachment, holding things back...it felt similar to the Boyles.

"I know, I thought the same, but we've gotten a bunch of complaints from the father over the years, all noted in the file. Apparently, the house was inundated with calls right after Kingsley was taken. They've changed numbers six times in the last nine years."

Nine years. He eyed the photo, the kid's round cheeks. Kingsley wouldn't look the same now; kids grew fast, especially between five and fourteen. But he'd be the same age as Gregory Boyle would have been, which felt like the point.

Petrosky reached behind him for his jacket, then remembered he was wearing a sweatshirt. No wonder Jackson had been looking at him funny—he'd hauled this beast from his trunk in the middle of the night: Michigan State. *Would Julie have gone to Michigan State?*

He cleared his throat and stood. "Let's walk Kingsley's photo down to Scott, see what he can do with age progression—I want to know what this kid would look like now." If there was any chance someone had actually seen Kingsley, they'd need to get his photo out to the masses—maybe they had a chance to save at least one victim. Maybe they'd find a way to bring him home.

But he doubted it.

# 23

THE HOME BELONGING to Kingsley Stinton's family sat just past the boundary for the school where Gregory Boyle had attended. In the few blocks between the district limits for Anderson and West Shores Middle, the houses had gone from moneyed quirkiness to smaller, uniform neighborhoods full of well-built colonials with cedar shingles.

The walkway up to the Stintons' house was lined with peach begonias, the grass edged in such fussy lines they might cut your foot if you stepped on them the wrong way. Petrosky dropped the brass door knocker and listened to the hollow tapping of footsteps and the throaty *clunk* of the deadbolt.

The woman on the other side of the door wore a knee-length red dress with a frilly white petticoat visible beneath. Red heels. Like a 1950s pin-up. Even her hair was from some long-ago year, coiffed and sprayed into a perfect Marilyn Monroe helmet.

"Mrs. Stinton?"

"Bonnie Stinton, at your service." She smiled with full lips painted the brilliant ruby of blood. "Can I help you?"

"We're here about your son."

Her smile did not falter, though her eyes dulled. "Roman?"

"Kingsley."

"Oh. Well…he's not here."

Petrosky and Jackson exchanged a look. Jackson flashed her badge. "No, ma'am, he's—"

"Bonnie! Who's at the door?" The voice was deep and laced with agitation, bouncing around the foyer with a force like thunder. Why was he yelling? Maybe they weren't used to visitors.

Still, Mrs. Stinton's—Bonnie's—smile remained, though her eyes widened like a foraging raccoon caught in a sudden flashlight beam. And just below her jaw…was that a touch of purple beneath her pancake makeup?

She turned to look over her shoulder—definitely a line of bruising from her jawbone to the back side of her neck. "Someone's at the door about Kingsley, dear."

The man who strode up the hallway behind Bonnie was shorter than his wife but had shoulders wider than her frilly skirt and the forearms of a guy who spent his life ambidextrously jacking it to beer ads. He narrowed already squinty eyes at them—at Jackson's badge—and frowned.

Bonnie's glorious but ridiculously fake smile remained plastered on her face. "Please come in, officers, we're always happy to receive guests."

Mr. Stinton sniffed, then turned on his heel—worn loafers, a hole in the side that should have been unacceptable for a guy this tight-assed. His wife followed, her red heels—lower than today's stilettos, but still probably uncomfortable—clicking against the tiles. Apparently, the perfectly put-together 50s vibe only applied to Bonnie. And inside…

Petrosky had never seen so much teal in all his life. The hallway walls were painted in it, as were the kitchen cabinets, visible through an arch on their left as they followed the Stintons deeper into the house. But not all of the kitchen was monochromatic; the fridge was as cherry red as the missus' dress, the floors a black-and-white checkerboard. *What year is it?*

They stopped at a family room near the back of the

house: teal carpet, a long yellow couch, a single yellow chair with straight wooden legs. A clock that looked like an oversized misshapen guitar pick hung on the side wall. Old, all of it, maybe original, except the flatscreen television that presided over the brick fireplace. Apparently, Stinton couldn't hold on to the charade where electronics were involved.

A boy in faded jeans, presumably Roman, slouched against an orange beanbag chair in the corner of the room, a video game controller in his hands. Sixteen or so, the beginnings of a meager mustache barely peppering his upper lip, long dark hair to his shoulders, covering half his face. The one eye Petrosky could see was locked on the black screen—the TV was off. Maybe he was just avoiding them.

"Can I get you a refreshment?" Bonnie asked, the perfect hostess no matter how she felt about their presence. Stinton just glared.

"No thank you, ma'am, we don't plan to be here long." He pulled out the notepad, the one Jackson had shoved into his hand as they exited the car. "When was the last time you received a call about Kingsley?" Petrosky asked.

For a moment, no one answered, and then the boy met Petrosky's eyes—large, questioning. Nervous. He turned away just as quickly, but not before Petrosky caught a glimpse of the long thin scar that bisected his cheek and vanished into the shadow of his neck. Jagged, but white, neat, made by something incredibly sharp. Had it been an accident? Petrosky stiffened.

"We get prank calls constantly," Mr. Stinton boomed, glaring at the boy in the beanbag chair.

*Jesus, does he yell all the time? You know what they say: big voice, small penis.* Petrosky eyed Bonnie's neck again. Glanced back at Roman. Petrosky's fist clenched around the pen, but he forced his hands to relax. One thing at a time. He'd get Child Protective Services out here, but without an exit plan, throwing around accusations was often the worst thing you could do in a domestic violence situation. The most vulnerable would pay for anything he said.

Petrosky tried again, lowering the notepad. "We understand you received a call not long ago. From someone claiming to have seen Kingsley."

Bonnie cocked her head, her lips turning to a friendly, curious pout. Her big brown eyes though—definitely confused. Mr. Stinton blinked. His eyes were brown too. Where had Roman gotten hazel eyes from? Maybe Mrs. Stinton wasn't as settled in her role as she wanted her husband to believe. Good for her.

Mr. Stinton's nostrils flared. "Nope, nothing, never anything useful from those whackos."

But Jackson had just called, and the person who answered had said… His eyes lit on the boy—Roman. He had answered the phone, right? And now the youngest Stinton raised his head once more, video game controller resting, forgotten, on his knee. "It's been a year, but they called, Dad; you know they did. I heard you talking to—"

Stinton turned on his son, eyes flashing. "Boy, you better remember your place."

Roman clamped his lips shut, but the fact that he'd spoken up so boldly… He wasn't afraid for his life, and the defiant way he was watching his father now was not the mark of a child who'd been attacked with a blade. And the kid certainly wasn't conforming to Daddy's wishes with his attire.

Petrosky leveled his gaze at Stinton. "And what about your place, Mr. Stinton? As Kingsley's father?"

The man whirled on Petrosky. "My place is here, as head of this household, and you'd do well to respect—"

"And you'd do well to respect that you're impeding a police investigation into your own child's disappearance." Petrosky stuck the pad back in his pocket and whipped out his cuffs. "Maybe you'd like to discuss it more down at the station."

Stinton crossed his arms, smug. "Like anyone would take

you seriously in your"—he gestured to Petrosky's sweatshirt —"outfit." Jackson glanced at his shirt, too, frowned, and looked away.

"Like anyone would take you seriously after 1952." He met the man's narrowed eyes. "Did you know they cured polio?"

Stinton's eyes widened, furious, but he pressed his lips together. One breath, and another, staring at Petrosky then at Jackson as if trying to decide whether it was in his best interest to answer—whether they could actually take him in. Finally, he sighed. "Fine, goddammit, fine."

Bonnie Stinton put her hands over her mouth as if she'd never in her life heard such language. Where had he found her? Was she playing a role, or was she really like this?

"Tell us about the call, Mr. Stinton."

"Nothing to tell. Some kid called—had that high cracking kind of voice you get around thirteen. Obviously a joke."

"Joke or no, what did he say?"

"He just said that he saw Kingsley. Then he started laughing."

"And then?"

"Then nothing. I hung up."

"He wasn't laughing." Roman rose from his beanbag, more gracefully than Petrosky would have imagined possible for a gangly teenager. "I was here, too, and he wasn't laughing, you would have said if he was laughing."

Stinton whirled on his son. "If I say it happened, boy, it happened." He sniffed. "Like you care anyway—he was always jealous of you, and you were just as bad with him."

But siblings didn't forget each other, a little rivalry or not. Roman looked away—at the blank television. "I just want to know where he is." His voice shook. Scared of his father, or grieving the loss of his brother?

"Mrs. Stinton, I'm surprised you aren't more forthcoming." Jackson stepped toward the lady of the house, whose hands were still clamped over her lips. "Aren't you worried about your child?"

The woman shook her head and dropped her hands, grinning again like a mannequin. "Oh, I'm sorry. I never met Kingsley."

"Come again?" Petrosky snapped, as Jackson said, "You didn't know Kingsley?"

"Oh, no, I just joined this lovely little family about six years back." She grinned again, but her eyes betrayed her—tense.

So…three years after Kingsley was abducted. How long had it taken Mr. Stinton to turn her into a truck stop poster? Had he groomed her the way someone had groomed the kidnap victims into leaving their homes? He wouldn't groom his own child to run away, but a child used to being told how to think, used to being controlled…that would have made Kingsley easier for someone else to control too.

"Where's the boy's real mother?" Petrosky asked.

Bonnie flinched enough to tug at Petrosky's heart, but Stinton cleared his throat. "Maisey had no idea what responsibility was. No notion of the importance of family."

"Yeah, I'm sure that was it," Petrosky muttered. Maisey must have been desperate if she'd left her two children in the care of a crazy person in order to escape her life of pin-up hairstyles and goofy dresses…and whatever her husband had done to her with his giant fists. His gaze flitted once more across Bonnie's neck and away again before the "head of the household" caught him looking.

"Do you know where Maisey is now?" Jackson said.

He shook his head. "No, she left the year before Kingsley did, probably changed her name or something. The police, they figure she came back and took him. Kingsley. Even put out a notice for the both of them. But it was okay—good riddance, that's what I say. That boy was trouble." He glanced at Roman as if daring him to deny it, but Petrosky's mind was elsewhere.

A runaway mother, a subsequent vanishing child. That was why the case didn't get a lot of press. The last detectives had a viable suspect in the abduction, and to be honest, if

Petrosky had gotten this call, he wouldn't have pushed it too damn hard. The cops had done their due diligence, put out an Amber Alert, tried to track the mother, but at the end of the day, if Kingsley was with his mom, he was likely better off than he was here with this joker. And yet...the odds that she'd leave Roman here and take Kingsley seemed slim. His gut tightened. With the similarities to Gregory Boyle's case, his money was on Kingsley being taken by someone else.

"Did Kingsley have any older friends, Mr. Stinton?"

Roman's eyes widened, realization dawning in his irises. Petrosky turned his attention to the boy. "What about you, kid? You know anyone else your brother was friends with?"

Roman opened his mouth to speak, but Stinton interrupted: "He had some friend out there, some girl. Wasn't in his class. Nobody in that class liked him."

"Then how did he know her?" Not like five-year-olds hung out at the bar trying to meet ladies.

Stinton frowned. He shrugged.

"Name?"

"Never said."

Roman sniffed. "Yeah, because you teased him about having a girlfrien—"

"He was trouble," Stinton repeated, as if a five-year-old could possibly be that awful—poor kid was probably just acting out because of his dickhead father. "And it's not like some little bitch girlfriend took him away."

Not if said girlfriend was also five, but if that "little bitch" was a grown up...

Jackson stared at the man, her gaze fiery. "What kind of trouble can a five-year-old possibly be, Mr. Stinton?"

"He was just wrong. You mark my words. Wrong like his mother." Which meant what? He didn't listen? He surely thought Roman was bad, too. Stinton sniffed again. "Thank the lord Bonnie knows better—knows what an honest woman looks like."

Bonnie's shoulders straightened, her hands clenched more firmly at her belly, a proud yet oddly defensive maneuver. Maybe it was defense—maybe all of her plasticky responses were self-defense, but she was in too deep to just walk out.

"When did you receive this call, exactly?" Jackson said.

Stinton marched around the couch and eased himself into the yellow chair across from Roman, eyes aimed at the blank television, a silent "fuck off" to his visitors. He had a bald spot on the back of his head. Served him right. "It was summer."

Jackson glanced from Bonnie to the back of Stinton's balding head—still watching the black screen? "We need a date, Mr. Stinton. We can't track a phone call just from 'summer.'"

Actually, they could, but it would take a lot longer to go through ninety days of calls. Petrosky sidled closer so he could see the man's face.

And what a show it was. Stinton's big cheeks had tensed, the muscles in his jaw working. "It was Father's Day. That little bastard ruined my morning, the one day people are supposed to leave me alone."

Roman was frowning, fiddling with the frayed ends of a hole in his jeans.

Leave him alone on Father's Day? But from the look in Roman's eye, the boy would be happy to leave Stinton alone every day of the week. No wonder Kingsley was so anxious to run off—the black sheep of the family. The bad one. Whoever took him probably just had to ask once, especially if they had asked nicely.

**24**

———

THE FATHER'S Day phone records were gloriously sparse—four incoming numbers. Looked like Mr. Stinton didn't have many friends, no one who wanted to wish him well, maybe because they knew he was a shit father and a shit human.

The first number was a telemarketing call. The next two numbers were still connected and easily verifiable as friends of the family—Roman's classmate for a whopping twenty-four seconds, and a longer call from the missus' parents.

And then there was one.

The residence linked to the landline was owned then and now by a woman named Marianne Bishop—no spouse listed in the records, not on the phone, not on the utilities, not on the mortgage, and a quick search showed a divorce ten years prior, just before the house was purchased. Her son Wes, presumably the boy responsible for the phone call, had turned sixteen last month.

*Hopefully, they'll be more normal than the Stintons—can't be more screwed up, right?* Petrosky stood on the Bishops' porch, a light breeze making the maroon leaves of the Japanese maple shudder in the front flowerbed. Less than two hours from the time they'd left the Stintons' place—it felt like an eternity, probably because this was the only real lead they had. If this didn't pan out... Jackson rang the bell.

Petrosky saw the woman's flaming orange hair, curly and wild, before he registered her face: slightly upturned nose, deep brown eyes the color of a good bottle of whiskey, a thin but welcoming mouth. But her smile fell when Jackson flashed her badge. "We're here about Wes." When Ms. Bishop's jaw dropped, Jackson amended, "About an anonymous call he made last year regarding a missing child."

She led them down the hall to a sun-drenched kitchen. A bowl of apples and oranges sat on the breakfast bar, their colorful skins reflecting rays of yellow afternoon, right out of a goddamn still-life.

Marianne Bishop stood at the counter near the farm-house sink; Petrosky and Jackson stood opposite her behind the barstools and listened to the heavy, clunky sound of teenage footsteps running down the stairs and heading up the hallway.

"Hey, Mom, what's up?"

Wes had deep brown eyes, too, but that was where the resemblance to his mother stopped: wide nose, full lips, straight, jet-black hair, olive skin. He towered over his mother as he stepped beside her. Six-two at least.

"These are detectives. They're looking for a boy you… called about last year?"

Wes's eyes widened. "Oh. Yeah."

His mother's jaw dropped—if the fruit was a still life, her face was a more realistic *The Scream.*

Jackson cleared her throat. "Can you tell us a little more about that, Mr. Bishop?"

"I saw him at the house on the corner, the one with the wooden fence."

"Did you speak to him, Wes?"

"I mean, a little, but…"

Ms. Bishop's shock finally seemed to wear off—she shook her head, eyes locked on her son. "Wes! You saw a missing child, right here in our neighborhood, and never mentioned it? Why didn't you say something?"

The boy dropped his eyes, not nervous like Roman—embarrassed. "I was scared, I guess."

"Of what? I'm on your side; you know that, Wesley. Anything that comes up, anything at all. I'm your mother; I can protect you, from…whatever." She shook her head, her eyes tight with hurt, or maybe disbelief. "I can help with whatever you're worried about."

If only it were so easy. If only parents could protect their children from the darkness in this world. The smell of Julie's charred flesh tingled in his nose and vanished.

Wes was shaking his head. "It's just…it's weird, okay? Their family was weird. The lady caught me peeking over the fence and yelled at me to stay away from her house."

His mother frowned. "You were scared of *her*? They were usually so…quiet."

But so was Jeffery Dahmer. Yelling at kids to get off her lawn, didn't mean the woman was a kidnapper—they couldn't even be positive the boy was Kingsley, not yet. But it sure did sound like the neighbor had something to hide.

"How can you be so certain the boy you saw was Kingsley Stinton?" Jackson asked. "Did he tell you his name?"

His forehead wrinkled. "No. But I'm sure it was him—totally positive. He had that weird thing on his ear. I saw it on the poster. Like…the top of it was split." He touched the cartilage at the top of his own ear.

Petrosky thought back to the image of Kingsley. There had been a line there, but he'd written it off to a blight on the photo itself. Was it an injury? Oh…maybe like the one Roman had, the slit from jaw to throat. It wasn't in the missing person's file, but if Stinton hadn't mentioned it, a scar might have been overlooked.

Jackson extended her hand—her phone. Kingsley's age progression photo on the screen. Wes nodded emphatically. "Definitely. That looks way more like him than the picture I saw—he was younger in that one."

*Here.* Kingsley Stinton was on this street last year, less than twenty miles from his own school. And…he'd been alive? But something else was bothering Petrosky. "How did you know to call the Stintons in the first place?" *Instead of the police?*

Wes shrugged. "I saw a poster up at the gas station with the phone number."

A poster? Stinton hadn't said anything about putting up a poster. If he was so worried about his house being inundated with phone calls, why put his phone number, his sixth phone number, out into the public again, and then not follow-up on every goddamn lead? It made no sense.

"Did Kingsley look injured?" Jackson asked. "Sick?"

"No, they were just...playing. They didn't really say anything to me, but they looked like they were fine. I kinda thought they didn't like me, though. Kingsley looked...mad."

Jackson's shoulders were rigid, her face strained as if she thought she could see right into Wes's brain if she concentrated hard enough. "Wes, you said 'them'—that 'they' were playing at the house on the corner. Do you mean the boy and his mother?"

Wes shook his head. "Yeah. I mean kinda." He shrugged. "I really meant him and his brother."

The room stilled; the air went electric, Petrosky's tongue itching with the subtle tang of metal. His brother. *His brother?*

But Jackson was already saying: "There was another boy there?"

This time, Ms. Bishop nodded. "Actually, I saw them a couple of times...walking with their mom when they moved in about eight years ago. All this time and I never got as close as Wes did, I guess."

They all turned to Wes.

"Yeah, there were two of them. I talked to them over the fence, the day she yelled at me—she was up in the house, though, so I couldn't really see her. But they were in the backyard, reading books on physics, one under the tree, and Kingsley kinda...just on the lawn."

"Physics?"

He shrugged again. "Some textbook, I dunno. He closed it

when I came up. Not sure exactly which book it was; they didn't go to my school."

Was the kidnapper teaching them? Petrosky's heart spasmed. Ponce had taught his "daughters" as well. They'd found a video of Ponce beating a girl with a belt, metal end first, for not knowing information he'd presumably taught his prior captive. "This other boy…what did he look like?"

"I mean…like Kingsley, I guess. I thought they were twins, the kind that don't look alike? But he wasn't on the poster."

Jackson had gone silent—tapping on her cell. Petrosky turned back to Wes. "Dark hair? Dark eyes?"

"Yes. Both."

Kingsley and…Gregory? Was that even possible? But with the bloody clothes, it was more likely some other abductee. How many kids had their perp taken? "If you thought they were twins, the boys must have looked to be the same age."

Wes nodded. "Well, kinda, but they said they were twins too. That's when the woman started yelling. I guess she heard them arguing."

"Arguing about…"

"The one by the tree said they were twins, and Kingsley got mad and told him to shut up."

He'd told him to shut up because they weren't actually twins—the only brother Kingsley had was Roman, and he hadn't seen Kingsley since he'd been taken.

*Huh.* For the woman to be passing them off as twins…that felt significant. But what kidnapper would let her stolen children sit in the yard when three words to a neighbor could blow her cover? *Was* she their kidnapper?

Petrosky turned to Ms. Bishop. "Did you ever see anyone else out there? A man, another woman besides the one you mentioned?"

Both Bishops shook their heads. "There was never anyone else there, never once," Ms. Bishop said. "The only people I ever saw were the woman and those two boys, and even then, not very often. Looking back, I suppose that is a bit odd, to never have friends over, no visitors. The lawn service came out once every two weeks to do the front grass for half the block—they work through the rental company. But I never saw her speak with them either."

One woman. One single female kidnapper—and killer.

Jackson held out her phone again—an age progression photo of Gregory Boyle. Petrosky hadn't even realized she'd had Scott do one on Gregory, but his heart suddenly leapt. *Please let this be something totally different from the Ponce case; please let him be alive.*

"Does this boy look familiar?" Jackson said.

Wes frowned. "No, that's not him. But I'd definitely know him if I saw him."

*Damnit.* Had he really thought Gregory was alive? But this was something, at least; they had Kingsley Stinton and another child. Was the other boy her biological son, or another kidnap victim they had yet to identify? There were so many similarities to the Boyle case, from a "friend" convincing them to run away, to the boys living less than ten miles apart, and their physical profiles were almost identical—same ages, unstable home lives... This had to be their kidnapper, didn't it? The same person who'd slashed Gregory Boyle's throat and dumped his pack at the landfill.

"Did either of you ever see a car out there?"

Ms. Bishop pursed her lips, then nodded. "You know, I did see a car a few times. A sedan. But I've never really been into cars, so I'm not sure about the type."

"It was blue, though," Wes said. "And like...old."

"Like a muscle car?" But he knew it wasn't. This was the car Mancebo's witness had seen. The car with the boy in the backseat talking to Gregory Boyle the day before he vanished for good.

Wes shook his head. "Nah, nothing cool. Just older."

"He says my car's old, too," Ms. Bishop said. "I have a 2005 Altima."

"Thank you, Wes, you've been most helpful." Jackson re-pocketed her cell and the notepad. He hadn't even seen her take it out, had he? "If you could point out the house for us, we can get out of your hair."

The house. Would they be reuniting families by dinner? But he didn't really want to bring Kingsley back to the Stintons'. If anything, he wanted to get Roman out of there.

Maybe he was more like their kidnapper than he wanted to admit.

Marianne Bishop was frowning, biting her lower lip.

"Ms. Bishop?" Jackson said.

"It's just…they moved out."

*Fuck.* "When?"

"A year ago, they up and…" She looked at her son. "It must have been right after you called. Did they move after she yelled at you?"

Wes swallowed hard. And nodded. "Did I screw up, scare them away? I tried to do the right thing."

"You did fine, son. Next time, just call the police." As if Wes would ever be in that position again. As it was, he'd scared their best lead away. Hopefully, there would be a mortgage, a rental contract, *something* that would lead them to at least one stolen child.

## 25

Jackson dropped her cell into the Escalade's console and fished her keys out of her jacket pocket. "Turns out it was the other kid, Roman—Kingsley's brother—who put up the poster. He's been doing it for years, puts up new ones every time they change their number."

No wonder each new phone number ended up with a million prank calls. "I'm surprised Daddy let him answer the phone again."

"Didn't. I called the station where Wes said he saw that poster." She shoved the keys into the ignition but didn't turn them. Instead, she stared at the Japanese maple in the Bishops' front flowerbed. "So, our kidnapper let Kingsley live—he was alive when she took Gregory. Kingsley might have even been the other child in the car. But why take a second kid at all?"

One child should have eased any maternal motivations. Was she taking a page from Ponce's book, using Kingsley as bait for new recruits? Would Gregory have been fine if he'd just cooperated? And…twins. *What the fuck is happening?*

Petrosky turned his gaze to the house on the corner as they headed down the road toward the place Wes had indicated. Two stories, wooden siding painted the pale yellow of two-day-old snot. The house was in good shape, but he would have known it was abandoned by the disarray in the front yard: crispy, ankle-high grass, weedy flowerbed, and hedges sporting snaky tendrils of evergreen, thin and bristly, twisting up to scratch at the siding.

Jackson crossed to the porch and tried the bell—"Just in case"— the thin *bing* filtering through the afternoon as Petrosky stopped by the sign in the front yard: Relenski Rentals. They waited. No activity inside the house.

The second-story windows glared down with glassy, gaping eyes. Faded yellow awnings above the two center windows turned the front facade into an agitated scowl. He imagined Ponce's cool blue gaze, his smile as he told Decantor: "I was their father. They all needed a father." Ponce's endgame hadn't been murder; killing had been a side effect, a stumbling block, what he'd deemed a necessary evil. What he'd wanted was…a family. Julie's face flashed in his mind. He shoved her away. Again.

Jackson was squinting at the house across the street now, the same "For Rent" sign in that front yard too. And there was another house up the street with a Relenski Rentals sign out front.

"Wonder what's up with these Relenski guys," Jackson said.

"Property values take a dive, companies like this buy up what they can at auction. Most of the people in this neighborhood probably worked at Edwards Tooling just a few miles from here before they filed bankruptcy." At least the rental company would have records. A name. A driver's license. Anything would be good.

They headed for the car, the grass whisking against his jeans and crunching under his soles—irritating. The little hairs on the back of his neck prickled as if the ghost of Gregory Boyle was scratching at his flesh.

Petrosky jerked his seatbelt over his shoulder. "It takes a hell of a narcissist to stay so close to the abduction sites all those years, especially with all the PI inquiries." But at least more victims should widen their suspect pool. The previous detectives had looked at school personnel, neighborhood personnel, but Kingsley and Gregory hadn't gone to the same school. Maybe they'd find some new shared connection. "We'll have to look at…shit, bus routes, the schools again. Any substitute teachers who crossed district lines." Petrosky watched the sky, his unease a steady tingling pressure at the base of his brain. A bank of clouds crawled south across the horizon, yellowed with the late-evening sun so that they appeared like bulbous gobs of hardened chicken fat. The house receded in the rearview. The tall privacy fence loomed in a sea of barren yards. And… He bolted upright, the seatbelt tightening against his middle. *The fence.* "Jackson, wait."

She pumped the brakes, eyebrows raised, and he put up a hand, his brain suddenly on fire with Corey's words, with what he'd said to the Boyles—"Little Greggie is dead." The Boyles had thought Corey meant the person he had been was dead, that he had come back changed. But Corey hadn't changed—he wasn't Gregory in the first place. Did he know Gregory was dead because he'd been a part of it, or was he a witness? *Seven years.* Marianne Bishop said the family had moved in eight years back. Kingsley and this other child had been living here when Gregory was taken—and stabbed. The bag and the shirt had been found, but not the boy.

Not the boy.

Petrosky opened his eyes. "Go back. I want to take a look at the yard." *And the basement.* It was probably crazy, they'd probably end up finding Gregory's body at the trash dump where Mancebo had found his backpack, but the yard was calling to him like a siren—what horrors waited beyond those planks? He opened the car door before it was fully parked and ran to the fence. And now it was Ponce's steely gaze in his head, the sick glitter in his eyes—*I wanted them close to me, I didn't want to bury them somewhere they had to be alone.* The wooden boards bit into his palms and pricked the pads of his fingers, but the adrenaline in his veins dulled the ache. He jumped, then heaved himself up over the fence, skinning his belly through his sweatshirt. His knees sang when he landed on the other side. Pain juddered up through his hips.

"Not bad, old man," Jackson called, already halfway over behind him.

The yard was small and overgrown like the front; it had likely never been particularly pretty. Yellowed grass, a big oak in the middle, an outdoor patio set rusting on the concrete slab beside the house.

Jackson dropped down beside him. "Is it everything you hoped?"

"Maybe." He scanned the slab—how long had it been there? Was there a child buried beneath; flesh and bone mixed in with the cement? The grass along the fence line looked as crunchy and angry as that in the front yard—nothing of interest there—and the flowerbeds were a snarl of bushy dandelions and milkweed. But... His gaze stopped on a section of the property near the tree, an oblong shape where the grass wasn't quite as yellow—definitely not the crispy mess that had been snapping under his shoes. Not because of the shade. It looked like something was...fertilizing it. "You see that? On the right side of the tree roots?"

Jackson's gaze darkened. "I guess we need a warrant."

"Or a few shovels." When she frowned, he amended, "I'll make a call."

"I'll take care of it. Got a judge who owes me a favor."

He raised an eyebrow. "Really?"

But she had already turned away, phone at her ear. He'd go ask Wes Bishop's mother for the tools. He'd buy her a new shovel if they ended up having to take it to the forensic lab.

---

Ms. Bishop had two shovels, given unquestioningly but with a horrified look in her eyes that matched the foreboding in Petrosky's chest.

He wasn't a fan of prayer, didn't believe in it at all, but he closed his eyes a few extra moments when he eased the shovel carefully into the ground.

*Please don't let Gregory be here.*

He heaved a shovelful of sod and earth behind him. Jackson did the same.

*Don't let me hit him.*

He dug, sweat dribbling down his ass crack. The underarms of his sweatshirt were soaking wet.

*Please don't let there be more than one.*

"The Relenskis are going to be pissed about what we're doing to their yard," Jackson panted beside him. She wiped sweat from her brow.

"We've got a warrant, let them be pissed." Petrosky slid the shovel back into the earth—*clunk*. Something hard.

Jackson withdrew her spade. And backed up.

Petrosky got on his hands and knees, carefully moving aside dirt and the occasional creeping earthworm. He slipped his fingers lower, lower, lower until he reached the spot the shovel had hit—hard. Cold. Dry.

"What've you got?"

He drew his hand back. His fingers were locked inside a child's skull.

**26**

———

JACKSON TOSSED a folder onto his desk. "The house was last rented to a Dakota Hodgson, under a social security number belonging to a woman of the same name who fell off a horse while on vacation in London about nine years ago. Skull fracture. No family, no friends, no funeral—sounds like her body was never even claimed."

She collapsed into the chair beside Petrosky and flipped open the folder, tapped the top sheet. "The rental agreement lists two children, Joey and James, both six at the time the rental application was completed—same age Kingsley would have been. Same age Gregory would have been, if…he was there." But Gregory had probably been there the whole time. Scott was confirming the forensics on the skull they'd found, but from the size of the skull, he'd have been around seven, the age Gregory was when he vanished. At least the Boyles would finally be able to bury what was left of their child.

Petrosky grimaced at the page—Joey and James. Dakota Hodgson. Surely all fake names—and that fake social for Mom. Was Roux in on it? "The social security thing seems coincidental after all that shit with Corey's stepfather."

"Roux got shipped back up to Maryland already, but the name Dakota Hodgson wasn't on the list of stolen identities, I checked."

So no evidence that Roux had ever been involved with the kidnapper—he probably really had seen Corey on television while down here for one of his scams and started blackmailing him. It fit the timeline. Corey had vanished from Fountainview Hospital in Windsor the night his mother died, same as Roux—but Roux had said someone was helping Corey, had "fed him information" and given him a place to stay. Corey'd gotten that tattoo. Then he'd made his way to the Boyles' and had been thriving by all accounts until Roux came back into his life. That's when he started falling apart, fighting, punching nurses and shit. And he'd become too much of a liability for the kidnapper. Petrosky could think of no one else with a stake in trying to get Mancebo to stop looking for Gregory, no one else who would be worried enough to kill Corey once he started acting out—no one else with loose ends to tie up.

He inhaled deeply through his nose. "So, what's our play?"

"I'm sending Kingsley's age progression photos to Acharya." When he balked, she raised a hand and said, "I know he can't post a story with them yet, or the kidnapper will know we're on to her."

"I just want to be careful, Jackson. If there's any chance Kingsley and this other child are still alive…" The kidnapper was not opposed to killing to cover her tracks.

"It's just so Acharya will be ready if we need him. Until then, we're going to backtrack, redo the work the original detectives did, look for common places, service people, anywhere the boys might have met a common adult—places Detective Harris didn't know to look. Might be a pediatrician, an eye doctor, a skating rink, the mail lady—the goddamn ice cream truck driver, who knows?"

"Did we check the computer? The online games Corey was playing?"

"Scott did. Nothing there, no chatrooms, no live feeds, and Corey didn't even have a headset despite the games—not a single social media profile. Nowhere he would have been communicating with the kidnapper. And Gregory wasn't online before he was taken. I'll make a call to the Stintons', but I can't imagine a five-year-old was online like that, especially not nine years ago."

Petrosky's heart was still throbbing painfully, but not as hard as before. The sharpness had dulled to a slowly vibrating pressure beneath his ribs. "I'll send an artist over to the Bishops', see if we can get a sketch of the woman who lived there. And the other boy Wes saw with Kingsley." And if this case was anything like the Ponce case… That lush grass behind the Relenski house. All those bones in Ponce's cellar. "We need to take a look at the rest of the property."

"Already applied for a warrant—the last one only covered the yard." Jackson's fingernails tapped on the desktop, echoing the thudding in his brain, amplifying the muted beating of his heart.

He sniffed, staring at the mound of papers on his desk—file after file of dead ends. "Maybe you should go back to your desk to work."

She snorted and rolled her eyes.

"It's been a long day, Jackson. I'm…tired of everyone."

"I know." She stood. "But I don't think this is about me. I think you need to go visit Linda."

He grunted but did not pull his gaze from the mess of case numbers and detective scrawl. "I don't need to do shit."

"Go see her anyway. You shouldn't be alone this week."

And now he did look her way—she was staring daggers at him, waiting for him to agree. Was she going to stand there all night? Probably, if he didn't say yes. He nodded, the muscles in his neck aching along with his jaw.

Shouldn't be alone right now?

*You don't know what I need.*

But he knew.

He did.

And, *oh god*, he was trying like hell not to do it.

HE CHAIN-SMOKED his way back toward his house, windows up, the dry acridity burning in his lungs. And his eyes. The first traffic light that stopped him was a bloody haze like fog in a red light district.

Maybe something would change his mind before he got home. Maybe the next light would turn red, and while he was waiting for green, he'd have an epiphany, or a random burst of resolve, Julie's voice whispering in his brain that he could hold on, that things weren't so bad, that it would pass, and his mind would change right along with the traffic signal.

Every light after the first was green. As if the universe was telling him it was okay to let go, to just stop trying so goddamn hard. To stop struggling.

The liquor store passed, bright and happy, the light fuzzy and diffused through the smoke in his car. He lit another cigarette. He had what he needed already.

The bottle was where he'd left it, middle of the coffee table, glowing in the dim lamplight as if it'd been waiting there all his life to offer him a few moments of reprieve—of *numbness*. The front curtains were already closed. The room was a sanctuary, hidden from the outside world.

*But not from yourself*, Dr. McCallum's voice whispered. But the shrink wasn't here to save him, not tonight. No one was here to save him.

No one but his buddy, Jack.

He stripped off his sweatshirt; it stuck to his back, and as he tossed it aside, he noticed the black dirt under his fingernails—dirt from Gregory Boyle's grave. He lowered himself onto the couch slowly. Maybe he should shower, go into the bedroom, see if he could fall asleep. But he could feel the steady pulse of the night-light from here, Julie's night-light, the one she'd probably have in her house, maybe in a baby's room if it hadn't been for him. If he hadn't been a cop. If he hadn't pissed off the wrong man. Julie had paid for his sins with her life.

The bottle was heavy in his hand, the glass cool.

Julie's face, her blue lips.

His palm tingled.

Julie's laugh, ringing through the living room.

*I'm sorry, baby. I'm so sorry.*

He cracked the bottle, hearing his daughter, hearing her begging, shrieking, high and desperate. How long had she screamed? How long had it taken her to die? Had she known it was his fault? Had she wished he was there?

He raised the bottle to his lips, the stink of it burning in his nostrils, his insides trembling. His mouth watered. His salivary glands stung, hot and—

*Bang! Bang! Bang!*

He jumped, a drop of the whiskey landing on his knuckle, a beautiful tiny drop of clearest amber.

*Bangbangbangbang!*

The door. And then a muffled voice: "Eddie?" The knock came again, and this time, another sound came with it—a bark.

*Go away.* He lowered the bottle, watching the liquid swishing inside it like waves, like the ocean, deep and full of promise, of the potential to drown. The drop on his knuckle slipped down along the back of his hand. His skin tingled as if trying to absorb the liquor through his pores.

"Eddie!" Billie was practically yelling. "Duke's been scratching at the door since he heard your car." *Bangbangbangbangbang!* "Open up!" *Bangbangbang!* "You okay?" Her voice was strained now, worried—definitely yelling. "I will break this door down, Eddie, so help me."

He set the bottle back on the table with a *clunk*. Heavier than it had felt just moments ago—his hand ached from where he'd been clutching the glass neck. "Coming! Just hang on a second, Jesus."

He capped the bottle and snuck it behind the couch pillow, then slid his sweatshirt back over his head—damp. His legs were heavier, too, as if all his energy had leaked from his flesh like sweat. Even the doorknob felt impossible to turn.

Duke bounded over the threshold the moment the door was open wide enough.

Billie cocked her head. "You busy?"

*Of course I'm fucking busy.* But when he met her blue eyes, that worried, fearful gaze, his anger eased—*What a piece of shit I am.* "I'm just tired. Long day at work. Hell of a case."

Billie's hair gleamed silver in the moonlight; the left side highlighted with the subtle yellow glow from the house across the way—he hadn't even turned his porch light on. He reached out and flicked the switch.

Billie blinked in the sudden brightness. Behind him, the living room felt exceptionally dim and hollow, like a gaping mouth that had grown teeth. Billie couldn't see the bottle of Jack behind the pillow—he didn't think. And if she could, what would she say?

But she wasn't looking into the room. She was staring at…him. Could she see the desperation in his gaze or the set of his shoulders? He straightened and plastered a scowl on his face as she said, "Want some pot roast?"

His shoulders slumped once more—his bones were too heavy. Duke nudged his hand, and he shoved it into his pocket. *I'm not good for you, boy. I'm not good for anyone.* "No thanks. I ate at the precinct."

"You can do better than the vending machine."

"I know, and I do appreciate it. I'm just tired."

Now she did peer past him, lips tight, looking for…what? A loaded gun sitting on the counter? No, he wasn't going there. He was down, but he wasn't that broken. Yet.

Finally, she shrugged. "I was thinking we could all play poker after dinner. It's been a while." And there was suspicion in her narrowed gaze.

"I really think I need to get some rest."

"Understood." But her eyes said more—*I get it, but I don't approve.* "We're here if you need us, Eddie, all of us. We've all been through some shit. And remember, Duke is counting on you. He really missed you today." She smiled past him, and Petrosky turned to see Duke sitting on the kitchen linoleum, tail swish, swish, swishing against the floor, patiently waiting for Petrosky to scratch his head, to stop being such a self-absorbed prick—he'd almost forgotten the dog was there. "Give him an extra scratch tonight, okay, Eddie? He's had a rough day too."

She squeezed his arm, smiled, and walked away, haloed in the porch lights and the silvered moon. Practically floating over the grass. Like an angel.

Much better than a red traffic light.

*I hear you, baby girl. I hear you.*

He closed the door.

Duke whined as Petrosky ripped the bottle from its hiding place on the couch, the pillow tumbling to the floor. The bottle clunked against the countertop. Duke followed Petrosky, his nails clicking against the kitchen tile.

The cap buzzed off.

Duke whimpered.

Petrosky's knuckles strained against the neck of the bottle. His hand shook. The bottom of the bottle teetered against the edge of the stainless sink.

*Drink it.* His mouth watered.

*Don't drink it.* Gregory Boyle's face rose in his brain, the smiling school photo, pale skin, dark hair, dark eyes, and then his flesh melted away to that awful gray skull he'd pulled from the earth just hours before. Then it was Corey Gagnon's purple tongue, his shit-stained legs. And there were other kids out there, kids he'd never find if he was plastered. Drinking was what he had done after Julie died. How many other girls had died before he'd found their killer?

Too many. Far too many dead because he'd failed. His gut clenched. Bile crept up his throat.

Julie laughed.

He upended the bottle over the sink, his mouth watering,

his eyes burning, the scent of the liquor in his nose welcome and vile and lovely and nauseating.

*I'm so proud of you, Daddy.*

He leaned over and rested his forehead against the faucet and let the liquor mix with his tears as it swirled down the drain.

**27**

---

THE SLAMMING of his car door reverberated through the lot, his elbow smarting with the force of it. Smoke clung to his jacket and the insides of his nostrils—leaked from his hair. He clutched the coffees so tightly he left fingerprints in the wax coating on the cups. But that was the least of his worries; his nerves were shot, excess adrenaline swirling through his system together with the warm pressure of exhaustion. They had at least two children in danger, the ones Wes Bishop had seen—if they weren't already dead— and leads in far shorter supply than he'd like. And their two kidnapping victims, Gregory and Kingsley, had gone to different schools, had no common teachers. They weren't even in the same grade when they were taken. How had they been targeted?

Jackson was already at her desk—*her* desk. An extra chair sat empty across from his own. She did not glance up as he slid into his seat and set the coffees on his desktop, but she'd be there soon enough to claim hers. Shame settled deep in his gut, the flesh on his back tingling—was she looking at him? Did she know how close he'd come to falling off the wagon?

That was paranoid, of course it was.

Across the room, Decantor typed at the frantic pace of a guy who'd just taken one too many hits of speed. *Click-clack-tap-clackclickclackclickclickclick.*

"Why are you so late?" Jackson plopped into her seat across from him and snatched the coffee he'd put in front of her spot, a drip spilling onto the sleeve of her navy jacket.

"Dunno. Why are you wearing blue?" Petrosky brushed his hand down his own navy jacket. "If I'd known you were going to steal my outfit, I'd have worn my Gucci." He straightened in his chair, catching a whiff of tobacco from his coat. A jacket and a shave made him feel less like he was giving up, but if he were being honest, he just wanted Jackson to leave him alone. She might not say much, but he had seen it in her eyes yesterday when she was looking at his wrinkled sweatshirt—he didn't want her to know that he was breaking. He straightened his lapel for good measure.

"Like you know what Gucci is," she said now.

"It's panda fur, right?"

She rolled her eyes, sipped her coffee, and stared him down.

"Fine, fine," he said, aiming for nonchalant. "Got our sketch artist setting up an appointment with Wes in the next day or two. And I walked the Bishop neighborhood all morning." Two hours of knocking on doors before people left for work, hoping the residents were still the same people as a year back when their suspect lived out that way. His calves were killing him. At least he'd gotten to wander and chain-smoke without anyone giving him shit about it.

"You smell like bad tobacco," Jackson said as if reading his mind.

"Better than booze." But his mouth watered even as he winced inside. *Smooth.*

She frowned. "Yeah, that's true," she said slowly, then: "No warrant yet on the property, but I think it'll come through by tomorrow." She cocked her head. "The Bishops' neighbors have anything?"

He sipped his coffee—tasteless today, though Rita's was by far his favorite place for a cup of joe. "A few people saw a woman with dark hair and two boys with dark hair, but no one ever went over to introduce themselves—not a single person in the neighborhood actually met her or her children, save Wes, and I'd hardly call that an introduction. Seems she was reclusive—distant enough that no one approached her. No one even saw her face. And both witnesses said she was wearing sweats; hard to guess on weight, but they think around five-four for height. Average." Not much help, except to confirm that she could be small enough to have a size six shoe. "Also got confirmation on the blue car," he said. "That PI dickhead was right, as was Marianne Bishop. But the neighbor across the road was more specific on the type: a Tercel."

"Okay, that's something." Jackson nodded. "I spent the morning scouring all the old notes on both the Boyle and Stinton cases. The bus drivers cycle through the district, high school, then the middle, then the elementary, but Gregory and Kingsley didn't share any of the same personnel, even substitute drivers. No full-time teachers, either, which we knew since they can't work at more than one school at the same time. The postal workers don't overlap—the Stintons were just over the edge into the next territory—and the kids didn't attend the same parks or camps or clubs. But"—she paused for dramatic effect, or maybe just to breathe—"there are personnel who traveled through both schools at some point while the boys were there and could possibly have met both—either who changed jobs to work at the other school, or who work different days at different locations throughout the district. Twenty-three possibles there. If you count substitute teachers, that number skyrockets to fifty-eight. And the shrink's one of them." Jackson drew the coffee cup back to her lips as Petrosky narrowed his eyes.

"The school counselor?" She was the right height, and Holloway had said she traveled between schools—that she was only at Anderson Middle School two days a week. Of course she visited the elementary schools too. But she'd been vetted; Harris had talked to her after Gregory's kidnapping.

Jackson set the cup down. "Before you say it, I know they looked at her—at everyone at the school. But I don't think they looked very hard. Why would they? They assumed Gregory was a crime of opportunity, not a planned abduction because Stevie never mentioned his brother's grown-up friend."

And now they knew better. Petrosky's heart ratcheted up. "That would explain why Corey refused to see another shrink. If he knew Holloway, if she was the one feeding him information about Gregory—"

"Right. And she's been with the county for the last ten years. No evidence that she ever met Kingsley, but the schools call her out by appointment, so she's always around. She'd have had plenty of time to groom them both even if she didn't treat Kingsley or Gregory before they were taken." She tapped the coffee cup lid with her fingernail. "I wish we knew who the third child was, the one Wes saw with Kingsley, but…"

Petrosky stared at his own coffee cup—still in his hand. If the divots in the side got any deeper, the whole cup would collapse. "But Holloway told us Gregory had threatened to run off, didn't she? If she convinced these boys to run away, why tell us that? Did she not think we'd connect it?"

"Why would we? No one was looking at Kingsley at all. His mother was already gone, so they assumed she took him. And the shrink is a smart woman, obviously. Even if she thought it was too big a hint, a little reverse psychology goes a long way toward confusion. Hence us talking about it now."

Petrosky ran a hand over his now smooth chin. Nancy Holloway. Flowered dress, deep, violet eyes—fake lenses. "She's the ginger, right?"

"I'm not sure you're supposed to call them that."

"She had dark roots, though." And the woman who had lived up the street from the Bishops had dark hair. What better way for a woman to hide her identity than a change in hair color?

"Something else interesting about Holloway, though: She's got two kids, according to the birth records, but they don't live with her. Both of her teenage sons live with their fathers, her second and third husbands, respectively. One of the dads has two DUIs—Mom doesn't have so much as a speeding ticket."

Petrosky frowned. Usually, mothers got custody—especially a shrink with gainful employment and no black marks on her record. Though half the time, shrinks were the most fucked up of anyone, and with three ex-husbands...maybe she wouldn't even need a secret identity, just enough last names to confuse the shit out of everyone. "You think she's trying to replace her own kids? Taking other people's?" Her boys were teens now, maybe close in age to Gregory, to Kingsley...

Jackson shrugged. "I've heard stranger. It's a bitch coming home to an empty house."

*Ain't that the truth.* The room fell silent for one far-too-sharp heartbeat, then livened up again, the typing of Decantor's keyboard across the way ticking in Petrosky's ears and tightening his jaw. "Holloway ever have a Tercel in her name?"

"Nope. And no evidence that she ever stayed at the place up the road from the Bishops. But there are ways around an auto registration." And plenty of ways to hide a car you didn't want connected to you; he'd once worked a pedophile case where the suspect kept a second vehicle hidden in a back alley ten miles from his house. Only picked it up when it was hunting time. Their suspect could switch cars every morning if she wanted to.

Petrosky stood. "Let's go have a talk with Nancy Holloway."

HOLLOWAY WAS WORKING at Southbend High today. They found her sitting behind a pine desk in a long pink skirt and a white blouse. She raised her head and her eyebrows when Petrosky and Jackson took seats opposite her.

"Is there more news? Did you find out who killed that poor boy?"

Petrosky watched her face, her steady gaze. The kidnapper, the killer, had panicked and murdered Corey, but did she believe she'd solved the problem? The world didn't know they'd unearthed a child's body—yet.

"We're looking into a few leads," Jackson said, "but we'll have to ask you to keep it quiet, for now. I'm sure you're good at that, being a shrink and all." But being a shrink hadn't stopped her from giving away a traumatized boy's secrets, release form or no.

Holloway nodded, and Petrosky leaned back in his chair. Her hair was fully ginger now; she'd done her roots. Her eyes were the same, though, that crazy violet, hiding whatever her real eye color was. "Have you ever owned a blue Tercel, Mrs. Holloway?" There hadn't been one in the parking lot, but their kidnapper had a hell of a reason to ditch the baby-snatch mobile.

She pursed her lips. "No, never. Why?"

"We have a witness who saw Gregory talking to someone in a blue sedan before he was taken. We think that person might have information on our kidnapper." He watched for a flicker of guilt—or abject panic—but aside from her tight mouth, he saw no hint of distress. Sincere unknowing? Or an unfeeling psycho?

"Oh dear." She put her hands on the table—strong, fleshy arms. Could she lift 140 pounds of dead weight, or would she need to leverage her weight against the couch?

"Anderson's principal had a blue car once, but I think it was a Corolla."

Nah, they'd looked at the principals—they hadn't changed schools, and none would have known both Kingsley and

Gregory. This felt more like deflection than trying to help. "Where were you the day before Gregory disappeared?"

"Here? I think? I'm not sure exactly when he—"

"May twenty-first, seven years back."

Her eyes narrowed.

"Just a question, ma'am. We're looking for anyone who might have seen the car that took Gregory. You know, just to verify." He laced his fingers in his lap. "So, where were you?"

Her gaze hardened. "Definitely not looking at any cars." Her voice was tight—agitated. Guilty, or just pissed at the veiled accusation?

Jackson cocked her head. "How can you be so sure, Mrs. Holloway?"

"I was in Hawaii."

*I wouldn't have been so certain unless I'd planned an alibi.* "You're awfully sure on those dates," he said slowly, his eyes locked on her face.

"Of course I am," she snapped. "The twenty-third is my anniversary, and seven years ago, I was getting married." She gestured to a picture on her bookshelf, the same one she had up at Anderson Middle School, the colorful one with her and the smiling bald man wearing flowered necklaces. The shelf was a touch crooked, just like the bookshelf at Nurse Ogden's boring white apartment. Why didn't people know how to use a level?

"You still married to him?"

"Yes." She drew her hands off the desk and rested them in her lap—leaning back, as far away from them as she could get. "What kind of question is that?"

Petrosky ignored her and said, "What about the night of August eighth, early morning August ninth. This year."

Now she sighed, leaning forward to glance at…a calendar. As he would have had to. "Oh, that was just this past Thursday. I was at home, dinner with my husband, then packing. Then…sleeping, I suppose."

"Going on another trip, ma'am?"

She glared at him—if she was innocent, he probably

deserved that. "No, for my office—getting ready for the school year. I moved my things in here and set up at a few other schools that week." She blinked those unnatural violet eyes, her irises spitting fire. "If I recall, you were there to witness that yourself."

They'd seen her unpacking over at Anderson. But how long did it really take to pack a box? Either way, the alibi should be easy enough to verify with her hubby.

"Do you remember Kingsley Stinton?" Jackson cut in, clearly tired of the alibi bullshit—which probably meant his partner believed Holloway.

She frowned. "No, I can't say I do."

"Little boy over at Garden Grove Elementary, about nine years ago."

"Oh, that would have been right after I started. With the parents' permission, I can pull files, but..." She shrugged her meaty shoulders.

"He was threatening to run away; the teacher scheduled a meeting with his dad, but he vanished. Just like Gregory Boyle."

Now her purple eyes widened. "Oh...yes! I do remember that. The police were over at the school then, interviewed everyone, asked me to run interference for the kids if any of them got upset. I never met the child himself, though. If I had heard about him threatening to run away before he disappeared, I certainly would have tried to..." Her gaze wandered over Petrosky's shoulder.

He turned. A girl in green camouflage pants stood in the doorway, her face half-covered by long curly hair dyed a pastel purple. The one eye he could see was wary. Suspicious. She and Roman would probably have a blast together.

Holloway waved to the girl and stood. "If you have more questions, we can talk again later," she said softly.

Petrosky's eyes lit on the photo on the wall. The flowered leis. An airtight alibi. And the neighbor had said the woman he saw with those boys was an average weight. Holloway was the right height, but bulky, strong—enough for a witness to mention. He'd forgotten that.

They still had fifty-seven possibles.

Fifty-seven chances to alert the kidnapper—no, the killer —that they were on to her. One wrong move, and Kingsley and the boy with him would be buried just like Gregory Boyle.

**28**

---

"ANYTHING BACK ON THE BODY?" Jackson re-pocketed her phone and slid into the vinyl booth, eliciting a squeak that sounded like Duke's butt after taco night. It was still quieter than the Elvis Presley tunes blaring from the faux-fifties jukebox and the noisy crowd that filled every other available seat.

"No DNA on the bones yet," Petrosky said, replacing his own cell. "But it's only been a day. Scott's still got Gregory's book bag and the bloody shirt from Mancebo, and he's working his forensic magic on the burial site, too…and the shovels. Woolverton did say that from the bones, the kid looks to be about seven when he died, so he's definitely not one of the teenagers Wes Bishop saw—almost certainly Gregory." He hated that, fucking hated it, but at least the Boyles would have closure. Not that it would stop the bleeding wound in their hearts. That type of wound never healed.

"But confirming it's Gregory Boyle won't help us find the murderer," Jackson said. "If we have any chance of saving Kingsley, we need to figure out where the kidnapper went after leaving the Relenski Rentals property—provided Kingsley and the other kid aren't buried somewhere in that yard, too."

With the forensic team on it, they'd know soon enough. At least Stinton wouldn't be heartbroken if the worst had happened—he thought Kingsley was bad anyway. But Roman…the kid had put up posters. He desperately wanted his brother to be alive. The boys would have bonded in the shared weirdness of that house, whether Kingsley was "bad like his mother" or not.

Jackson laid her palm on the stack of manila folders dead center of the table, glancing briefly at the salt and pepper shakers she'd balanced on top of the napkin holder to make room. "Out of the fifty-seven suspects we had left, fifteen had alibis for Corey's murder that we can verify without inter-views. Credit card alibis." She removed the top set of folders and set them aside. "This stack is out. Now can you tell me why we drove forty-five minutes to get to this diner? You didn't get enough of that fifties vibe at the Stinton place?"

Petrosky glanced at the black-and-white checkerboard floors, same as the Stintons had in their kitchen, then at the long, brilliantly red bar, the matching swivel stools, all currently filled to capacity. "Let's call it a side project."

"Hey, you do you. As long as this place has burgers, I'm good."

"Burgers and fries and malted milkshakes." Just like you'd expect from a diner called The Soda Shop. "So we're down to forty-two possibles," he said, rubbing at a sore spot at the base of his skull. Forty-two people, any one of whom could have the boys.

But where to look? The kidnapper needed a house to hide them, either in a neighborhood where people were used to looking the other way or a place somewhere more secluded. But maybe she had learned to be more careful after having to hightail it out of her rental. Did she even let the kids outside anymore? He was hoping against hope that after keeping Kingsley for nine years, she'd try to keep him just a little longer—that she'd bonded with him. Mostly, he was hoping their investigation didn't push her to do something more drastic to keep Kingsley from being discovered—no one stayed quiet like the dead. Petrosky flipped open the top file folder in Jackson's stack: Gloria Miller, a music teacher who had worked at both schools…and three other elementary schools in the area. Then Raquel Albertson, a woman who had once taught art at the high school, but had ended up substitute teaching in all the elementary schools in the county after funding was cut. Their kidnapper was probably a woman, based on whom they'd seen connected with Kingsley—and Corey if she was the woman outside the tattoo shop. But most of the school personnel for both boys were women, so that didn't help much. "What do those forty-two possibles look like? Kids, families? Housing situations?"

Jackson tapped her fingernails on the tabletop. "None of our forty-two have overt connections to both Gregory and Kingsley, not that I could find," she said. "These are all just people who might have *met* both. And most of them have children, but I looked extra hard at any who've experienced loss—something that might trigger them to replace a child. One janitor who spent time working in both schools lost a boy to leukemia three years ago—sad, but doesn't fit the timeline. And we've got a few divorces with shared custody, but nothing nasty."

Petrosky stared at the page until the words blurred. "What about…twins?" He set the folder aside. "Wes Bishop said the boys told him they were twins. Clearly they aren't, but they're being raised as twins—they were listed on the rental agreement as both being ten. If she had two that she lost, she'd be likely to take two—she'd take Gregory even though she already had Kingsley." And twin births, and subsequent deaths, would be easier to track.

But Jackson was already shaking her head. "No one with twins at all in this pile, let alone dead twins."

"Bummer."

Her eyes narrowed. "Yeah…bummer."

"You know what I mean. If someone had twins who died the week before Kingsley vanished, we'd go snatch them up."

But Jackson wasn't looking at him anymore; she was staring at the waitress, eyes wide.

"Well, detectives, isn't this something?"

Petrosky followed Jackson's gaze. Bonnie Stinton was wearing blue today but still had on the same blood-red lipstick. And the same fake smile that was supposed to keep what she really thought under wraps. Like any good fifties housewife, or any waitress at the height of a lunch rush.

He forced his lips into what he hoped passed as a smile. "Mrs.….Stinton, is it?"

"You remembered. I'll have to get you an extra piece of pie for that." She glanced over at Jackson—his partner had gone silent, her eyes on him now, a smirk on her lips.

"So, what'll it be?" Bonnie asked.

Jackson nodded to him. "You know this territory better than I do."

"Two cheeseburgers, both with fries," Petrosky said. "And chocolate malts all around."

"I'll bring those right out, Sugar." Still smiling, she headed for the counter on her shiny red heels.

Jackson was still staring at him. "How'd you know she worked here?"

"Side project, Jackson."

"I'm just saying, of all the places—"

"One: Money's tight for them—he lost his shirt in the market a few years back, as evidenced by his worn loafers. And Bonnie plays this role better than anyone else who works here because she plays it at home too."

Jackson crossed her arms. "This isn't the only diner, Petrosky."

"Stinton's ex-wife worked here. It was in Kingsley's file." *And I might have made a call up here to see when Bonnie was working.* He winked.

"You're a maniac."

"It's part of my charm."

The clink of forks on plates and the drone of conversation from other tables drifted over them. Finally, Jackson cleared her throat. "If this kidnapping deal is a maternal thing, someone trying to replace a lost kid or two, do you think Kingsley is alive?"

*I sure as shit hope so.* "We have no way to know, that's the problem." He sighed. "But probably. If she's a pedophile, she'd have gotten tired of them by now. Plus, she's educating the children she has—that points to raising them as opposed to just taking them for another reason. But if she sees them as her children now, her twins, she'll do anything to keep from losing them. And if there's resistance…look what happened to Gregory, to Corey." This kidnapper had no problem killing when she thought it necessary—and they had to assume it'd become necessary if she thought they were getting close to catching her.

"We should talk to McCallum," Jackson said.

Petrosky grabbed another folder and paged through it, the words a blur, then met her eyes over the top. "He's not in this week."

"Really?"

"Having surgery or something."

"Didn't he call you the other day?"

"Yeah, just to keep me up-to-date. To let me know he'd be back soon."

She frowned. "But you said he was on vacation."

"Had to use vacation days for surgery, you know how that goes." Petrosky blinked, seeing the whiskey swirling down the drain. The shrink had a right to be worried. And so did Jackson. But the week was almost over—a few more days of pretending, and Julie's birthday would pass just like every other year, and he'd forget. Again.

He pushed the files aside, as Bonnie returned carrying a platter laden with grease and meat and carbs and thick, frosty chocolate malts. The salty stink of it made his mouth water—*finally, some real food.* Bonnie glanced at him as she set the plates down, but turned away once the last dish was delivered.

When Bonnie had sashayed back to the counter, Jackson

picked up the top file again. At least she'd dropped the idea of seeing McCallum. "A dozen on the list are single," she said. "Only two have additional properties in their name, and those places are out of state—doubtful they're keeping kids there, but we can make sure." She slid a few more folders from the stack and set them aside. "I think there are another twenty we can rule out based on other people living in the house—specifically, kids who attend school. I don't see how they'd be able to keep it quiet if there were abducted children hanging out in their bedrooms while they sat in algebra."

"So we're down to twenty-two?"

She nodded. "Twenty-two."

He drowned his sorrows in grease and salt, letting the burger slide down his gullet. *Amazing.* Why had he ever stopped eating like this?

Jackson shoved a fry into her mouth and chased it with the shake. "But this is where it's going to get harder—everyone on this list looks legitimate. They have jobs, families, obligations that wouldn't allow them to stay home with a pair of kids. And all of the social security numbers from these twenty-two are valid—nothing wonky like what we saw with that rental property, with Dakota Hodgson. No connections to Canada. The school counselor license numbers are right, teaching certifications are connected to the right numbers, and not one of those numbers has a death certificate attached to it—fingers crossed our kidnapper just used the fake for the housing rental."

He sighed. The more research they did, the more it felt like they were heading in the wrong direction, especially since so many on their list had been vetted when Harris was working Gregory's kidnapping. *Even Mancebo probably looked at them.* "We'll have to talk to the Boyles when the forensics come back."

Jackson tossed her half-finished burger onto the plate. "I'm just glad they already know Corey wasn't their son. It won't make it easier, telling them we found Gregory's body, but..."

He grabbed his malt—cold and slippery against the pads of his fingers. "Yeah. They were raising a Canadian. The constant niceness should have been a dead giveaway."

Jackson frowned, eyes far away. "Maybe there's something to that."

"To what? I'm sure they felt better when he started punching people. It's the American way."

Jackson ignored him and snatched a fry off his plate—hers were gone. "We don't know exactly how Corey ended up down here, but we do know he was Canadian. That has to be where he met the kidnapper—he moved into the Boyle house a month after his mom died, and before then, according to Roux, he was living with someone who was feeding him information on Gregory. Maybe he came down here with our suspect." They couldn't be certain of that, it could have been someone who just wanted to help Corey out of his situation, but that person would have no reason to harm him. Only someone with something more serious to hide would kill to protect that secret—kidnapping Kingsley, stabbing Gregory? Those were definitely worth killing over…well, if you were a desperate murdering psycho.

Though… "We considered that already, the kidnapper going up there to recruit a replacement."

"But the kidnapper might have lived there at some point —had a life there," Jackson said. "Before she moved down here and started stealing kids. Not like she just walked up to a stranger and said, 'Hey, want to pretend to be a teenager and live with a new, weird family?'"

He gulped his malt, a headache stabbing at his temples, then waning as he plied his mouth with his last bite of burger.

Jackson wiped her hands on her napkin. "We'll see what we can find out from our neighbors to the north—the Canadians should have something by now. I'll take a closer look at Corey's school, too, but if we get nothing by tomorrow, maybe I'll give Acharya a call. He might have sources up there the way he does down here. Come on," she said, as he furrowed his brows. "We don't have much on our kidnapper except that she's a remarkably average brunette, and every one of our possibles meets that criteria."

"Yeah." Petrosky swallowed his last fry, the food sticking in his suddenly dry throat. "Tell Acharya to watch himself, though. Any hint that we're on to her, and she'll panic." If she had killed Corey when he showed instability, how long would Kingsley last when his mere presence would prove her guilt? If she was cornered, would she want the boy to live without her? Would she want to live without him? She was obviously a whack job, and he wasn't about to risk it. He suddenly felt it in his guts, the weight of impending doom—nearer, nearer. He was tempted to call Acharya himself. He reached for his wallet instead.

Jackson waved his hand away. "On me today, you got last time." She tossed thirty onto the table.

He nodded but slipped an additional fifty from his wallet, then his card. Jackson eyeballed him. "You going to take her home? Let her live in your woman stable?"

"It's just a house." He scribbled a note on the back of his card, along with his cell number. "But if she needs that…" He shrugged and reached for the stack of file folders. "Let's get out of here before she comes back."

"You scared of Marilyn Monroe?"

Petrosky shrugged. "Who isn't?"

# 29

---

"FUCKING CANADIANS." He slammed the phone back into the cradle. Hours of research, what seemed like hours of phone calls. His head throbbed. Outside the precinct windows, the sun was half-hidden behind the horizon; the clouds orange and red and the sickly purple of a bruise. Another day over, the bleak void of darkness edging ever closer—everything felt heavier at night. "The officer, Mountie, whatever you call them, is going to call me back, and she was so goddamn sweet it made my teeth hurt."

Jackson set a napkin-wrapped bear claw on his desk and settled in beside him. "Got you this as a midnight snack, but if you're having dental issues—"

Petrosky grabbed the pastry and took a bite for good measure—sweet, sugary perfection. "Kick off, Jackson," he said with his mouth full. Then: "All they had in the file was what they already sent us. Nothing on the school, nothing on Corey's last few days up there, no adult females hanging around, including his mother. Corey was eighteen, so his disappearance wasn't really investigated. The principal didn't know anything either, though he made it a point to say that Corey was a loner—didn't have friends that anyone knew about, one of the reasons he worried about the kid. Made him sound like the kind of kid who might commit suicide."

*Which might be why the kidnapper picked him.* If only they had a sketch of this woman—the principal was looking at his employee files from the school, was going to send down lists of teachers, descriptions, and the like, but that probably wouldn't amount to anything. She'd proven adept at flying under the radar. They'd have to go up there while Kingsley got precariously closer to becoming fertilizer. Like Gregory. He shoved another bite into his maw, crusted sugar raining down on his shirt. So were they dealing with a Canadian kidnapper or an American? It still had to be someone the kids knew, someone with access to groom them into running away...but maybe they were wrong about that, too. Maybe their kidnapper just knew the kids had disturbed home lives. Maybe the runaway thing was a coincidence, an expected reaction to a shitty family.

But he didn't like coincidences. And the blue sedan—the house. Even if the kidnapper had started out in Canada, she had definitely lived here for a time. Had she gone back north, taken the boys? If so, how the hell would they ever find them? That place was huge, and the whole family could just hide behind a moose or some shit.

"If she went back across the border, the boys have passports; can't get around that these days," he said. They might be able to look at passport scans from the boys crossing, but she wasn't likely using their real names, and they weren't sure when any of them had gone over. Too much traffic to wade through, especially on a short timeline.

"The easiest way to get passports is with a birth certificate," Jackson said, her gaze on the darkening window. "Two in this case—twins, right? I think that's our best bet."

He nodded, the sugar burbling in his guts—oily, but satisfying. They'd already checked their twenty-two suspects; most of them didn't have passports at all, but that didn't mean they weren't using a name besides their own.

"I'm going to make some calls," Jackson was saying. "We need to see how many twin births, and more specifically, deaths, there were in Canada and the Detroit metro area in the few years before Kingsley was taken. It makes sense that losing a child would be a trigger since the motivation appears more maternal—plus, that twin thing. Acting like they're related. Maybe she's trying to forget that she lost a kid at all."

"Yeah." Petrosky set the remaining half a donut on his desk, his stomach sour. *Dammit.* He'd need to eat five donuts a day until he built his tolerance back up. "Hopefully the kidnapper wasn't dealing with infertility." If she'd never had a child of her own, or she wanted her own biological kid to have a live-in friend, that'd be harder to track.

"Hopefully. Either way, there has to be a reason those boys are being raised as twins. I'm not buying that she just likes matching turtlenecks." She sipped her coffee—wait, had she brought him any?

Nope, no coffee to wash the sugar from his mouth—no water either. His belly churned; he swallowed hard and reached for the phone. "I guess I'll call those friendly dickheads back, see what they can pull."

Jackson shook her head. "I've got it. You go home, Petrosky. There's nothing else we can do here tonight, and I'm better at people than you. If anyone could piss off a Canadian..." She looked at him pointedly.

He shoved the rest of the pastry into his mouth, then pushed himself to standing. "Knock yourself out, Jackson." Just the thought of talking to the Canucks again made the throbbing in his brain pulse anew.

She cocked her head. "Where are you off to?"

"Home, you just said—"

"You should go see Linda."

*Nope.* He tried to swallow, but his tongue had gone dry. "I already sent her an email about the Stintons so she can follow up, get Roman into a safer situation."

"Well, maybe you can bring her some dinner, thank her for her trouble." Her eyes were on the file in front of her, but he averted his gaze anyway as if she might see something in her peripheral vision that he wanted to hide.

"That's her job, Jackson, like this is ours. Besides, I'm sure she's busy."

Silence filled his ears. Then: "But isn't it—"

"Isn't it what?" he snapped. A hole had opened in his chest, a jagged throbbing chasm. Bile rose in his throat. *Jackson and all this meddling bullshit.* He didn't need to be anywhere but home, didn't need to burden anyone else with this, especially not Linda—she'd borne enough for him.

"Nothing." Jackson stood suddenly and headed for her desk, but glanced over her shoulder halfway to her seat. "If you get bored later, Lance and I are ordering in. If you need us."

He turned for the stairwell, his guts rancid, his ribs painfully small. *I won't.* He was going to go home and forget.

---

Sweat dripped down his back, his heart throbbing in his throat—burning, acidic. Duke's happy panting hissed against his thigh. His kitchen had smelled like liquor though he'd scrubbed the sink, and Julie's night-light had been buzzing, buzzing, buzzing, buzzing, so loud and insistent he was half certain it had somehow been infiltrated by swarming insects, though no bees crawled from the glass or clung to the switch beneath. The night-light was off, he was certain it was off, but he felt its presence like an electrical current running through his veins.

So he'd run away. Taken Duke, and taken off.

His cell vibrated—again—and he slowed enough to retrieve it, Duke matching his pace. Three messages from Linda stared back...and the date.

*August 15th. August 15th. August 15th.*

McCallum always said the only way to get through all the bullshit, all the pain, was to face it head-on. Linda was doing that tonight.

*No, she's celebrating Julie's death.*

He shoved the phone back into his pocket and ran on,

harder, faster, trying to numb the rage that burned over the sick feeling in his belly. Was this who he wanted to be, who he really wanted to become? A man who couldn't even think about his little girl on her birthday?

*She's fucking dead; she doesn't have any more birthdays.*

The fury waned, replaced with a trembling ache—that hollow yet jagged hole pulsating in his chest. Linda wasn't celebrating Julie's death; he knew that. He just wanted an excuse to hate her. That's what Dr. McCallum would say. McCallum would also say Linda was trying to celebrate Julie's life, so she didn't forget her, so she would always remember their daughter, could forever imagine the amazing young woman she might have become.

What kind of father was he? His mouth watered, craving the gentle burn of Jack Daniel's in his gullet. Would he make it through the night without a drink? Probably not. But he couldn't jog all night.

*Be a man. Stop hurting that poor woman who was unlucky enough to marry your sorry ass.*

He ran harder, sweat dripping into his eyes, burning, burning. Was Linda in more pain without him there? Would holding her hand for a night, the way he should have held her every night after Julie died… No, he couldn't make up for that.

The donut burbled in his guts. He couldn't make up for being an asshole. But he could try not to hurt Linda more. His breath hissed in his ears, a stitch needling his side.

*Is this who you want to be, Daddy?*

He stopped, panting, wheezing.

Duke whined.

---

*THIS IS STUPID; what am I doing?*

The night outside his car was bleak and dark, full of street signs and other vehicles he barely registered, his chest too tight to do more than wheeze. Linda would be sad, like he was, but she wouldn't have liquor, not anywhere he could find it. They'd sit on the couch and look at Julie's old teddy bear, or her middle school yearbook—he had her night-light in his bedroom, so surely he could look at a teddy or whatever other things Linda had unpacked from her attic boxes. *Of course I can do that—of course.*

They'd drink coffee. They'd cry. He'd go home. For once, he wouldn't let her down. Maybe he'd even stay sober. Maybe he'd ask her more about the case—they could talk about Roman Stinton, too.

No, he shouldn't bring that up.

A package of chocolate sandwich cookies sat on the passenger seat—Julie's favorite, something he never thought about, ever, but it had hit him on the way up the road, a memory of her at the kitchen table, twirling one side off, smiling, dunking. He should have picked up milk. Why hadn't he picked up milk?

Linda's house was dark inside save for a subtle blue glow somewhere beyond the front windows. TV? *Thank god.* Maybe Linda needed a little distraction, after all, same as he did. He'd open with the case—nothing broke the ice like a kidnapping.

He rubbed at his breastbone—his heart ached.

Linda opened the door in a pair of jeans and a yellow T-shirt, her eyes so puffy they were almost sealed shut. And beyond her, in the living room—laughter.

His gut clenched. Not just laughter—Julie's laugh.

He peered past Linda into the room. On the screen, a colorful Happy Birthday banner waved, strung across the trees; their backyard in the old Ash Park house. And below the banner... His chest compressed, lungs hot as if someone had taken a flamethrower to them.

*Julie.*

She sat below the slowly waving banner beside a haphazard pile of brightly wrapped gifts, grinning at the camera. Linda said something off-camera, and Julie—

*—laughed, laughed, laughed—*

Bile rose in his throat, and his face burned, everything so *hot*.

He'd missed it, that party. He'd been working a case. He couldn't even remember if he'd gotten a dry piece of leftover cake because there were too many missed birthdays to sort out.

The package of cookies hit the porch with a plasticky *thrink*. "I have to go."

Linda stepped closer, over the threshold, onto the porch, hand outstretched, but he was already backing up, stumbling down the porch steps. "Ed, please—"

"I can't do this."

"Ed, you can, it's been—"

"It doesn't matter; it doesn't fucking matter how long it's been! She'll always be my child."

"She's my child, too! We can't just pretend it didn't happen! We have to be honest with ourselves, we have to—"

"You want honesty? I'm sorry I failed you as a husband, that I fucked up as a father, that I fucking killed our child, but I can't sit here all night and think about how I'll never see her again!"

He ran.

Again.

He barely heard Linda calling through the night after him.

---

PETROSKY RANG THE DOORBELL, some fancy song like the jangling of an ice cream truck. No noises from inside. But the glow, that glow from the television...blue and hazy. Maybe they were inside watching videos of Julie, too, maybe it was all a conspiracy to screw him up.

*This is wrong; this is a bad idea, I just need to find a bar, stop fighting so goddamn hard.* One night, right? Just one night wouldn't hurt him. His chest—*fuck*—his chest.

He raised his hand and slammed his fist into the front door until his knuckles throbbed as painfully as his heart.

The door flung wide open, Jackson peering into the night like she was ready to punch someone in the mouth. He held up a bag. "I got cheese puffs and the new Road Warriors game. Is Lance busy?"

She appraised him, maybe trying to see if he was drunk, but apparently, he passed scrutiny because she stepped back and gestured to the living room. He heard the tapping before he entered, the incessant button-pushing of a hand-held video controller. The boy was sitting on the couch, headphones on, in front of a flatscreen that probably cost more than every electronic Petrosky had ever owned. Even in Jackson's luxurious SUV, it was easy to forget she'd been some Wall Street big-shot before her elder son died—before she joined the academy. You couldn't forget it here, in this house, even if the burlap pillows and the suede couch made it feel homey.

Lance didn't look up as Petrosky entered—*taptaptaptaptap*—did not look over as Petrosky sat down on the other end of the sofa. Petrosky kept his eyes on his knees and held the game up, halfway between them. The tapping of the controller stopped.

Lance shifted his weight. The game vanished from Petrosky's fingertips and into the console. Lance pushed a controller into Petrosky's hand.

The kid kept his eyes on the screen. *Taptaptaptaptap.*

Petrosky kept his eyes on the screen. *Taptaptaptaptap.*

The ache in his chest eased. He opened the cheese puffs and set them on the couch between them, hoping Jackson wouldn't come in and tell them there was no food allowed.

Sometimes moms just didn't understand.

## 30

———

JACKSON PLOPPED into her chair at his desk, pulling a sheaf of papers from beneath her arm. "You okay?"

"Your couch sucks donkey balls." Petrosky rubbed at his neck muscles, but at least his chest felt better—achy but not painful.

She dropped her gaze and flipped through her stack. "Yeah, yeah. I'm sure it was the couch and not the family-sized bag of cheese puffs you scarfed down with my son last night."

He frowned. "Does Lance have a backache from the snacks, too?"

She stopped rustling the papers, something not quite a grin touching her mouth—satisfaction? Relief? It'd been so long since he'd felt either. Maybe he couldn't recognize them anymore.

"Actually…Lance seemed pretty happy this morning."

"Good. He's my favorite." The kid knew what it was to just relax into the moment. To not have to chat about every goddamn thing. Petrosky had never been much of a video game guy, but he didn't mind it as much as he'd always imagined. In the game, there was just you and your car, you and your gun—no time to think.

"The feeling's mutual." Jackson appraised him silently for

a moment, but Petrosky kept his eyes on the file in front of him until she set her sheets on his desk. *Don't think, just work.* "We got an email from the Canadians," she said finally. "They're looking into the school personnel for us—principal sent the info there instead of here because of jurisdiction. And they already interviewed Corey and Rosalie's neighbors, looking for any strange women who might have gone to the apartment, anyone matching our suspect's description, but nada—not a great part of town, so people might be more apt to mind their own business."

"We'll have to go up there, jog their memory."

She groaned. "Yeah, we'll have to make the trip." Their suspect wasn't perfect—someone, somewhere, had to have seen her.

"Nothing on Canadian twin birth or death certificates yet either," Jackson continued, "but without knowing exactly which area to look at..." She shrugged. "They'll get back to us if they find deceased twins or cases where only one twin survived."

Dead ends. All dead ends. He leaned back in his seat. "I ruled out one more from our stack of twenty-two—a substitute teacher who's only a hundred and five pounds; a friend was teasing her online for wearing a size five shoe." His left leg weighed more than she did. More importantly, her feet wouldn't fit in the shoes that made the prints at the Boyles' house.

"Where are you on the twins?" Jackson asked. "Or close in age brothers?"

Joey and James, both ten, had been listed on the Relenski Rentals lease agreement. They knew one of them was Kingsley, but whether the other was the kidnapper's real child remained to be seen. But Wes had said they told him they were twins. No one just decided to be twins. He nodded. "That's what I've been working on all goddamn morning." In the five years before Kingsley's abduction, there were too many cases—too many dead kids—but narrowing it down to Caucasian twin births who'd be the same age as their boys helped some. "I kept to Detroit and the Ash Park metropolitan area, but there's no way to tell where the kidnapper came from; she might have moved here from literally anywhere." He ran a hand over his face—prickly. Again. At least he'd stopped at home for a blazer. "I wanted to narrow it further to dark-haired boys because of the similar physical profile, but that's not as easy—the information isn't listed on a death certificate. And it's tricky because we don't know if she lost two children or just one—the boy with Kingsley could have been her biological. All the cross-referencing…it's a bitch."

"I can help with that. How many are there?"

"Thirty sets of twins where one or both died, either at birth or before age six. Didn't even get to the close in age siblings, the so-called 'Irish twins'—I have a feeling there will be too many to count, or to investigate properl—"

"Shit!" Deep voice, rumbly.

Petrosky and Jackson both looked up to see Sloan at his desk across the bullpen. Decantor's very Irish, very stocky partner shoved his thumb in his mouth.

Petrosky straightened. "Sucking your thumb, Sloan? I might have a spare diaper if you need one."

"You would," Jackson muttered.

The man's gravelly voice came back, "How 'bout a bandage? Got a rogue screw in the side of my drawer, little bastard."

"If it's that deep, go get a tetanus shot," Jackson said. "Otherwise, suck it up." Jackson slipped from her seat, but Petrosky could not take his eyes off Sloan. Thumb wrapped in a napkin now—and laughing as Jackson tossed a box of bandages across the room, hitting Sloan on the side of the head. Laughing. Not in pain. And not afraid.

Not afraid.

The world pulsed around Petrosky in time to his heart, words echoing in his brain, too many to tease apart, a jumble of tangled yarn when you knew the right color was in there somewhere—one loosened knot, and it would all unravel.

"Petrosky?"

Jackson was back. He turned slowly. "Corey...Corey vanished from the hospital the night his mother died, right?"

"Yeah, that's old news. Why?"

His head was spinning, one fact after another slamming against the sides of his skull. "He wasn't afraid of needles."

"What?"

"Gregory Boyle was afraid of needles. But Corey wasn't."

"Well, right, but Corey knew that Gregory was scared because someone was passing him information. So he pretended."

Pretending was all well and good, but the needle thing hadn't been in the papers. Petrosky'd heard it for the first time from Holloway when she said that Imposter-Greg had responded violently. "How many people would have known that to pass it along? About Gregory's phobia?"

She shrugged. "Parents, doctors—but Kingsley and Gregory had no common medical personnel, we checked. And the kidnapper would have known—she was Gregory's best friend in the world, right?"

Right. The kidnapper knew Gregory himself. His chest deflated. "Corey reacted so strongly, though, too strongly for someone trying to keep a low profile."

"He was an imposter. He had to make sure he didn't get stuck with a needle."

But...the nurse. She hadn't been testing his blood—hadn't even swabbed his arm. And what better person to meet Corey at the hospital where he'd vanished than... "The nurse worked at both schools—Kingsley's and Gregory's." And she'd gotten punched in the face for her trouble just last year when Corey started acting out—punched by a boy who had no issues with needles. Was Corey really that good an actor, or had he hit her for another reason?

Jackson shook her head. "Nurse Ogden's not even on our list. Harris looked at her, and we did too—she doesn't fit the physical profile."

"Because she's blond? Hair's easy to change."

"She's on the taller side, too, though; five-six at least. And there's no evidence that Ogden ever met Kingsley. Everything she said about transferring to the middle school after someone else retired checked out." Jackson hurried over to her desk for a file and returned, squinting at the tiny print. "Her nursing license number is valid, same with her social security number—no connection to Canada. And she has no children, alive or dead. And we were in her apartment—no sign of kids there."

"She own any other property?"

Jackson squinted. "Nope. And she drives"—she flipped a page—"a tan Civic. Not a blue Tercel."

But that didn't mean much for a woman with a penchant for fake names; a dead woman was the name listed on the Relenski Rentals house. "What if...is it possible she worked at that hospital up in Canada? That's the last place Corey was seen before he showed up down here." But how could she be working here in the states and up there at the same time? And be monitoring two children?

Jackson looked as skeptical as he felt, but Kingsley had been with his kidnapper for nine years—if he was still alive. The boys could be brainwashed enough that she could trust them not to run off. Or she had cages. And locks. Probably the latter.

Jackson was still frowning. "So you think she just met Corey at the hospital and said 'Hey, want to slide into a new family?'"

"Maybe? Let's play dumbass devil's advocate for a sec. Maybe she worked for the school district while she was moonlighting at the hospital over in Windsor. Once she realized the PI was still poking around, talking to folks at the school, she decided she needed an out. Might have been dumb luck that she watched this abused kid lose his mother. And Corey was a frequent flier at Fountainview, same with the mom. They were probably well-known to the staff."

Jackson drummed her fingers on the desktop. "Our kidnapper was surely desperate for the PI to stop looking for

Gregory, and Mancebo'd have no reason to keep poking around if the kid was home. But she didn't know he'd found the backpack and the shirt, that he knew Gregory was dead. Or that Adrian knew Corey was an imposter."

Petrosky nodded. "Right. And things seemed okay there, for a while—Corey seemed to fit in, and neither the PI nor the parents voiced any suspicions. Then the bottom fell out. Maybe she got nervous because Roux was blackmailing Corey, or maybe the stress from the book publicity got to her. Or it might have been on Corey's side—maybe he wanted out. Could have been the friction from Adrian Boyle who never really accepted him as hers, or simply depression and grief from his mom's death, his severe trauma history. Whatever it was, he flipped, threatened to tell, an argument ensued—"

"And he punched her in the face." Jackson's voice was hollow. "But if that's true…did she hack into the system, change her social on the state licensing documents? That's almost impossible."

"Maybe she didn't have to. She could have used someone else's nursing license number, taken their identity." And with working at the hospital… "How hard is it to delete a death certificate?"

"Someone should have come for it eventually—for the body."

"Unless they had no family." Like Dakota Hodgson, their skull-fractured horse rider whose name was on the rental house, a woman who'd died in…London? "Dakota…did she die in London, England, or London, Canada?"

"I…Canada." Jackson met his gaze, shaking her head. "Fuck. And she didn't even die in London—that was just where she was vacationing at the time of her death, which is why they listed it in the reports. She was on her way back to the states, stopped at a bed and breakfast in LaSalle, ended up under a horse instead of on it."

LaSalle was near enough to Windsor that she might have been taken to Fountainview for treatment, the hospital where Corey was last seen. Death certificate was irrelevant if there was no one to miss them—to look for them. Dakota Hodgson's body had still been hanging out in the morgue while their kidnapper was signing that lease agreement, and the rental company wouldn't have looked too deeply into her past, definitely wouldn't have bothered double-checking for a death certificate—if it had even been filed yet. And Ogden worked at the school. Easy enough to bring a pair of those skater shoes home during that marketing push Scott mentioned.

"I keep thinking about her house," Jackson said. "It was so *tidy*, but she knew we were coming. And we didn't search the house—we stayed in the living room. The kitchen."

Petrosky scowled at the pages—at Ogden's driver's license photo. Blond hair curled just under her chin. That sweet smile. "Is the Canadian hospital within driving distance?" he asked.

"It's an hour, maybe an hour and a half out. If she was there part-time, just working one or two weekend shifts a month..." She stood. "Give me twenty minutes. I'll call the hospital, see who I can address the email to, make sure it gets into the right hands—I'll send Ogden's photo, and we'll check for a death certificate under the same name. Then we'll head out to Ogden's apartment. Just to make sure."

And this time she wouldn't know they were coming.

**31**

——————

"BAD NEWS." Jackson clicked her cell off. "And good news. Shit, I don't know."

They needed good news—Nurse Ogden hadn't shown up for work today, which seemed like an ominous sign. He squinted through the Caprice's windshield, the haze of old tobacco glowering in the afternoon sunlight. "Out with it, Jackson."

"First, Scott called. Got the DNA back on our skeleton: not Gregory Boyle. This kid's information isn't in the database anywhere, nor are any close relatives.'"

*Shit.* How many victims were there? Maybe Gregory's body was still in the trash dump after all—they'd find out in a week or so once the cadaver dogs got out there. *What are you betting on, old man? You think they'll dig a kid's bones from beneath years of kitchen waste?* His fingers tightened on the wheel. "What's the good news?"

"That was the hospital administrator—we officially know who the kidnapper is." She shifted in the seat, eyes narrowed at her cell phone screen. "Ms. Janna Ogden, an American-born nurse, died at Fountainview Hospital more than ten years ago—right before our suspect came to work in the states. Sounds like the real Janna Ogden stayed with a friend in Windsor after her cancer diagnosis, so no paper trail that would have alerted us. Our Fake Ogden's real name, at least the name she used when she worked at Fountainview, is Phoebe Tozer, according to their records—another nurse. But though the hospital administrator is sure the real Janna Ogden is dead because he knew her personally, there's no death certificate registered anywhere." She scrolled through the rest of whatever she was reading, foot tapping on the floorboards. "And...yes, Tozer was working the night Corey's mother died—the night he vanished. She only did two midnight shifts a month, tops; they just called her in when they needed her. But she officially resigned two weeks after Corey stopped showing up to school. Now, Corey didn't show up at the cemetery claiming to be Gregory for a couple more months, but my bet is she brought him home with her the day his mother died and spent the next month preparing him."

"I doubt she had to try very hard to convince him." Corey was a just-turned-adult who'd never had a real childhood or a good education, and he had nowhere else to go, no other family outside his shitty abusive stepfather. He wouldn't have had to be tricked; he just had to be an opportunist.

"Yeah." Jackson glanced out the window of his Caprice, then back at the phone in her hand, nose wrinkled in disgust. "Why the hell are we in your car again? It smells like a stale tobacco farm had sex with a bag of moldy pretzels."

"Because she knows your car, smart-ass." Petrosky hit the gas. If Tozer saw the car from the second-floor apartment, would she run off? Would she hurt the kids the first chance she got? Had she hurt them already? Or had they vanished, the way they had after Wes caught the boys in the backyard? He sucked in a breath, but his ribs were too tight to allow it. He coughed instead. Her sad smile. The tears—real tears—about Corey's death. About Gregory. And Corey had attacked her, punched her in the fucking face. "How did we miss this, how the hell—"

"Shut up and drive. But not like you did in that game last

night." She elbowed him in his sore ribs. "Lance says you're awful."

The apartment building loomed. Jackson peered up through the windshield, and he followed her gaze—the window. Nurse Ogden, Phoebe Tozer, whatever her name was…her curtains were drawn. Of course they were. They took the side entrance and the stairs instead of the elevator.

He was wheezing by the time they reached her door, but that didn't stop Petrosky from pulling his Swiss Army knife from his back pocket. "You hear screaming?"

"You didn't even knock, Petrosky." Jackson reached around him—toward the door. She paused with her fist poised above the wood.

He righted himself, clenching the tool so hard the metal bit into his palm. "What are you doing, Jackson?" he hissed. "She didn't go into work. She's nervous, she's gotta know we're still looking—and if she's friends with Holloway, if the counselor told her we were there…" She'd already killed at least three people trying to keep her secret safe—Corey, bloody-shirt Gregory, and the John Doe child buried in her old backyard. They couldn't risk her getting ahead of them—couldn't risk her locking herself and those boys in the bathroom, blowing their brains out while he and Jackson were still out here knocking. The element of surprise counted for something. Sometimes it was the difference between life and death.

Jackson lowered her fist.

He jammed the blade into the space between the door and the jamb and wiggled. "Don't worry, ma'am!" he said, too quietly for anyone on the other side to hear. "I'm on my way!"

"Doesn't matter what you say, no one's going to believe you heard—"

"Don't tell me what I heard, Jackson."

The lock popped with a hollow *clunk*.

Petrosky pulled out his gun and held it ready, easing the door open with his toe. Listening. The whistling of the air conditioner whirred in his ears. Nothing more except the thudding of his own heart and the tentative clumping of their footsteps as they crept into the living room—the same room where they'd interviewed Tozer. Had it been only eight days since this case began? It felt like forever ago.

The room was exactly as he remembered it, neat and tidy, paperbacks stacked in the slightly crooked bookcase, not a single item out of place. They rushed through the living room to the hallway—light beige walls adorned with a single landscape in a gilded frame. No family photos, no stray baseballs, no backpack left haphazardly on the floor.

The bathroom was white, sterile—no surprise there—and the spare bedroom was empty, too, with a single twin bed with a navy comforter dead center, flanked by a cheap pine nightstand on one side and a rocking chair on the other. Closet door open: empty. Not so much as a hanger.

Jackson was already in the second bedroom when he entered, gun at her hip, peering into the closet on the far side of the double bed. An end table identical to the one in the first room sat on his side of the bed, a vase of fake sunflowers on the top.

Jackson glanced over her shoulder. "Closet's empty. Looks like they left town already."

He opened the top drawer of the dresser. Nothing. How much of a head start did she have? She'd been at the school just yesterday, they'd checked. But not today. She hadn't even bothered calling in.

They made their way back up the hall to the living room, but Petrosky paused at the entry to the kitchen, eyes narrowed at the counters, then at the bistro table. Clean, everything was tidy and in its place, but was that… He ran a hand along the countertop and rubbed his fingertips together: dust. His fingers left little trails on the linoleum. *Huh.* It was one thing to have dust on a bookshelf, even on the coffee table, but on the counter? Surely she'd eaten in the last week, and the amount of dust here was from a lot longer than that. She hadn't *left* this apartment—she didn't *live* here.

She'd met them here because this was her front, and she was too smart to keep just one place or just one name. Wherever those kids were, it was somewhere no one would know them. Where no one would see them.

But she'd skipped work—she had to be feeling the pressure. And people under pressure did crazy things in the name of survival.

They needed to get to those boys before she did.

**32**

———————

"I LOOKED INTO HER BACKGROUND, but there isn't much that'll help us find her," Petrosky said as Jackson returned to his desk with a pair of coffees and another file folder. It had been an hour since they'd left Tozer's apartment, and every minute had felt like an eternity. Where the fuck was Tozer? So far, he'd found dick that would lead them to her now, though he had managed to dig up her past. "Born in Canada, good grades, came down here to attend the University of Michigan for nursing school. No history of mental health issues or hospitalizations that her co-workers knew about. Parents deceased. No marriages, no father listed on the birth certificate for her twins—one child deceased." He stretched his arms over his head, trying to ignore the way his shirt pulled tight across his gut. "At least she's actually a nurse. I'd hate to think she spent all those years treating kids with no medical background." As if that was the worst thing she'd done this week. His lungs tightened. "And the address she gave the hospital for her tax forms was a bust—the building was demolished six months ago, but she might not know that."

"I'm sure she doesn't know we have this either." Jackson laid down the cups and dropped a sheet on his desk. One

235

page. A xeroxed news article from a printed paper—old school. "From Acharya. Better late than never, I guess."

They both peered at the clipping.

### One Dead In Toronto Crash

Twin sons, age four, both injured—one dead on arrival the year before she'd kidnapped Kingsley. *If only Acharya had come back with this a week ago.* Tozer's Oldsmobile had been T-boned by a van belonging to another mother whose blood alcohol level was well over legal. The article did not have names, but the photo was enough: a brunette Tozer screaming by the side of the smashed car as if she was trying to call her child back, and he felt the burning in his throat, the ache in his lungs as if it were him beside that car. In the days and months after Julie's death, he'd done his share of screaming—at Julie's room, at her night-light, at the ceiling, at himself, at Linda—and it had done no good. He'd never be able to scream loudly enough for his baby girl to hear him. He'd done all the screaming too late.

"So one boy dead, and one made it," Jackson said. "The other boy Wes saw has to be her surviving son, Sterling. And she abducted Kingsley, then Gregory, and who knows how many others trying to replace the one she lost."

"Exactly." But why take so many children to replace a single boy? She'd already had Kingsley when she took Gregory. Then again, nothing could ever fill the void of a dead son or daughter. Maybe she still felt that aching hollowness of loss and thought that if she took another, the "right" child this time, the pain would finally ease.

Jackson's brow furrowed as she went on: "In a case like this, the kidnapped kid being a replacement, her own child might be able to live a normal life, even go to school, while the kidnapped child, or children, stay home to fill some sick, delusional void. But— She shook her head. "No child by that name—Sterling Tozer—is registered at any school in the state." And Mom would be unlikely to let him out when one wrong word about his "brother" would bring the cops to her doorstep.

Jackson sighed. "We have the why and the who. We just need the where." Same question over and over, the one question they couldn't seem to answer.

Petrosky's phone buzzed—text. He pulled it from his pocket, mouth tight. "Damn."

She raised an eyebrow. "Whatcha got?"

"I had Scott run Ogden's credit cards, hoping that she'd get groceries or incidentals nearer to wherever she's keeping the boys, but it looks like she even shopped around the school—she bought gas here, did her grocery shopping near Anderson Middle or her fake-ass apartment." He drew his fingers to his suddenly throbbing temples. "She's smart. And really careful." By far his least favorite kind of criminal—and the most dangerous.

Jackson had quieted, face pensive.

He dropped his hands. "What?"

"Just so you know..." She finally dragged her gaze to his. "I told Acharya to run with his article—with the pictures of the boys and our perp."

Petrosky's jaw dropped. "What the—"

She put up a hand. "Chief's orders. This woman is going to run, maybe flee the country, and then we'll never find those boys—if they're still with her at all. This is our best chance to stop her. We don't know where to start looking." Jackson grimaced at the desktop. "Acharya said he's working on the article now, already has the age progression photos of Kingsley and photos of Phoebe Tozer—he should have it out to the public within a few hours."

The bullpen felt suddenly smaller, stuffy. A lump settled in Petrosky's throat. *Fucking Acharya.* Their timeline had just been cut down. He forced out: "Her place *has* to be somewhere nearby, close enough that she could commute to her job at the school—the Relenski house would have taken less than twenty minutes."

Jackson nodded, still watching him, maybe waiting for

him to lose it over Acharya, but they didn't have time for that, not now. "To commute, she needs to be two hours from Anderson on the outside, but probably less than one."

And with her being gone all day…was there any way she sent the boys to school? Highly unlikely, but what kid read a physics book on his own? "We should check the homeschoolers. Is there a database or something?" Their perp liked everything to look good on paper—she might be using different names, but she'd have a paper trail if anyone ever asked.

Jackson shook her head. "That one will be tricky. I looked into it for Lance, before I realized how much he needed the structured environment. You don't have to notify the school district of your intent to homeschool, don't have to withdraw your kids from classes, don't have to report grades or curriculum. There's no way to tell how many kids are even homeschooled in this state—they aren't accountable to anyone." She shrugged. "It makes it harder for us, but it's their right."

Yeah, maybe it was a parent's right, and most of them had the best of intentions. But he wasn't worried about parents—he was worried about kidnappers. Child abusers. Not that they were known for being rule followers. He drew his fingers back to his head, pain pulsing through his brain with every heartbeat—*thud, thud, thud*. Hopefully, the age progression photos of the boys and their sneaky nurse would yield some results while they still had living kids to locate. Because if she panicked… Corey's bloated purple tongue swam into his brain. No, there was no telling how far she'd go to escape her sins. And he couldn't risk the lives of those boys on the off chance that she cared too much to hurt them.

Love or self-preservation—that was no choice at all.

## 33

———

"GOT A HIT." Jackson practically ran to his desk, her coffee sloshing from the side of the cup and onto her leather shoes.

"From Acharya's article or the Amber Alert?" Hopefully, the Amber Alert; he hated it when journalists found clues that they couldn't. Those slimy fuckers had more luck than Petrosky ever managed. He shoved aside the giant list of homeschool co-ops he'd spent the last three hours emailing, hoping to god at least Sterling saw other humans once in a while. After all, she'd trusted Corey out in public with her secret. Until she hadn't.

"From Acharya." Jackson slugged back the remaining coffee and tossed the cup into his trash bin. "Someone recognized them from a school over in Rock Creek." She slapped a driver's license photo on the desk, her face bright with excitement...or desperation. His heart throbbed wildly—*please let this be it.* "Mother is Andi Harper, seen here," Jackson said. "Fraternal twin boys, Johnathan and Joe, fourteen years old, according to the school records—pretty close to Joey and James, the names she put on the Relenski lease. And they transferred into the district the year after Tozer left her Relenski Rental behind."

After she caught Wes Bishop hanging over the fence, talking to her children. At least one of whom she'd stolen.

Petrosky stared at the picture. Blond hair, like Tozer, thin nose, heart-shaped face. But this woman was wearing far more makeup, like one of those before and after internet makeover videos. The thin nose could be contouring. Her lips looked different, too, bigger, but they were painted a deep shade of maroon that might or might not have followed the outline of her real lips. One of the things he'd always loved about Linda was that she looked the same when she woke up as when she met him for dinner—a little mascara didn't hide her face. This, what this woman was wearing…it seemed dishonest. But like a beard, it was the ultimate disguise. Most people didn't realize how significant those differences could be. How much eyebrows mattered.

And Shae McCartney, the tattooist who had inked the birthmark on Corey's thigh, he'd seen a woman outside…and said she wore lots of heavy makeup. And a cap.

"And get this," Jackson was saying. "She works at Riverside."

"The hospital?"

"She's in administration, not nursing, but it's not a stretch to think she might be sticking to a similar occupation. If she had experience in nursing, getting a job with the hospital HR department would be easy."

"But…she works in the schools, or did until yesterday. How in the world could she be working two jobs?"

"Lots of people work two jobs, Petrosky. Check your privilege."

"It's not privilege—it's logistics. She can't work two jobs at the same time during the same hours."

Jackson stood. "Grab your jacket. I want to find a judge who'll let us take their DNA before they get out of school. She might leave town without the kids if she knows we're there with a warrant, but I don't want to walk into that school with nothing, or she could just send a proxy to pick them up and be well within her legal rights. At least if we have the DNA already, we'll know for sure in another day or so—and we can follow the kids until then."

He looked up. "They're at school?" But Ogden-Tozer hadn't shown up to work today—she was probably ready to take off the moment the boys got home. If she realized what they were doing, she'd either race to the school to get the kids, and they'd take her away in cuffs, or she'd leave without them as Jackson said—and the boys would finally be safe. "I've got this one, Jackson. I have a judge in my pocket, too."

She chuckled. "Do you now?"

Petrosky sniffed, and her smile fell. "Yeah. I do." The bastard just didn't know it yet.

<hr>

ROGER MCFADDEN, Shannon's fuckweasel of an ex-husband, had somehow ended up on the bench—then again, maybe sharks like him were bound for positions of power. It was a narcissist's dream to be able to sit behind a desk higher than everyone else in the room and pass judgment. Knowing that this bastard held the cards made Petrosky want to punch the sonofabitch, and if that hadn't been enough, Roger's Ken-doll physique would have done it.

Petrosky nodded to the man's secretary, knocked, and pushed the door open without waiting to be admitted.

"Well, look what crawled out of the gutter." Roger sat behind an enormous mahogany desk with a carved front facade, grandiose enough to belong in the Oval Office. Maroon leather on the just-as-pretentious armchairs. Bookshelves full of leather-bound legal texts that Petrosky would have bet a testicle Roger had never read.

*Legal-Eagle-Barbie motherfucker.*

Roger straightened his already straight tie, a hint of a smile playing at the corners of his mouth. No more wrinkles than the last time Petrosky had been in here—asshole probably got Botox. "How's Shannon?"

*She's called me eight times in the last five days, so she's probably on her way here to punch me in the kidney.* "Shannon's fine."

Roger's nostrils flared. "I hear she's out in Georgia."

"Yeah, she is." *You possessive bastard.* But the man had loved her, dickhead or not.

"She seeing anyone? I should give her a call." Roger grinned, smug, and fury rose, hot and wild in Petrosky's throat. His surfer-boy partner, Morrison, Shannon's late husband, hadn't hated anyone, not really—except for Roger. And now Morrison was gone, and Petrosky had to hate Roger enough for them both. Not that it was hard.

He swallowed a snarky comeback and said, "I'm not sure, but I can ask for you if you do me a favor."

Roger crossed his arms. "I don't need you to ask her if she's seeing anyone. I can find out for myself."

"But, you do need me, Roger." Now Petrosky smiled, showing as many teeth as he could. "How's your new wife?"

Roger narrowed his eyes. "Lindsay's fine, thanks for asking."

"Good." Petrosky leaned over the desk. "How's Annice?"

Roger's cocky grin faded. "You following me?"

Petrosky shrugged. He'd seen the law clerk leaving a valentine under Roger's windshield wiper six months back—and he might have stopped in at Roger's favorite hotel a couple weeks ago, asked a few pointed questions. "It's always good to have a little grease for the wheels in your back pocket, Roger."

"Man, I used to think it was the booze, but..." Roger's eyes narrowed. "You haven't changed at all, have you?"

Petrosky met his gaze. "Not yet."

## 34

"You should have seen him, Jackson. It was a thing of beauty." Roger and his pompous ass. They probably could have gotten a warrant anyway—maybe—but Petrosky hadn't wanted to wait. And he'd wanted to see Roger's face.

Jackson raised an eyebrow but kept her gaze on the windshield—her Escalade this time. She'd pretended to stick a finger down her throat when he'd offered to drive again. They'd already stopped at the house listed on Andi Harper's driver's license—no one there. But the Rock Creek principal was certain the picture he'd seen in Acharya's article, emailed to every principal in the area, was the woman they were looking for.

"Don't you sniff at me like that, Jackson. I get very little joy in my life. You will not take this away from me." And the world did feel a little lighter today, didn't it? Maybe it was the lead, but his chest didn't ache near as much as it had in the past week.

The Rock Creek High principal met them in the hallway, a dark-haired man of indeterminate race in a blue suit and a purple tie. He ushered them up the hall to a door marked "Nurse." The skin between Petrosky's shoulder blades prickled uncomfortably.

The hinges squealed.

Inside, two boys sat by the far wall, slouched over a smartphone. The one on the right looked up as Petrosky entered—he lost his breath. Kingsley? The progression wasn't perfect, but the thin nose, the freckles across the bridge, the upturned inner edge of his eyebrow... Kingsley Stinton. *Alive*. And right down the road from where he was taken. His rib cage loosened—he hadn't even registered it being tight without the pain that had been his constant companion in the last few days. Petrosky glanced at the other child's head, still bent over the phone—dark hair, no other discernible characteristics from this angle. Was this Tozer's biological son, Sterling?

The hinges squealed again. The slight woman who entered behind them wore lilac purple scrubs and glasses to match. Her lipsticked mouth twitched up at one corner as her gaze darted from them to the principal, to the boys. The name tag on her breast pocket read, "Adelia King, Nurse."

"Has their mother been contacted?" Jackson asked.

*Mother*. The word felt harsh in his ears.

"On her way," the principal said, his face drawn. "I told her we were having a problem with the boys."

"We didn't do anything wrong."

Petrosky turned. The second child—not Kingsley—had raised his head, the cell forgotten on his knee. Big blue eyes, straight Roman nose, the high cheekbones of a boy band member. "Are you, Joe?"

"No, I'm Johnathan." He jerked a thumb at the boy beside him. "He's Joe." His voice had an edge to it, the odd mix of defiant and perpetually confused that only an irritable teenager could pull off.

"I thought his name was Kingsley."

Joe—Kingsley—cocked his head and smiled. "A case of mistaken identity." He laughed, and his brother joined in.

"At least we got out of class." Boy Band Johnathan—Sterling, had to be—grinned wider with straight white teeth. "If he pretends to be Kingsley, can we stay through physics?"

Physics. The book the boy was reading. This was too

perfect. But Petrosky's back was still tight, and it took him a moment to figure out why. Kingsley…his ear was intact. Not split. Had it been repaired? But he couldn't tell; plastic surgery these days was pretty advanced, and if she was worried about Kingsley being identified, fixing the injury would have been a simple procedure. Fuck—he should have checked into that. A plastic surgeon might have had an address.

"How's your ear?"

Boy Band Sterling reached for his ear, not even the correct one. Kingsley just raised an eyebrow. *Huh.*

Jackson stepped up, the DNA test kits in her hand. "All we need from you is a quick cheek swab."

The nurse frowned. "Do you have authorization to—"

"This is a murder and kidnapping investigation, and we're working against the clock," Petrosky snapped.

"Also, yes." Jackson produced the warrant and passed it to the principal, who barely glanced at it before tucking it into his jacket. Jackson shot Petrosky a brief glare that said, *why do you have to make everything more difficult than it needs to be?*

And it was a valid question. Just not one he felt like answering.

Jackson knelt in front of the kid who looked like Kingsley and unscrewed the Q-tip from the little glass vial. "Open your mouth."

The boy glanced at the principal, then the nurse. Then his brother.

"Kid, the sooner you do this, the sooner we can all go home," Petrosky said. But they weren't going home, at least not to the home they knew. Not if their mother was a kidnapping murderer.

The boy frowned, but he opened his mouth.

*Screeeeee.*

"What the hell is going on here?"

A woman burst into the room. Average height, shiny blond hair, even lighter than her driver's license—platinum. She dropped her oversized purse on the chair near the door.

"You get the hell away from my kids right this second." Glasses obscured the top part of her face—this woman was clever disguise on top of clever disguise. And was her hair longer than it had been earlier this week?

Jackson placed the Q-tip back into the vial and screwed the top closed as she turned, standing in a defensive posture in front of the boys. The kids had put the phone aside and were now sitting, rigid in the chairs. "Andi Harper?"

"What are you doing to my children?" Her walk...it wasn't right. Ogden had been proper, stiff; this woman had a slouchy, shuffling gait, the kind you get from a bad hip or a knee injury.

"We have a warrant for their DNA," Jackson was saying, but her words were less certain now.

"What in the hell for?" The woman tore off the glasses.

Brown eyes, deep wrinkles at the corners. Giant sticky-looking lashes. Bags that even makeup couldn't hide.

They didn't need the DNA test.

This woman wasn't Phoebe Tozer.

**35**

———

THAT WAS IT. Nothing else from any other school or homeschool co-op. They'd called, sent pictures, asked around about kids who might fit the profile, asked about mothers, asked about school nurses and nurse parents. And while there were a few sibling pairs that had seemed promising, closer investigation—and school ID photos—had ruled them out.

They'd spent yet another hour at Anderson Middle, the school Corey had attended, talking to Nurse Ogden's co-workers, the principal, even a few kids who'd spent a little more time than average in the nurse's office, but none reported any wrongdoing on the part of Janna Ogden, AKA Phoebe Tozer. None of the staff had ever hung out with her after work, or knew where she lived—none of them believed she had children. And the kids said she was kind to them but not overbearing; she let them ride out stomach aches, but didn't ask questions about their home lives, she didn't give them treats or try to make them feel special.

Because she wasn't looking for anyone else to take—perhaps she had completed her little kidnapped family by the time she sent Corey Gagnon to live with the Boyles.

So, where were they? Children, living children, were

harder to hide than dead ones. They needed groceries. Medical care. Education. *Fuck.*

Petrosky usually loved silence, but the ride back to the precinct was steeped in an awful kind of disappointed quiet.

What did they have? Age-progressed photos? The pictures weren't enough—they didn't have any pics of Sterling, and while Kingsley's and Tozer's photos were on cellphones nationwide as an Amber Alert, no one had called in that seemed credible.

Jackson's brows were furrowed, the afternoon light catching the sharp planes of her cheekbones through the windshield.

Those kids were alone. Alone, maybe hurt. And now there was an Amber Alert out for the boys—for their killer. Had Tozer seen it?

That skull in the backyard. Corey's bruised and cracked ribs. Kingsley's ripped ear.

*His ripped ear.* "Jackson, if you saw a child with an injury like Kingsley's...would you worry about them?"

She pursed her lips, finger tapping on the steering wheel —she was beating up that wheel far more than usual. Was she just anxious about the case? "If it was healed, maybe not. But if I was already suspicious of the family..." The tapping stopped. "You're thinking someone might have called it in recently? That'll be a bitch to track."

It would. But what choice did they have? They'd need to look at all cases—who knew what social securities or identities she was using now. And they'd find nothing unless she'd allowed someone else to see the boys after her mistake with Wes Bishop. "It's a long shot," he admitted. But she had let the children outside before Wes. Would she switch tactics, lock them up, disappoint her own children, children she surely needed to love her? After all, this kidnapping shit was about her emotional issues—not about the kids. She might be more susceptible to anger and guilt from them.

"We should call Linda," Jackson said, pulling into the station. "She'll have more access to those files." She was right

—half of those cases weren't in the computer, he knew that from experience. Social workers were notoriously over-worked, and not all offices had electronic record keeping, just two of the reasons kids sometimes fell through the cracks. But he didn't want to call his wife. *Ex-wife*.

A memory came unbidden: Julie, five or six years old, her face pressed against the window, him coming up the walk from work. Longing to see him…or for someone to let her out. How his heart had hurt then.

Was he willing to let two more children suffer because he didn't want to take the quickest means to an end? Didn't want to admit he needed Linda? Didn't want to have to apologize for running from her house last night?

Petrosky slipped his cell from his pocket with shaking hands, and listened to it ring, swallowing his pride. It went down like razor blades. "Linda." His voice cracked. He coughed to clear his throat. "I need your help."

---

LINDA FOUND twelve possibles that specifically mentioned ears or the more broad "facial lacerations," but they ruled out ten of them based on forwarding addresses and driver's licenses. Of the last two, one listed four sisters in attendance. No one had ever mentioned seeing girls. And the other…

He snagged the top three pages that Linda had faxed over. The call had come in about eight months ago; the neighbor claimed she'd seen the boy when the family moved in and was concerned about an injury on his face. Because it was healed, she'd let it go. But when the children hadn't come out of the house for several months, she'd finally picked up the phone. The social worker had found nothing to suggest neglect or danger—the interviews showed "polite, seemingly well-rounded children, no evidence of trauma, past or present." The mother, Sydney McCain, had produced evidence of proper homeschooling, and the worker had noted that the children seemed to be above their grade levels. There was one additional bit of information that seemed odd, but Petrosky was going to get to the bottom of that, too.

Linda had come through for him, as always. He pushed the guilt way down into his guts.

He'd failed her, and he'd failed his daughter. And himself.

Petrosky shoved the seat back so fast it tottered, but he grabbed it before it fell, and wheeled it over to Jackson's desk. She looked up at him in surprise.

"Got a hit...maybe. The xeroxed driver's license from the social work file is blurry, but the general characteristics seem right. I can't find her actual license in the database, though, not like the others—no record at all under Sydney McCain. No birth certificate that matches the date of birth on the license, but no death certificate either that I can find." The words had come out like vomit, a pressured stream that hadn't stopped until the final word had fallen from his lips. Jackson had gone still, watching him with wide eyes. Was he even right? They'd already been wrong once today, and this woman...

Sydney wasn't even a nurse. According to her rental paperwork, she was a freelancer, whatever that meant. They were looking for a woman so careful she'd been able to hide right in front of their eyes for the last nine years, working at the very schools from which she'd groomed and kidnapped and murdered her victims. Did they really think she'd be careless enough to trigger a CPS call?

He set his cell on Jackson's desk and hit the speakerphone button.

"Hello?" The voice was high and softly optimistic, what you'd expect of an elderly woman picking up a call that might be a grandchild.

"Mrs. Abagnale? This is Detective Petrosky with the Ash Park Police Department. I have a few questions for you about your neighbor, Sydney. And her boys."

Silence. Then: "They're wonderful people."

*Wonderful people?* He and Jackson exchanged a glance.

"Aren't you the one who called Child Protective Services on her?"

"Oh, that." The woman snorted. "It was just a mistake. I didn't know there was such a thing as homeschool. Back in my day, you sent them to school with a proper teacher. But Sydney, she's a smart one. Figured she could do it better herself, even if she does have to work during the day."

"Sounds like you've made quite the turnaround, Mrs. Abagnale."

"You have to understand, I didn't know them back then—didn't know her. But after the investigation was over, she came and introduced herself, brought some cookies. Introduced me to the boys."

*Cookies.* Sugar was the way to anyone's heart.

"One of them had an injury, too, right?" Petrosky said slowly. "I can understand why you might've called." He was trying not to lead her, to make sure she could identify Kingsley from his ear, but it was clumsy, and he felt it.

"Oh, well, that's not why I called—by the time we met, it was healed up nicely." *A healed injury—Kingsley, had to be.* "Dog bite right to the face, can you believe it? Just awful. He's lucky he made it."

Wait, the face? Not the ear? "Where was the injury, exactly?"

"Oh, up around the cheekbone. Most of the side of his face, really."

*Shit.* "What about his ear?"

"Yes, probably his ear, too." She paused, and when she spoke again, her voice was suspicious. "Don't you already know this, being the police and all?"

Kingsley didn't have facial injuries, just his ear. Maybe Sterling? While they knew Sterling had been injured in that car wreck, the hospital records weren't back yet. And the ear was specific—that would have been confirmation. His heartbeat throbbed in his neck, vein pulsing like a writhing anaconda. Petrosky cleared his throat, trying to keep the disappointment out of his voice. "Another thing in the file seemed a little strange to me—did you accuse this woman of killing your cat?"

Jackson reared back and jerked her face to him, her eyes wide.

"No, of course not," Abagnale snapped.

"But you told the worker who came out that someone had killed your cat, did you not?" This was the other anomaly in the file, aside from everyone being stone-cold innocent. "Sounds like a veiled accusation."

"I did say that, but I wasn't trying to say it was *them*. I just wanted someone to do something—the neighbor on my other side found her cat cut to ribbons just the week before, but the police did nothing. And those boys deserve to be safe. No one wants a maniac running around."

*Ain't that the truth.* He'd thought perhaps Tozer was trying to stifle violent impulses by harming other innocents, but now he wasn't even sure this Sydney was their kidnapper. Something wasn't right; this didn't feel ri—

"When was the last time you saw Sydney or her boys?" Jackson cut in.

"We were supposed to have dinner tonight, but she had to cancel. Said she had to go away for a few days."

Now *that* was definitely suspicious. Jackson leaned forward over the desk, her eyes locked on the cell like it held the key to eternal life, and maybe it would help two boys live just a little longer.

"Did she tell you why she had to leave?"

"Her mother died." But her voice was less certain now. "She's driving out to Nebraska for the funeral."

But Sydney had no license. Sydney had no American social security number, let alone a mother who lived in the states. This had to be her. "I see. And what time did she call, Mrs. Abagnale?" If she'd called this woman from her cell phone, maybe Scott could triangulate her position from the towers. Morrison had done that once, hadn't he?

"Oh…I'd say about an hour ago. Brought me a lovely bottle of merlot, though, as an apology. My favorite."

The world stopped spinning.

Jackson found her voice first. "Are you saying she was home an hour ago?"

"I believe she's home now," the woman said slowly. "I can go talk to her, ask—"

"No!" Petrosky and Jackson said together, so loudly that Decantor looked over from his desk across the bullpen. "Stay where you are," Petrosky said. "She might be very dangerous, do you understand?" The silence stretched. "Ma'am?"

"Are you sure about this, young man?"

*No.* "Just stay where you are, Mrs. Abagnale. Please? I'd hate to see you get hurt."

"Aw, hell. I knew it." Abagnale sighed. "I just knew it."

## 36

---

JACKSON KEPT the siren off and her foot on the gas.

Petrosky clutched the door handle so hard his knuckles ached. This Sydney McCain, she'd befriended the person who turned her in. It made no sense for anyone to do that—to even speak to the woman who'd called CPS—unless they were trying to hide something more sinister than child abuse by playing the perfect mother. "If you were wrongly accused of child neglect, would your first reaction be to make dinner plans with the person who called CPS on you? Or would you give her dirty looks and then slice up her cat?"

Jackson side-eyed him. "Are those the only options?"

"They are for me."

"You'd take that cat home, and you know it." Jackson hooked a left into the neighborhood, squinting through the windshield. "I can't believe she's still here."

*If it's even her.* And the tension in Jackson's voice betrayed her concern that they might be wrong—again. But they had reasonable suspicion to enter the house based on their conversation with Abagnale. And with the Amber Alert and the likelihood that their suspect would panic once she saw it, they were on a truncated time table. Then there was Abagnale. Hopefully, the woman would mind her own business for once and stay at home—hopefully, she wouldn't warn their suspect.

"She's obviously a whack-job, maybe a narcissist," he said. "Figures if she shows everyone what a good person she is, what a good mother, a good nurse, they'll never suspect her."

Jackson nodded, fingers too tight on the wheel to do that nervous tapping thing. "And they never did suspect. Even the neighbor who called CPS ended up believing she'd been mistaken. I bet she gets some sick satisfaction from being able to trick the people around her. Gets off on watching the Boyles, watching the police scramble. Watching Mancebo look for her year after year, knowing she's sitting right in front of him."

Tozer had snowed everyone, manipulated the people around her the same way she'd groomed those kids.

*And us. She snowed us too.* Petrosky could almost see her prim little smile, her cold, calm eyes—calm like Ponce. "Are we right about this?"

"Yes. I mean…I think so."

Her eyes were still tight, uncertainty tugging the corners of her lips down just a little, but her jaw was set. They were almost sure, but the only way to be positive was to see her. They'd go into that house and get the boys out before those kids got hurt. And if they were wrong… They'd worry about that later.

Petrosky watched the street as Jackson turned onto the block one down from their final destination, more like an alley—weeds and crumbled asphalt and enough broken bottles to dissuade children from playing here if they wanted their bike tires to stay intact. Probably great for a couple of hidden children.

Would the boys be in there when they arrived? Maybe this house would be as dusty and empty as her apartment.

*She's here; she has to be here.*

Jackson wheeled the SUV to the curb near the corner and nodded to the back of the house—a brick bungalow halfway up the block, barely visible from here, but Petrosky would have been able to pick it out without the address. The place sported a high wooden privacy fence while the rest of the houses along the alley had cheap chain-link.

"I'll sneak in through the back," Petrosky muttered, easing out of the car. No back gate, but the wooden fence looked to be about six feet high, and the cigarettes hadn't eaten all his stamina—yet. "Backup on the way?"

"Decantor's already out in front with Sloan—they'll knock in a few. I'll go around the back fence opposite you."

He squinted up the road, trying to see past the house. Decantor's Charger sat parked up the way in front of an aluminum-sided one-story, the engine running.

The neighbor's grass brushed against his shoes; the chain-link fence clanked dully on its posts as he opened the gate and hurried through. No guard dogs next door, thank god, and the neighbors had a swing set, the monkey bars close enough to the side for him to reach the wooden fence—he just wanted to peek. When you were dealing with a killer, it was always good to look before you went barreling in. Or so he'd heard.

Petrosky climbed, his heart hammering, breath too hot in his lungs. His knees ached from his leap into the Relenskis' mini-graveyard the other day. The arches of his feet smarted, but he was already two rungs from the top—then he was there.

He balanced precariously on the top rung and peered over the fence.

A boy sat twenty feet from him at the base of a birch tree, hunched over the book in his lap. Dark hair. Lanky. Might be Kingsley, might be Sterling, but Petrosky couldn't see his ear...or his face. Would he alert their suspect once he saw Petrosky? Better to have the element of surprise.

*One.* He leaned against the top of the fencing, the wood abrading his belly, a cold, thin breeze slipping down his spine. *Two.* He clenched the wood harder, palms on fire. The boy did not look up. *Three.* With a grunt, he hoisted himself over, thigh muscles singing, the already skinned flesh on his belly scraping against the fence. He landed hard on ankles that felt extra angry that they'd been forced to catch his fat ass, but he righted himself quickly and kept moving, hurrying toward the boy.

The kid turned.

Petrosky's heart stopped throbbing. His lungs ceased to work. Even the breeze against his face paused as if someone had flipped a switch.

Wes had been wrong—he hadn't seen some random kid in the backyard with Kingsley. But Petrosky had been wrong, too. This child wasn't Tozer's—no way—and they weren't dealing with a case like Ponce, where they were going to find a dozen bodies stashed under the porch.

The child looking back at him was Gregory Boyle.

## 37

———

THE BOY SCRAMBLED to his feet, gaze jerking past Petrosky as Jackson hit the ground inside the fence line on the opposite side of the yard.

"Who are you?" But the words were delivered with a slight lisp—muddled. *Shit.* The kid's face. "Go away!"

Petrosky put a finger to his lips, but his hand shook—the boy's mouth was split down the side, tiny bumps like evenly spaced whiteheads visible along his upper and lower lip, though the wound was long healed—the needle marks from rough stitches. She'd sewn him up herself, probably while he struggled. Another slash split his cheek, veered back to a spot behind his lower jaw, then zagged down over his neck. *What'd she do to you, kid?* No wonder Wes hadn't recognized their photo, why he'd said: *I'd definitely know him if I saw him.* Why hadn't Wes mentioned the kid was sliced to hell?

"It's okay, we're the police," Jackson said, approaching quickly and far more nimbly than Petrosky felt—his limbs were weighted, the muscles too weak to support his bulk.

The boy's eyes widened. "No! Mom!" He ran for the sliding glass door just as Petrosky reached out for Gregory's shoulder. Jackson was already at the kid's side. "Hey, kid, it's okay," she said, "We're here to—"

Gregory threw an elbow that hit Jackson square in the

258

nose; Petrosky heard bone and gristle crunch from where he stood, saw the explosion of blood in the center of her face.

She blinked water from her eyes and snatched at the boy's shirtsleeve.

Petrosky put his palms up, showing Gregory his hands. "It's okay; we're cops. We're here to help."

Gregory shook himself free of Jackson's grasp and staggered back toward the door. Three steps from the glass. *Come on, kid, don't make me wrestle you.*

"No!" Gregory screamed, eyes wide with terror. "No police, go away, you get out of here!"

Brainwashed as shit. They'd expected it, but damn. What had she told him to make him so terrified?

Gregory stepped back again, one step to the door. Petrosky lunged. The kid fell toward the glass—*oh god, he's going to fall through it, we'll have to tell Greg's parents that we found him and he bled to death on the living room floor*—but Jackson got her hands around the kid's upper arm, Petrosky grabbed the other, and they both pulled at the same time. Gregory reeled forward, gasping, onto his belly, and Jackson leapt onto his back, red pouring from her nose, her chin bearded with blood.

"Go!" she snapped at Petrosky. "Go!"

He threw open the sliding door, drawing his weapon—quiet. His sneakers made a subtle *eek, eek* against the linoleum in the family room. Couches, bookcases, a coffee table, everything he'd expect, but something was wrong… No television. That was strange, wasn't it? Then again, if you wanted to make sure your wards didn't get brave or start to think the police were the good guys, you probably needed to make sure they had as little contact with the outside world as possible.

He hurried into the kitchen, listening, back against the wall. White paint, the surfaces as clean and tidy as the apartment, but here there were signs of life—the remnants of a peanut butter sandwich next to the sink. A cup on the dining table. A green hoodie thrown over the back of a chair.

But no people. The downstairs was deserted.

He took the steps two at a time, his footfalls muted by the thick beige carpet. When he reached the top, he hooked a right, pressing his back against the hallway wall, listening to the silence. Two doors on this side. The first was a bathroom; three toothbrushes in a cup, a flowered shower curtain pulled back, revealing a damp washcloth over the faucet, and two bottles of shampoo. No people.

The second door was closed. He tried the handle. Locked.

His Swiss Army knife was heavier than usual in his shaking hand, but it made quick work of the lock, which gave with a tiny *clunk*. Petrosky toed it open slowly. Less than thirty seconds from entering—would another thirty see him leading the other child out?

Two twin beds inside, a closed suitcase on the left one, a pile of books stacked on top of it. On the right bed, sat another suitcase—open and empty. And between the beds stood a dark-haired boy.

The kid's back was to the door, his eyes on the far window, a pair of rolled socks in his hands. He tossed the socks into the air and caught them, tossed them again. Petrosky crept forward, gun raised—was anyone else in here?

The boy paused as if only now realizing he was being watched and turned slowly. Kingsley, definitely Kingsley, the slit in his ear dark like an angry mouth beneath the thin film of hair that hadn't been captured in his ponytail. The boy frowned and said, "Well, fuck." A bizarre reaction, almost as strange as Gregory Boyle's had been, but not as bizarre as the transformation of his face. As Petrosky watched, the boy's eyes filled. His lip trembled. "Please don't make me go. I told her I'm not moving again."

Petrosky listened to the hallway for a moment, then the boy's harsh sniveling, gaze drifting to the window, then the open bifold closet doors, weapon ready to take Tozer out if she leapt into his line of sight. But he heard no one else. Saw no one else. "Where's your mother, son?" *Mother.* The word was bitter. Hopefully, she wasn't here at all—hopefully, he could lead the kid out without incident.

"I'm not sure where she is, but I'm scared, I'm so scared."

As he should be. Petrosky could practically feel the skull from the Relenskis' backyard, cold and heavy in his hands. *Grab him now, run him to the car, save him.* They'd already lost too many children—he would not lose another. The hairs on the back of Petrosky's neck prickled, but he lowered his weapon and reached out a hand. "That's okay; we'll get you out of here, and—"

"No!" Kingsley stepped back, his eyes wide. "I mean, I don't want to leave, she keeps us here, and the outside seems so scary."

The words made sense—what kid wouldn't be terrified of sudden freedom after being locked in a house for nine years —but the intonation was wrong. Flat. And the boy wasn't looking at Petrosky anymore. Kingsley was looking past him.

Something creaked at his back.

"Get away from my son."

Petrosky turned. Tozer, weapon in hand. His memory might not be perfect, but there was no mistaking that brow line, her thin nose, the shape of her jaw. But now she had an earring in her right nostril, and her hair had gone a brilliant shade of orange-red, like a bloody sunset, and this felt somehow like a premonition—laced with finality.

She cocked her gun and aimed at Petrosky's head.

38

———

"You don't want to do this," Petrosky said, backing into the room, against the side wall where he could see both the boy and the woman who'd deemed herself his mother. He kept his gun trained on the woman in the doorway. Why hadn't he called down when he found Kingsley? He should have called Decantor. Sloan. Jackson. *Someone*. It had been only minutes since he'd walked inside the home—two, tops. Were the others even in the house yet?

"How would you know what I want?" she said. But the gun trembled, and her breath was coming way too fast—panting.

"I know you don't want your son to watch you bleed out on his bedroom floor."

She glanced at Kingsley, then back at Petrosky, nostrils flaring, the one with the earring in it swollen—new. Another disguise, ready to start over. "It was never supposed to be like this."

"I'm sure it wasn't. Why don't you tell me what it was supposed to be like, and we can assess it together?"

Her eye twitched. "I'm a good mother to these boys."

"I'm sure you are."

"They're better off here than where they came from."

In Kingsley's case, that was possibly true, but it didn't give her the right to steal him.

Her hand steadied, her eyes clearing—gaze cool and earnest. "They needed me. They still need me." One corner of her mouth turned up, more a spasm than a smile. "Just let me take care of them. I promise, you'll never see me again."

Manipulative—and she really believed it. Even believed it would work on Petrosky. "I bet you say that to all the fellows."

"Ask him." She cocked her head toward Kingsley. "Ask him if I'm a good mother."

"I can ask all I want, but you're not their mother." From below—a *thunk, thunk, thunk.* The door knocker?

Tozer appeared not to hear it. "I *am* their mother!" Her cheeks went a furious maroon. "I'm the one who fed them, clothed them, taught them. I am the one who stayed up all night stroking their hair when they got sick." The knock came again. Her earnest eyes had gone wild. Panicked. Her hand trembled once more, finger twitching against the trigger. *She's going to shoot me by mistake.*

From the corner of his eye, Petrosky saw Kingsley edging toward the mattress. "Don't move, kid." The words felt hot on his tongue. Petrosky's lungs ached.

Kingsley climbed onto the mattress on his knees. Mere feet from Tozer, from the gun. "I'm just—"

"Quiet. And don't fucking move."

Kingsley ignored him, still shifting nearer over the comforter, nearer to Tozer. Was he going to try to protect her? But of course he would—he was her son now. "Please, just let us go, Mister Officer, don't hurt—"

"Shut the fuck up, kid, Jesus Christ." In the silence that followed, he heard a crash—the front door.

The woman kept her gaze on Petrosky, a hard expression fixed on her face. But Kingsley's gaze darted to the door. His eyes glittered, shoulders straightening.

*Don't be stupid, kid.*

Kingsley lunged at his mother. Her eyes widened as she

fell sideways into the wall, the weapon faltering, but neither went down.

*Bang!*

A bullet whizzed by Petrosky's ear—electric, zinging, burning the hair at his temple—and buried itself in the wall in a hail of plaster.

*Bang!* The noise ricocheted around Petrosky's brain. He hit the ground behind the bed, his breath leaving him in a whoosh that he barely felt over the frantic vibration of his heart. His temple was on fire. The side of his head was wet with blood. *Where the hell is Jackson?*

He rose to his hands and knees and peered under the beds, checking Tozer's position, trying to see Kingsley. The boy was still wrestling with his mother, their shoes a blur of activity. *Why is he attacking her?* He'd just said he was afraid of the outside. But maybe he hated her; maybe he felt like a captive and was ready to shoot her in the face for taking him.

Petrosky understood. But death was too easy for a kidnapper, for a woman who'd murdered Corey, who'd killed the anonymous child buried in that backyard.

Petrosky crawled closer to the foot of the bed, ears ringing, and peered around the footboard. They were still near the door, grunting, both of their hands on the weapon, and… his shoes. Kingsley was wearing a pair of skater shoes almost identical to the ones Scott had shown him. *What the--*

*Bang!*

Tozer made a thin, high-pitched noise, and hit her knees. Petrosky leapt to standing, gun aimed. "Drop the weapon!"

The gun stayed clenched in Kingsley's fist—aimed at Petrosky. Blood spattered the boy's arm.

"Put the gun down, kid."

"I'm a hero, right?" His cheek was speckled with blood, too, like crimson freckles. A thin gurgling sound came from the floor, but Petrosky could not look. He watched Kingsley, his face burning. The boy did not lower the gun.

Thudding on the stairs—backup. *Oh, thank god.*

"She took us; she hurt us. She was awful." Kingsley's eyes

were watery, but there was something in the set of the kid's mouth that made the hairs on the back of Petrosky's neck vibrate more furiously. *He's faking.* Petrosky would have bet his left arm on it. *And the shoes, he's wearing the shoes...*

"I know you've been through a lot. Just put the gun down so I can help you." The gurgling continued, the sick, desperate squelching noise one makes when they're losing the battle to draw breath. The noise stopped. Petrosky dropped his gaze—one second, but that was all he needed. Her eyes were wide to the ceiling, a halo of blood soaking the carpet around her head, hands limp near her shoulders. Kingsley had shot Tozer in the throat.

"You should leave," Kingsley said quietly. "I want to stay here, alone. I don't want to go back."

No one would want to go back to the Stintons', and for Kingsley to remember whatever he'd witnessed upwards of nine years ago, it must have been horrific. But...

Petrosky blinked, trying to take in the room in his periphery—the door, the woman on the carpet, the blood splattered along the baseboard, along the wall. Her rib cage wasn't moving. And then Roman's face blinked in his head, Kingsley's brother, the jagged scar along his jaw. It wasn't the same as Gregory's injury, but it was a hell of a coincidence. What if...

Petrosky met the boy's eyes—cold, dead—as Roman's words echoed in his brain: *I just want to know where he is.* Roman's shaking voice. He hadn't been putting up the signs because he'd wanted his brother home—he'd wanted to have warning if the kid was nearby.

"I'll make sure you don't have to go back home, Kingsley," Petrosky said slowly. "You won't have to go back to your father's. Just put the gun—"

"Is Roman there?"

"If you want to see your brother, I'll arrange it. But you have to put the weapon on the floor." Petrosky's own gun was slick against his palms, burning as if the metal was slowly going molten.

"I don't need a brother," he spat.

"Is that what happened to Gregory?" *Wrong question*—he knew it the moment it left his lips. Tozer had wanted a son, and she'd gotten a monster.

Kingsley's face hardened. "She shouldn't have brought him here!" His voice had risen with each word, high-pitched and insistent, but the gun stayed trained on Petrosky's face. "I was enough!"

Footsteps. In the hall, now—close. It had been less than five minutes since he'd entered the house, probably less than one since Kingsley had first pulled the trigger, but it felt like hours.

The boy glanced at the woman at his feet. Blood had pooled around her head, painting the carpet, matting her hair. Kingsley smiled, looked up at Petrosky, and caught himself—his smile fell. His lip trembled once more, but his gun hand remained steady, and his chest rose and fell so slowly... He was calm, calmer even than a cop after his first kill. He didn't step back, didn't seem to mind the blood soaking into his navy skater shoes. Petrosky had seen some bizarre grief reactions, but this lip thing, the smiling, that wasn't grief or even shock. Kingsley had been a psycho like his father when he was taken, and he was a cold-blooded psycho now.

"Please, Officer, I'm just a victim here. She kept us here, didn't let us leave—"

"How'd you get out last week?" *To kill Corey?*

His tears dried in an instant. The barrel of the gun was a black hole ready to suck Petrosky's life away, but it wasn't nearly as empty as Kingsley's gaze.

Footsteps again.

Jackson's face appeared outside the door, just past the doorframe. Her back against the wall between the room and the hallway—one shot through that plaster, and she was dead.

Petrosky drew his eyes back to Kingsley, trying not to alert him to Jackson's presence, but it was too late. The kid smiled. Kingsley jerked the weapon up, away from Petrosky, aiming at the wall, aiming right at Jackson's fucking head—

*Bang!*

*Bang!*

*Bang!*

Kingsley dropped to his knees, mouth gaping in shock. Red on his lips.

Blood bloomed on his shirt.

In the hallway, Jackson hit her knees, crawled toward the doorway, gun drawn, but she froze when she saw the bloody boy on the floor. "What did you do, Petrosky?" She lunged for Kingsley, yelling, but he could barely hear Jackson's voice over the throbbing of his heart. "What the fuck did you do?"

## 39

---

*Bang! Bang! Bang!*

Someone was shooting at him. Petrosky covered his head and rolled, landing hard on one side, and his face…wet. Why was his face wet?

Duke whined.

Petrosky opened his bleary eyes—the dog's giant tongue slimed his cheek again, missing the bandage where they'd sewn his grazed skin back together. Two people dead, one of them a child, and he'd gotten what amounted to little more than a piercing gone awry.

He blinked at…the floor. Was he in his living room?

Yes. As he had been for the last week.

The death of Kingsley Stinton had rocked the Ash Park community. Dead kids got headlines, and the fact that he was a missing child, that Kingsley Stinton, a kid so much like Little Greggie Boyle, had been gunned down, made for great media. No one cared that the kid'd had a gun. That the kid was a murderer. At least Acharya had actually taken Petrosky's side, but not the family. Kingsley's father, crazy fuck that he was, had even gotten in on the action. He'd threatened to sue.

*Do it, asshole. Take it all.*

Petrosky was on leave until they sorted it out. He didn't deserve to wear a badge. Or have a gun.

Or have a life.

*Bang, bang, bang, bang, bang!*

Not gunshots. The door.

He shoved himself to his knees, then his feet, muscles aching, the room spinning like he was in the middle of a tornado. A half-empty box of donuts, the only food he'd had in three days, lay on the kitchen counter, the waxed paper dark with oil. The remaining pastries were probably hard enough to use as projectiles. And…

The Jack. He hadn't cracked the bottle, but it was there on the kitchen counter, waiting. Tonight was going to be the night; he could feel it.

The door creaked open, and he leaned against the jamb.

Linda—eyes narrowed. Worried. "Can I come in?"

"It's not a good time."

Her face twitched, hurt—*what did she expect?*—but she nodded. "Okay. I've been calling you all week."

*I didn't want to talk to you.* "Phone's dead." That part, at least, was true—he'd let it die after listening to Shannon's voicemail the day before. She'd sounded worried, too, and maybe a little mad at him for ignoring her calls, but all she'd said was, "Evie misses you. Call us, okay?" The mere mention of Evie's name drove a knife through his heart. And he didn't need their pity. He wasn't good for either of them—he had to let them go.

"Jackson said she talked to you," Linda said now.

*Because she broke into my house and poured out all my booze.* But he'd gotten more an hour later. Another bottle to watch.

There was always more.

"I don't recall that." He gripped the door tighter, pressing it against his shoulder so she couldn't see past him—he hadn't even bothered hiding the liquor. Duke snorted from the tile behind his heel. "I'm sure Jackson has better things to do than talk to me. Only idiots suffer fools."

Linda half-smiled, though it looked strained. "Sweet talker."

They stared at one another until she said, "I talked to the...women next door. Becky said you refused lasagna. That isn't the Ed I know."

*I guess you don't know me, then.* "Billie."

"What?"

"That's her name. Not Becky. Billie."

The silence stretched. Somewhere in the yard, a bird shrieked, then again, softer as if it had taken flight, and he was suddenly jealous of that ability, to just scream and fly away—what did a bird have to scream about anyway, those lucky assholes? He could shriek all day, and it wouldn't be enough.

"The Boyles are in the news again," Linda said, bringing him back. "Looks like they're really doing well—Gregory is doing well, readjusting. Roman, too. I visited him in his new foster home today." Roman had admitted his father had sliced Kingsley's ear as punishment for not listening to him— "If he can't listen, why have ears at all?" The wounds Kingsley inflicted on others seemed to be part payback for an abusive childhood, and part desire to have his parental figure all to himself.

"You saved those kids, Ed."

"You helped Roman, not me."

"You're the one who called me, the one who—"

"I didn't save anyone. Gregory was doing okay where he was." And so was Kingsley, until he'd gone in there and shot him. He regretted it, but he still wasn't sure how much he should, not after what Gregory had told them—what Gregory had seen, and what he'd heard from Tozer as part of a cautionary tale.

Kingsley had been the first child she'd taken, a new twin for her biological child, Sterling. But Kingsley hadn't liked being one of two any more than he had at home. The difficulties she'd attributed to his abusive beginnings had cost Sterling his life. She'd found them in the bathtub when they were both seven, her biological son blue beneath the water, Kingsley's hands still around his throat. She had buried her son in the backyard.

By then, it was too late to get rid of Kingsley—she couldn't bring him back. And despite it all, she loved him. More than that, perhaps, he knew her secrets.

It sounded as if she ranted about other mothers—like the drunk driver who'd hit their car—more than most. She seemed to believe that bad parents didn't deserve to have children, and, more critically, that God had given her two— she deserved to have two. She'd picked up Gregory after school on a street one block over from his usual route, rather unceremoniously. But Kingsley had attacked him almost immediately. Tozer had stitched Gregory up and dumped the backpack in the trash, probably figuring they'd assume he was dead, then started locking Kingsley in his room when she went out. And Gregory began sleeping in her room. If she'd allowed Kingsley out, Petrosky had no doubt Gregory would have ended up dead as well.

Then there was Corey Gagnon. She'd met him at the hospital in Canada as they'd thought, during one of her few overnight shifts. When his mother died, she'd brought him home, intending to care for him—maybe she thought Gregory and Corey would be her two boys, and Kingsley just a bad mistake. But one day, Corey vanished. Tozer had panicked until Kingsley told her where Corey was, the boy in a jealous rage, according to Gregory. She hadn't been the woman at the tattoo parlor, after all. Had Corey come up with the idea himself, or had Kingsley? That much remained unclear, along with how Kingsley had finally managed to sneak out the night of Corey's murder—he'd probably waited years for that opportunity.

One thing was sure: Phoebe Tozer had known how off Kingsley was—how sick. Gregory said she often prayed before bed, three words over and over:

*God save me.*

Because the kid was bad. How many lives had Petrosky saved by getting rid of Kingsley? Was he a child-murdering hero? Perhaps he, like Kingsley, had no frame for right and wrong. Perhaps he'd shoot another child if given half a chance.

He was a murderer.

A child killer.

Linda was still staring at him. He'd almost forgotten she was there. "Ed, you did all you could. This isn't your fault."

He cleared his throat. *Bullshit*. That was the main reason he was here, hiding from the world. He was tired of hearing everyone say it wasn't his fault. *It is.* Another child dead, the same age Julie had been when she died. Another child he'd failed, another child he'd killed. "I'm tired. I think I'll go back to bed."

"It's two o'clock."

"Hence *back* to bed."

She appraised him. "When are you meeting with Dr. McCallum?"

*I'm not.* "I'll find out tomorrow."

"Why don't I stay here until then? I can even drive you up there. I've been meaning to pop in and say hello to him anyway." But she made no move to touch the door—perhaps she could feel the agitation radiating off him. Maybe she knew he was dangerous. Or maybe she knew better than to try, to really try—maybe she didn't want to help him at all.

"I'm fine. I have things to do. Got a lot to catch up on around the house."

"Like what?"

*Staring at the bottle of Jack by the kitchen sink.* "Just odds and ends."

"I don't believe you."

"I don't fucking care." He stared her down.

She stared right back, eyes fiery. "You can't keep doing this to yourself, Ed. Stop punishing yourself for things that aren't your fault."

"It was my fault." The words were hot and thick in his throat—he nearly choked on them.

"Julie wasn't your fault either."

*She was.* But he couldn't force the words from his lips. He couldn't say anything at all—like he had a tennis ball stuck in his gullet. He swallowed hard and croaked, "I have to go."

He closed the door and leaned his head against the wood. Duke whined.

He turned the deadbolt.

**Petrosky's not done yet!** *Composed* **is the next novel in the Ash Park series.** *As gruesome killings terrorize the citizens of Ash Park, detective Edward Petrosky struggles to overcome his own demons. But when the chief of police—Petrosky's only ally—is abducted, can Petrosky pull himself together to catch the killer and save his best friend?*

## *COMPOSED*
## PROLOGUE

The walls are thick with black, the kind of dark that blocks out the world—as it should. Everything feels so loud when it's bright. Creation takes quiet, he knows that now. It takes darkness. And once you pare your craft down to its most fundamental and achingly perfect form, you can release it out into the universe.

But not until it's ready. Finished products are a labor of love, of sweat—of blood.

Finally. Years of musing, of failed attempts, but it's all led here. And he's ready for it, though his hands shake, though his belly feels queasy as if he might vomit. He has already. Twice.

*No, I'm ready.* And he has an audience waiting.

He looks back down at the sleek magazine in his hand. The pages flip with a plasticky sound, each model practically screaming with the type of confidence acquired through a surgeon's blade. They are but poorly rendered sketches, more Barbie-esque than beautiful—matte and smooth. But those women can't speak.

They're not real—they probably don't exist at all.

He squints at the page in front of him, at her long legs, blond hair, creamy skin the color of a frog's belly. He frowns and reaches for the floor beside him. For the blade.

He starts with her upper eyelid.

The first incision goes smoothly, the hiss of steel against flesh—against paper, fair, but it doesn't sound that different from flesh, not really. Or maybe it's that it doesn't feel so different in the wrist. It's hard to tell sometimes what he really means until he writes it down. He's never been great at interacting in the moment, the pressured way his words rush out, half of them not even close to what he wants to say, but just give him a pen.

Or a scalpel.

He traces the gentle slope down to the tear duct and watches as it ruptures, the white of the eye, the glorious blue iris freed from its prison. The room is hot, though when the temperature rose, he isn't sure. Maybe there's something wrong with him. Is he sick? He might be sick.

He moves the blade to the lower lid. And begins again.

Sweat drips from his nose and onto the page—*plip*. He barely notices. In this moment, he's a surgeon; he's a harbinger of perfection. He's a better version of himself.

*Hissssss.* The blade pauses as if of its own accord. He sets the tool aside with a clink, but neither that nor the hissing can cover the sound of crying. He ignores it and peels the lower lid away, then swallows hard over a lump that even now rises higher and harder in his throat.

*No going back now, no going back.*

He tosses the magazine aside, listens to it rustle like the wings of a hundred agitated bats then suddenly cease as if the entire flock has dropped from the sky, just more victims of a world gone mad.

That line, even only in his head, is lovely, but he can't focus on it for long, can't relish it, because from somewhere below him, the cries accelerate, keening and high-pitched and desperate.

He stares at the tiny eyeball in his hand, feels its realness in the pads of his shaking fingers. Sweat drips down his spine. The screaming comes again, cutting the silence.

No, these women staring at him from the pages are not real.

But *she* is.

**GET *COMPOSED*
on https://meghanoflynn.com**

---

**To save herself, she'll have to face the world's most vicious serial killer. She just calls him Dad.** Fast-paced, electric, and barbed with nerve-shredding thrills, the Born Bad series is perfect for fans of Gillian Flynn, Caroline Kepnes, and *Dexter*.

### *WICKED SHARP*
### CHAPTER 1

I HAVE a drawing that I keep tucked inside an old doll house —well, a house for fairies. My father always insisted upon the whimsical, albeit in small amounts. It's little quirks like that which make you real to people. Which make you safe. Everyone has some weird thing they cling to in times of stress, whether it's listening to a favorite song or snuggling up in a comfortable blanket or talking to the sky as if it might respond. I had the fairies.

And that little fairy house, now blackened by soot and flame, is as good a place as any to keep the things that should be gone. I haven't looked at the drawing since the day I brought it home, can't even remember stealing it, but I can describe every jagged line by heart.

The crude slashes of black that make up the stick figure's

arms, the page torn where the scribbled lines meet—shredded by the pressure of the crayon's point. The sadness of the smallest figure. The horrific, monstrous smile on the father, dead center in the middle of the page.

Looking back, it should have been a warning—I should have known, I should have run. The child who drew it was no longer there to tell me what happened by the time I stumbled into that house. The boy knew too much, that was obvious from the picture.

Children have a way of knowing things that adults don't—a heightened sense of self-preservation that we slowly lose over time as we convince ourselves that the prickling along the backs of our necks is nothing to worry about. Children are too vulnerable not to be ruled by emotion—they're hardwired to identify threats with razor's-edge precision. Unfortunately, they have a limited capacity to describe the perils they uncover. They can't explain why their teacher is scary or what makes them duck into the house if they see the neighbor peeking at them from behind the blinds. They cry. They wet their pants.

They draw pictures of monsters under the bed to process what they can't articulate.

Luckily, most children never find out that the monsters under their bed are real.

I never had that luxury. But even as a child, I was comforted that my father was a bigger, stronger monster than anything outside could ever be. He would protect me. I knew that to be a fact the way other people know the sky is blue or that their racist Uncle Earl is going to fuck up Thanksgiving. Monster or not, he was my world. And I adored him in the way only a daughter can.

I know that's strange to say—to love a man even if you see what terrors lurk beneath. My therapist says it's normal, but she's prone to sugarcoating. Or maybe she's so good at positive thinking that she's grown blind to real evil.

I'm not sure what she'd say about the drawing in the fairy house. I'm not sure what she'd think about me if I told her that I understood why my father did what he did, not because I thought it was justified, but because I understood him. I'm an expert when it comes to the motivation of the creatures underneath the bed.

And I guess that's why I live where I do, hidden in the New Hampshire wilderness as if I can keep every piece of the past beyond the border of the property—as if a fence might keep the lurking dark from creeping in through the cracks. And there are always cracks, no matter how hard you try to plug them. Humanity is a perilous condition rife with self-inflicted torment and psychological vulnerabilities, the what-ifs and maybes contained only by paper-thin flesh, any inch of which is soft enough to puncture if your blade is sharp.

I knew that before I found the picture, of course, but something in those jagged lines of crayon drove it home, or dug it in a little deeper. Something changed that week in the mountains. Something foundational, perhaps the first glimmer of certainty that I'd one day need an escape plan. But though I like to think I was trying to save myself from day one, it's hard to tell through the haze of memory. There are always holes. Cracks.

I don't spend a lot of time reminiscing; I'm not especially nostalgic. I think I lost that little piece of myself first. But I'll never forget the way the sky roiled with electricity, the greenish tinge that threaded through the clouds and seemed to slide down my throat and into my lungs. I can feel the vibration in the air from the birds rising on frantically beating wings. The smell of damp earth and rotting pine will never leave me.

Yes, it was the storm that kept it memorable; it was the mountains.

It was the woman.

It was the blood.

**GET *WICKED SHARP***
**on https://meghanoflynn.com**

**Seven people. A locked storm shelter. Inevitable starvation. What could you do to survive?** *A refuge turns into a nightmarish prison in this chilling thriller.*

## *THE FLOOD*
## CHAPTER 1

Victoria could almost see it: the way the cotton pillow would pucker around her fists as she clamped it over his face, how the misshapen lump beneath would wriggle as he tried to force air through the goose feathers, how everything would lapse into silence, nothing to break the stillness but her hushed exhale of relief. On any normal evening, at least. Now, the night breathed wetly, almost as loudly as he did, a thick swooshing against her eardrums. Viscous. Raindrops *plink, plink, plink*-ed against her soaked hair. The shingles caught the skin on the backs of her legs sharply no matter how she tried not to move, like being slowly ground to dust by sandpaper, and water stung in every scrape. Victoria inhaled in the soupy night, stifling her gag reflex when the musky, acidic stench of shit hit her. Her muscles cramped harder. The sound of the rain against the lake of sewage around them was a constant reminder: they were going to die.

Three days they'd been stranded so far, sitting on top of Chad's family home, separated from the nearest dwelling by a mile of farmland and animal pastures. Three days of not eating, of her belly twisting and angry. Three days of filling her hands with rainwater to avoid dying of thirst.

Three days on the roof with the husband she'd been planning to leave.

The forecasters had said it was a long shot, the storm hitting here, and an even longer shot that the enormous storm systems out in the Atlantic would build in strength and aim themselves at their little low-flood-plain section of Louisiana. *That would be ridiculous,* they'd insisted, *unprecedented.* And they'd all been wrong, especially that twit on the news with his gray hair, his eyes an odd purple-blue that didn't exist in nature—"Probably won't be more than a category two, and a little rain the week after," he'd said. Bullshit. And now all the people who'd stayed were fucked. Totally, one hundred percent fucked. *We should have left.* That would have been the rational thing to do, *honey*, the logical thing.

Her heart seized, her stomach cramping too, a burning knot of hunger. Her lungs were far too small. But panicking made you stop thinking clearly—it could only make things worse. She forced air through her mouth as loudly as possible, drowning out the sound of the storm and Chad's equally labored breath. But not his words.

"Are you okay, Vicky?" He said it in a high voice, almost sing-song, the kind of voice he'd use to ask one of his students about a skinned knee.

Victoria wiped her wet hair from her forehead and tried to relax the painful knot in her guts. Raindrops tapped against her flesh, incessant, like a petulant child. The gray of Chad's irises seemed darker than usual in a world haunted by yesterday's storms and pregnant with electricity and anticipation of the second hurricane. She wished they had a radio, a cell phone to check the status of the upcoming storm, but their electronics had been impossible to keep dry. Their phones were sitting on the roof somewhere near the chimney, useless. *Why the fuck did I listen to you?* She turned away from Chad. Couldn't stand to see the guilt in his eyes, like she was supposed to make him feel better.

Chad always felt awful if he gave someone bad advice—he'd once teared up when he realized he'd given a stranger the wrong directions—but he had this way of convincing people not to bitch at him by making them feel guilty or sorry for him. That wasn't going to last. If they stayed on this roof much longer, he was going to get an earful.

In her peripheral vision, off the edge of the roof, the shitty, brackish water rippled like the skin of an enormous serpent, oily scales shivering with the anticipation of finishing them off. Half a block down, the broken post that used to hold their street sign stabbed through the surface of the filth. And to her other side loomed the muscly bulk of the chimney, topped with the grate she'd installed to keep the animals out, now ripped open like snapped metal ribs—some creature had been at it. Maybe whatever had clawed it apart was still there, lurking in the brick tunnel, drowned and bloated, tenderizing in the sea of bacteria.

Her throat closed. She forced it open. Her black leather work boot tap-tap-tapped against the soggy shingles. She tugged on her cut-off shorts, then the hem of her favorite black T-shirt, so dark she couldn't see the film of dirt and wet. The water was still rising, the red of the shingled roof so dark it looked like drying blood, and some of it probably was—Chad had a gash across his shin from a torn aluminum gutter. Behind Chad, the expanse of sky darkened, threatening, and the rush of rain on water seemed suddenly louder; she felt sure he wouldn't be able to hear her unless she yelled. But she said nothing. There was nothing to say.

If only they lived somewhere else, somewhere higher, somewhere the earth wasn't perpetually soggy from April to August, somewhere with some semblance of civilization. All they had in this section of Fossé, Louisiana was the community college, but that was over an hour away by car—and the levees had failed, leaving the paved roads leading to the college impassable by car or truck. The college itself would be underwater too before the week was out, especially if this storm didn't move on, or the second hurricane hit as hard as they'd been saying. And if the next storm hit while the citizens of Fossé were on their roofs... The winds would rip over the flooded streets, tearing shingles and people alike from the tops of their homes, flinging them against the treetops, impaling them on the remains of fences or drowning them in the sewage from overflowing septic tanks. Even if it did pass quickly, the water table was so high that people would be stuck for weeks. No power. No food. No drinkable water once the rain stopped. These might be her last days on this earth, and she and Chad should not be living their final hours together.

They'd been inhabiting their own little worlds for months now, independent planets merely circling the same sun. Even now he was staring out over the water, waiting passively for someone else to come to their rescue, though for once, she had no other ideas herself. They weren't going to swim twenty miles, and the waste products from the farmland—pig and chicken shit—were rife with E. coli and salmonella and other antibiotic-resistant bacteria that would spread through their injuries into their blood before they got to safety. Sepsis. That'd be a fun way to go out. Better than drowning though—she'd done that once, and once was enough.

The rain spit, water on water. The wind howled, an angry beast bellowing from the sky. The expanse of water pulled her gaze, but she refused to look at it, like it was a monster that could only exist if she let herself notice. Victoria shivered.

"Is there more peroxide?" Chad said.

"It's gone."

She sat back on the gritty shingles and turned away from him, squeezing her eyes closed, forcing the sound of the rain and the image of the storm from her mind. But in the blind starbursts of light behind her eyelids, she saw her parents' Chicago apartment and the square of afternoon sunlight that hit the living room floor when the sun snuck between the neighboring buildings. She and her twin brother Phillip used to sit on that little spot whenever they could, which wasn't often—usually the room was occupied, her father out there screaming at her mother, or screaming at Phillip for stealing money, and later for taking their mother's painkillers. Once she'd tried to help and ended up in the emergency room with a broken rib. Phillip had held her hand the whole way there, sung her songs, refused to let go even when the nurses came to ask her questions about her "fall."

*Why the fuck am I thinking about this now?* But she always

thought about Phillip when she was stressed. He was like…a teddy bear, the memory of his voice somehow comforting. Illogical, sure, but everyone was entitled to one foolish, illogical thing. Better than Chad's foolishness—his was going to get them killed.

She leaned back, resting her head against the sandpapery shingles.

*You're going to be okay, Victoria, you know that.*

Her brother had said that just before he left Chicago for good. That was why she'd come to Louisiana in the first place, Phillip's last known address—she'd hoped their twin connection would help her do what a PI couldn't. She'd been wrong, yet she'd stayed—too long. Ten years now, fourteen since she'd seen her brother. She did get occasional postcards from him, pictures of historical spots around Louisiana, little notes on the back like "I hope you're doing well. I'm still working on 'well'. See you when I manage to get there." Those cards ripped her wounds open every time, kept her up hearing the words in her brain, his voice whispering to her while she tried to sleep. She could help him. If he'd just fucking *call.*

"Hey!"

Her eyes snapped open. Chad scuttled to his feet, the grating sound ringing through the night as he slid on the gritty roof tiles. The sky was pitch as tar, not even a glimmer of haze on the horizon. Oh god, how long had she been out? Was the next storm here? She'd slept through the last dregs of light leaving the sky. But she didn't feel the harsh gusts of wind, didn't see flying debris, only Chad's silhouette, and she'd not have seen him at all were it not for…

*The light.*

Far out over the water, a hazy circle swept first one way, then the other, the rippling muck glittering like yellow diamonds in its wake.

Victoria pushed herself to standing, but the roof was slick despite the grit; her foot slid from beneath her and she went down hard on her knees, scrabbling at the tile with her fingernails, cursing under her breath at the wretched shingles.

"Hey!" Chad cried, waving his arms. "Over here!"

The light glided back and forth, back and forth, and only then did she realize the whoosh of rain was muddling the noises around them. She'd become so accustomed to the patter and slap of rain that it had all but vanished from her awareness, but now, looking over the water…the night was *loud,* the wind screaming, the rain hissing into the muck around their little island of house. They'd disappear into the landscape if they couldn't overcome it, and…the water was higher than it had been just hours ago, the ripples licking at the base of the gutters. A few more hours and the nasty water would creep over the shingles, and then—

"Help!" she yelled, still on her hands and knees. The roof and the water went black again as the light swept away off to her left, then to the far side of the boat—the opposite direction. *They can't hear us.* She planted her feet. *Stand up, stand up! Yell louder!* She inhaled once through her nose, put her hands on her thighs, and heaved herself to standing. "We're out here!"

"This way! Hey, help us!"

"Over here!" Her throat ached, her eyes stinging with rain and unshed tears, but the light swept toward them once more. The beam hovered—and stayed. The sound of a motor cut the night.

They were coming to help. Hopefully, they had a place to ride out the storm.

**GET *THE FLOOD***
**on https://meghanoflynn.com**

<u>PRAISE FOR BESTSELLING AUTHOR
MEGHAN O'FLYNN</u>

"Creepy and haunting... fully immersive thrillers. The Ash Park series should be everyone's next binge-read."
~*New York Times Bestselling Author Andra Watkins*

"Full of complex, engaging characters and evocative detail, *Wicked Sharp* is a white-knuckle thrill ride. O'Flynn is a master storyteller." ~*Paul Austin Ardoin, USA Today Bestselling Author*

"Nobody writes with such compelling and entrancing prose as O'Flynn. With perfectly executed twists, Born Bad is chilling, twisted, heart-pounding suspense. This is my new favorite thriller series." ~*Bestselling Author Emerald O'Brien*

"Visceral, fearless, and addictive, this series will keep you on the edge of your seat." ~*Bestselling Author Mandi Castle*

"Intense and suspenseful...captured me from the first chapter and held me enthralled until the final page."
~*Susan Sewell, Reader's Favorite*

"Cunning, delightfully disturbing, and addictive, the Ash Park series is an expertly written labyrinth."~*Award-winning Author Beth Teliho*

"Dark, gritty, and raw, O'Flynn's work will take your mind prisoner and keep you awake far into the morning hours." ~*Bestselling Author Kristen Mae*

"From the feverishly surreal to the downright demented, O'Flynn takes you on a twisted journey through the

**deepest and darkest corners of the human mind."**
*~Bestselling Author Mary Widdicks*

**"With unbearable tension and gripping, thought-provoking storytelling, O'Flynn explores fear in all the best—and creepiest—ways. Masterful psychological thrillers replete with staggering, unpredictable twists."** *~Bestselling Author Wendy Heard*

**LEARN MORE ON**
**https://meghanoflynn.com**

# Learn more about Meghan's novels on
# https://meghanoflynn.com

# ABOUT THE AUTHOR

With books deemed "visceral, haunting, and fully immersive" (*New York Times bestseller, Andra Watkins*), Meghan O'Flynn has made her mark on the thriller genre. Meghan is a clinical therapist who draws her character inspiration from her knowledge of the human psyche. She is the bestselling author of gritty crime novels and serial killer thrillers, all of which take readers on the dark, gripping, and unputdownable journey for which Meghan is notorious. Learn more at https://meghanoflynn.com! While you're there, join Meghan's reader group, and get a **FREE SHORT STORY** just for signing up.

**Want to connect with Meghan?**
**https://meghanoflynn.com**